A matter of trust—
and a chance at love . . .

Alexandra wanted to trust him. Like it or not, she had spoken marriage vows that included "until death do us part" and the four glorious days they had spent together in Kent had been the happiest of her life.

When he reached for her hand, she smiled and twined her fingers in his. Maybe if she made a concerted effort to overlook his odd eccentricities . . . and maybe once they reached that magnificent medieval castle of his . . . but she had enough to worry about in the present. She would let the future take care of itself. . . .

ENJOY THE OTHER
REGENCY ROMANCES BY
NADINE MILLER

The Unlikely Angel
The Madcap Masquerade

The Barbarian Earl

Nadine Miller

A SIGNET BOOK

SIGNET
Published by New American Library, a division of
Penguin Putnam Inc., 375 Hudson Street,
New York, New York 10014, U.S.A.
Penguin Books Ltd, 27 Wrights Lane,
London W8 5TZ, England
Penguin Books Australia Ltd, Ringwood,
Victoria, Australia
Penguin Books Canada Ltd, 10 Alcorn Avenue,
Toronto, Ontario, Canada M4V 3B2
Penguin Books (N.Z.) Ltd, 182–190 Wairau Road,
Auckland 10, New Zealand

Penguin Books Ltd, Registered Offices:
Harmondsworth, Middlesex, England

First published by Signet, an imprint of New American Library,
a division of Penguin Putnam Inc.

First Printing, December 1999
10 9 8 7 6 5 4 3 2 1

*To Mary Henson, my beloved goddaughter,
who is one of the joys of my life;
and to Frances Sonnabend, who supplied me
with such incredible information on smuggling
during the Regency period, the scenes almost
wrote themselves.*

Prologue

"You've a fine way of wrapping your tongue around the King's English . . . for a bastard and a smuggler." The Earl of Stratham slumped deeper into the armchair that cradled his wasted body and surveyed Liam Campbell with hard, lead gray eyes. "Properly clothed, you might even pass for a gentleman."

Liam shifted from one foot to the other, strangely unnerved by the old man's scrutiny. He'd been warned by the earl's solicitor that Stratham was dying. Still he found it difficult to equate this emaciated shell of a man with the barbaric, red-haired giant he had once likened to the Viking warlords in his boyhood history lessons.

"I've been told you can read and write as well," the earl continued when Liam failed to comment on his first observation. "How so?"

Liam shrugged. "I was tutored by the local vicar. He also taught me to cipher—a skill even more useful in my profession."

"I thought as much. Your mother, as I recall, was comely enough, but no brighter than any of the other tavern wenches I bedded."

"Devil take you, old man, leave my mother out of this," Liam warned. Nothing had changed. After all these years, he still felt the same bitter resentment toward the nobleman who had seduced his mother, then callously abandoned her and the son he'd sired. If the evil old lecher wasn't already dying, he'd be tempted to ring his scrawny neck.

A caricature of a grin spread across the earl's forbidding countenance. "Just what will you do if I insult the sainted slut?"

he taunted. "Will you pelt me with rocks as you did when I rode through your village some twenty years ago?" He touched a bony finger to the jagged scar that defaced his gaunt cheek. "Don't try to deny you were the ragged brat who gave me this. I remember your pretty face all too well."

"I had no intention of doing so," Liam declared. "Throwing that rock was one of the more rewarding moments in my otherwise bleak childhood."

He stared down at the pitiful remnant of the powerful nobleman and wondered what had possessed him to make this futile pilgrimage to The Aerie, the medieval fortress that had been home to the Earls of Stratham since the Middle Ages. The answer, of course, was the fifty pounds the solicitor had offered to any of the earl's male bastards who visited the dying man.

Six months earlier, Liam would have scoffed at the offer. But with the war ended and Bonaparte safely imprisoned on Elba, normal trade with France had quickly resumed. Smuggling French brandy was no longer a lucrative profession, and Liam found himself sadly short of the ready.

Impatiently, he pushed a stray lock of flame-colored hair off his forehead—his only legacy from his noble father. "I assume this tender reminiscence we've just shared puts paid to my collecting the promised fifty pounds. Therefore, I shall bid you farewell, my lord, and let you get on with your dying. But I promise I shall offer up a prayer that you get your just rewards in the afterlife." Without further ado, he turned on his heel and headed for the door.

"Not so fast, young hothead. The offer stands—unless I make you a more generous one."

Liam stopped in his tracks, torn between his distrust of the unscrupulous earl and his pressing need for fifty quid. "How much more generous? And why would you make such an offer to me?"

"The answer to your first question is 'a great deal more generous.' The answer to your second is 'I have no choice.' From what I've seen of the motley collection, it appears you are the only one of my bastards who is literate enough to pass for a member of the nobility."

"Me? A high-and-mighty milord?" Liam's laughter echoed off the walls of the earl's paneled book room. "I fear your illness has addled your brain, my lord."

"The fact that you are a handsome devil and, my solicitor tells me, a legend with the local wenches is an added bonus," the earl continued, ignoring Liam's protestation. "Now that I think about it, I can see you will fit nicely into my plan."

Certain the old man was a raving bedlamite, Liam took another step toward the door.

"Wait!" Stratham raised a hand shaking with palsy. "Hear me out. Then if you have no interest in my proposition, you are free to leave, fifty pounds richer than when you arrived."

Intrigued in spite of himself, Liam took the chair the earl indicated. "Just what would I have to do to earn this 'more generous offer'?" he asked warily.

"One thing at a time. To begin with, I am the last of my line. I have no legitimate heir—not even a distant cousin. Therefore, I must resort to naming one of my illegitimate offspring heir to my title—"

"And that's your idea of a generous offer?" Liam leapt to his feet. "You have the wrong bastard in mind, my lord. The last thing I want to be is a bloody earl."

Sparks flared briefly in Stratham's dull, gray eyes. "Sit down, you young fool, and let me finish. Have you any idea how rich I am?"

The question took Liam aback. "Not really, but I've heard rumors you're rich as Croesus, and I suppose you must be to live in a pile of stones as big as the mad king's castle."

"Croesus? That piker?" the earl scoffed. "It so happens I am richer than God. If I name you my heir, you will spend the rest of your life as one of the wealthiest men in all of England, provided you meet my one requirement."

"The devil you say!" Liam sat down. The idea of never again having to risk life and limb just to fill his empty belly was too appealing to dismiss lightly. "And just what might that one requirement be?"

"Within six months of my death, you must marry a certain young woman of noble birth—Lady Alexandra Henning, the only daughter of Viscount Hardin."

"Never!" Once again Liam bolted from his chair. "There's not enough money in all of Christendom to tempt me to leg-shackle myself to some milk-and-water aristocrat. I saw enough of the spoiled little darlings on one walk through London's Hyde Park to last me a lifetime. My taste runs to lusty tavern wenches—as did yours when you were my age."

The earl's hooded eyes narrowed. "Try not to act the complete fool," he said with biting sarcasm. "You need spend only enough time with the silly chit to get her to the altar. All I ask is that she become your lawfully wedded wife and that you consummate the marriage so it cannot be annulled.

"Do with her what you will after that. You need not worry about producing an heir. Will the estate to one of your bastards if you wish, or let the title and fortune revert to the crown. It matters not to me."

"Then why do you require me to marry her if not to carry on your line?" Liam asked, pacing to the fireplace and back. He could see the earl was tiring fast, but he wanted this business between them settled one way or another before he took his leave of the old man.

The earl pressed his fingers to his temples and closed his eyes. "Because she is her mother's daughter, and Henrietta Henning, Viscountess Hardin is the woman I once thought to marry."

Again Stratham's answer surprised Liam. Was it possible the acid-tongued old reprobate actually harbored tender feelings for some woman? He raised a skeptical eyebrow. "You amaze me, my lord. You do not appear the sort of man to wear the willow."

"Wear the willow?" Stratham's eyes popped open. "Hogwash!" Spots of angry color flared in his pale cheeks. "For your information, I haven't a sentimental bone in my body. 'Tis plain and simple vengeance I'm after.

"I traveled to London when I was three and thirty for the sole purpose of taking a wife of noble birth. But the stiff-rumped bitch I chose turned me down flat when I offered for her. Called me a 'hideous barbarian' and made me such a public laughingstock, no other woman of quality would consider marrying me either, despite my wealth and title.

"I was young and hot-blooded and full of anger. One thing led to another, and her noble father, may he rot in hell, left me with a bullet in the knee and these as a reminder of my foolishness." He indicated the pair of crutches braced against one arm of his chair.

"I have waited more than twenty years to take my revenge

on that bitch and take it I will through you. I can think of nothing that would horrify her more than to be forced to accept the by-blow of 'the hideous barbarian from Exmoor' as her son-in-law."

The earl leaned forward in his chair, a malicious gleam in his rheumy eyes. "So what say you, my lad? Are you game to play for the highest stakes you'll ever be offered?"

It occurred to Liam that of all the coils the fates had devised for him, this was surely the most ironic. It was a testimony to Stratham's lack of sensitivity that he failed to consider that even a bastard might find it galling to be deemed such an undesirable *parti* he could be used as a tool for revenge.

His first inclination was to consign the old man and his ugly retaliation scheme to hell and be done with it. But times were hard and he was uniquely unqualified to make a living as a farmer or shopkeeper. In truth, with smuggling no longer profitable, the only profession he could see open to him was that of highwayman—and he had a distinct aversion to ending his life dangling from a gibbet.

The more he thought about it, the better the incredible proposition sounded. Still, something about it bothered him. "You act as if my convincing this aristocrat to marry me is a sure thing," he ventured. "How can you be so confident? She might well be as high-in-the-instep as her mother—in which case it is unlikely she would agree to wed a bastard and ex-smuggler—even a rich and titled one."

"I am counting on your handsome face and charming manner to win her over," the earl replied. "And naturally, sufficient funds will be made available to you to court the chit properly. However, what Lady Alexandra thinks of you is relatively unimportant in the long run. The daughters of English aristocrats have little to say about whom they wed. That is a decision left up to their noble fathers."

A calculating smile crossed Stratham's rough-hewn face. "Ergo, you need only offer the viscount a large enough marriage settlement and I guarantee he will see to it she becomes your obedient bride. The fool has been sailing the River Tick for some time now and his ship is about to sink. He is, in fact, but a breath away from being clapped into debtors' prison."

Liam was appalled at the thought of forcing an unwilling woman to marry him. But, he reasoned, it surely wouldn't come to that. His success with tavern wenches and innkeepers' daughters was indeed legendary, and he suspected all women, including bluebloods, were much the same when it came to a toss between the sheets.

"Well, that's that then," the earl declared. "I shall order my servant to prepare a room for you, and first thing tomorrow morning I'll have my solicitor draw up the necessary papers to put my plan into motion. For what it's worth, the title and The Aerie are yours regardless; the fortune only if you marry the chit I've designated. Otherwise it reverts to the crown." It was obvious, from his triumphant expression, he believed he had made an offer his chosen bastard could not refuse.

As indeed he had. For if the helter-skelter life Liam had led had taught him nothing else, it had driven home the truth that the practical men of this world were the survivors. And no practical man in his right mind could turn down such an offer, no matter how reprehensible the man who proffered it might be.

He felt a brief stab of regret that the viscountess's innocent young daughter must be involved in the earl's revenge, but he quickly dismissed it. If what he'd heard about the marriages of the nobility was true, the chit would be no worse off as his wife than if she were caught in parson's mousetrap with one of her own kind.

And as for her pinch-nosed mother—if, as the earl predicted, the thought of a bastard son-in-law horrified the old besom, then she just might have to develop a taste for crow.

He told himself his reasoning was sound; he assured himself his conscience was clear. Then why, he wondered, did he have the feeling that he had just managed to sell his soul to the devil?

Chapter One

London, England—March 1815

Lady Alexandra Henning had grown accustomed to the admiring looks cast her way by the eligible bachelors of the *ton*. She was, after all, an acknowledged beauty on the verge of her third London season, as well as the richly dowered daughter of a viscount.

With so many of this year's incomparables not yet in town, she had received more than her share of attention at Lady Rutherford's ball, which traditionally opened the London season. But the tall, red-haired man leaning against one of the pillars in the elegant ballroom didn't just look at her. He literally undressed her with his eyes.

The cheeky fellow discomposed her—especially when the pattern of the minuet she was dancing with Freddie Hawthorne led her close to him and she realized his strange, gold-flecked eyes held the same feral gleam as the restless lion she'd watched prowl a cage in the Tower of London. This shocking discovery caused her to stumble back.

During the first waltz of the evening she remembered where she had seen hair that color before. The Duke of Bellmont had escorted his controversial new bride to the little season's opening performance at the Royal Opera House in September, and every other woman in the theater had seemed pale and colorless beside the spectacular redhead.

Her mother had taken one look at the duchess, and tight-lipped and silent, had stalked out of the theater before the curtain was raised. Just thinking about that bewildering evening caused Alexandra to trod heavily on young Baron Fitzwalter's toes during a sweeping turn—an inexcusable faux pas since the baron was far and away the best dancer in London.

The last note of the waltz had scarcely died away before her disgruntled partner escorted her to where her best friend, the Honorable Miss Elsie Trumbold, waited at the edge of the dance floor. Bowing stiffly, the baron quickly disappeared, leaving Alexandra humiliated and seething with impotent rage.

"Who is he?" Elsie whispered behind her fan.

Alexandra had no doubt which "he" Elsie had in mind. "I have not the faintest idea, but I can tell you this much—he is no gentleman, despite his elegant attire."

"He does appear frightfully bold."

"Bold?" Alexandra gritted her teeth. "The insolent devil looked me over in the same manner I've seen men appraise the light-skirts parading their wares outside Covent Garden."

Elsie sighed. "But you must admit he is excessively handsome. Such speaking eyes . . . and all that gorgeous flame-colored hair."

"I admit no such thing. I despise red hair. And what man with the slightest sense of what is *au courant* would wear his so long it brushed his shoulders? As for his 'speaking eyes,' I find the message they project insulting in the extreme."

Elsie's pale brows drew together in a frown. "Why is it the exciting things always happen to you?" She shivered dramatically. "I wish some man would look at me like that."

"For your information, it is not at all pleasant. I swear I felt as if I were dancing that miserable waltz in my shift."

Elsie giggled. "Oh, Alexandra, you do say the most outrageous things. Your mama would be so shocked."

At the mention of her mother, Alexandra sent a nervous glance toward the row of chairs reserved for the chaperones. It was obvious from the sour expression on the Viscountess Hardin's face that she had witnessed the stranger's shocking perusal of her daughter. So, no doubt, had everyone else in the ballroom.

Alexandra breathed a sigh of relief that her most ardent admirer, Sir Randolph Twickingham, had not yet arrived. He might have felt compelled to challenge the boorish fellow to a duel, and she suspected that dear Randy was more adept at wielding a pen than a pistol.

Ignoring the babble of voices around her, she peeked over her fan toward the spot where the annoying stranger had stood, only to find he was no longer in sight. Relief washed through

her. Yet, at the same time, she felt an odd sense of disappointment. Elsie was right. It had been an exciting moment in her
otherwise perfectly ordered life.

Why, she puzzled, had the brazen fellow singled her out in
such an insulting way? Could that intense look in his strange
eyes have reflected the lust her mother had repeatedly warned
her lurked inside every male? If so, it was her first encounter
with the raw emotion, and she couldn't imagine what she had
done to inspire it in a man who had never before laid eyes on
her.

Standing on tiptoe, she searched the crowded ballroom for a
glimpse of a head of glossy red hair. None was in sight, and she
had to wonder where he'd gone, and why, if he lusted after her,
had he made no effort to approach her? Not that she would have
given him the time of day. But it infuriated her that he should
make her the subject of tomorrow's gossip in every fashionable
drawing room in London, then vanish before she could give
him the set-down he deserved.

Out of the corner of her eye she caught a glimpse of her
mother advancing toward her through a sea of gawking onlookers. "Well you've done it this time, my girl," the viscountess
hissed as she drew Alexandra and Elsie into a shadowed alcove
behind a huge urn of snowy plum blossoms.

Between the heady fragrance of the blossoms and the cloy-
ing scent of her mother's French perfume, Alexandra found it
impossible to draw a deep breath. From the small, snuffling
sounds Elsie was making, it appeared she suffered from the
same problem.

Not so the viscountess. Wagging a finger in Alexandra's
face, she launched into a lecture on her favorite subject—her
daughter's sad lack of social decorum. "If I've warned you
once, I've warned you a hundred times your hoydenish ways
would one day land you in serious trouble. Well, that day has
come. Have you any idea who it was you were flirting with, my
girl?"

"No, Mama, and I was not flirting with him."

"The Earl of Stratham, that's who. I'd heard he was in London. It just never occurred to me he would have the audacity to
show his face in polite society, despite his connection to the
Duke of Bellmont. But there is no mistaking him. Both he and
that bold-as-brass sister of his inherited hair the color of the

flames of hell—and appropriately so, considering the devil who sired them."

Elsie's eyes grew round as teacups. "That handsome fellow is an earl and the brother-in-law of the Duke of Bellmont?"

The viscountess sniffed. "By default only. Wouldn't you know that evil old reprobate, Dierk Wolverson, would pass his title to one of his bastards."

Alexandra gasped. Her mother's unusually blunt speech shocked her even more than the stranger's insulting perusal. She had to ask. "Surely you are not implying the Duchess of Bellmont is a . . . is a—"

"A bastard? Of course she is. Why do you think so many doors in the *ton* are closed to her—mine included?"

Alexandra couldn't remember when she had been more shocked. She swallowed hard to clear her constricted throat. "But why would the duke marry such a woman?"

"Lust." Her mother spat the word out as if the very saying of it defiled her. "How many times have I told you men are ruled by their carnal instincts. The Duke of Bellmont is living proof of that." She shuddered. "His poor mother must be turning over in her grave.

"But enough of that. It is the scapegrace earl who concerns me at the moment—not his sister." The viscountess glanced about her as if to make certain no one was within earshot. "Speaking of which, there is something I must tell you, Alexandra," she said in a voice fraught with emotion. "And since Elsie is your dearest friend and constant companion, it is best she, too, be made aware of the danger of attracting the attention of a man like Stratham."

"Danger?" Alexandra and Elsie exclaimed in unison.

The viscountess nodded grimly. "Hear me and hear me well, Alexandra. Under no circumstances are you to step out of the town house without a footman accompanying you for as long as that man remains in London."

"But why, Mama? What could he do to me?"

The viscountess gestured impatiently. "If you will stop interrupting me, I shall tell you." She swept Alexandra and Elsie with a chilling gaze. "But first, you must both promise you will never repeat a word of what I am about to say."

"I promise," Alexandra said solemnly.

"And so do I," Elsie echoed.

The viscountess took a deep breath. "To begin with, the Earl of Stratham developed a . . . a mad passion for me the year I made my come-out."

"He did?" Elsie stared at her with obvious disbelief. "But he looks so young!"

"Not this Earl of Stratham, you peagoose." Alexandra cast a disparaging look at her dense friend. "Mama is obviously talking about his father." Elsie had the grace to blush.

"He was a dreadful fellow," the viscountess continued, seemingly unaware of the interruption. "A great, ugly brute from the wilds of Exmoor, with the manners of a jungle savage and the morals of a gypsy. Having him lust after me was the most terrifying experience of my life. You can imagine how distressed I was when I saw his whelp ogling my daughter."

Alexandra felt as if she were truly seeing her mother for the first time. No wonder Mama was so obsessed with the subject of male lust.

The viscountess pressed a hand to her heaving bosom. "First the fool stole the miniature I'd had painted for your father. Then he tried to kidnap me when I rejected his suit. He would have succeeded, too, were it not for Papa's vigilance. If Papa had had his way, he'd have seen Stratham hang. But, of course, my reputation would have been ruined if word of the kidnapping got out, so Papa had to let him go." She cleared her throat. "After he shot him in the knee."

Alexandra gasped. "Grandpapa actually shot the earl?"

Elsie giggled nervously. "Good heavens, how gothic!"

"This is not a laughing matter, young lady," the viscountess declared in a voice edged with ice. She caught Alexandra's arm in a viselike grip. "You should never have encouraged that man's attention. From his performance here tonight, he could very well be the same kind of madman his father was."

"I did not encourage him, Mama. I ignored him—and, as you can see, he has already left the ball," Alexandra declared with a confidence she was far from feeling. "He is apparently more easily deterred than his father. I doubt very much I shall ever see him again."

"I pray you are right. The earl drove off all my other suitors for one entire season. God help us if this by-blow of his does the same to you. Your father has already stood the cost of two very expensive seasons in which you rejected every man who made an offer. Unless you accept one of your suitors soon, he will choose your husband for you. You are one-and-twenty, for heaven's sake—already too old to attract many of the *ton's* most eligible bachelors. If you waste another year, as you've wasted the past two, you will find yourself permanently on the shelf."

"I promise you I shall be betrothed before this current season is over," Alexandra said, thinking of the plans she and Sir Randolph had already discussed. She leveled a silencing look on Elsie, who was privy to those plans.

"Thank goodness." A satisfied smile softened the viscountess's sharp features. "The sooner the better, in case the young savage should get any ideas about following in his father's footsteps. Granted the son is more pleasing to the eye than the father, but I doubt he is any less a barbarian. I shudder to think what agonies a gently bred girl like yourself would suffer should she fall into the hands of such a creature."

Alexandra's eyes widened in alarm. She had never been the missish sort, but now that she thought about it, there had been something undeniably menacing in the red-haired earl's single-minded contemplation of her.

"You need a husband to give you the protection of his name, Alexandra—preferably a very wealthy one," her mother continued, as if reading her thoughts. "But choose wisely. With your beauty and impeccable bloodlines, you can have any man you want. I've noticed the Marquess of Nettleford has been paying you particular attention lately. I can think of nothing I'd like better than to see my daughter a marchioness."

"But Mama, the marquess is two-and-seventy and has already been thrice married," Alexandra gasped.

"Exactly. The ideal husband to my way of thinking." The viscountess brushed away a blossom petal that had fallen on her sleeve. "I'll give you girls the same advice my dear mother gave me when I was your age: 'Choose a man as rich as a nabob and old enough to leave you a wealthy widow while you are still young enough to enjoy your independence.' I wish to heaven I'd had the sense to heed her words."

She glanced toward the crowded dance floor and frowned thoughtfully. "Unless I am mistaken, your partners for the next set are looking for the two of you. Act as if nothing untoward has happened and, above all, answer no questions put to you about the bastard earl.

"Meanwhile, I shall attempt to diffuse the gossip already circulating throughout the ballroom. There are those in the *ton* who would be only too happy to find some scandal they could tie to me or mine." Without further ado, she edged round the urn and strolled with studied nonchalance toward the row of chattering chaperones.

Elsie made a few vigorous swipes with her fan to rid the alcove of the viscountess's perfume. "I must say, it has been quite an evening."

Alexandra nodded. "Amen to that. If nothing else comes of it, I have a better understanding of why my mother bears such hatred toward men."

"That business about the kidnapping was a bit of a shock—I mean, your *mother* for heaven's sake." Elsie frowned. "I don't know about you, but what with one thing and another, I find I've lost all interest in dancing—especially with Oliver Kingston, who is my partner for the next set. His palms sweat and I've no desire to have his handprints on my new silk ball gown. Let's slip out the French windows to the terrace. I am badly in need of fresh air."

"So am I, but Mama will be frantic if I disappear from the ballroom. She'll think the Earl of Stratham had kidnapped me." But even as she said it, Alexandra picked up her skirts and made a dash for the nearest French window.

Elsie followed her at the same reckless pace. "The handsome devil can kidnap me any time he wants," she panted once they reached the terrace.

Alexandra laughed in spite of herself. "Brave words, my friend. But I wonder what you would do if you ever really came face-to-face with the lusty earl. For that matter, I wonder what *I* would do."

"You would turn tail and run, the same as I would." Elsie sighed. "Your mother is right, you know. Barbarians are not for the daughters of English aristocrats. But then neither are penniless poets. She will have a tizzy when she learns you mean to marry Sir Randolph. He is nothing like her description of the ideal husband."

"But he fits mine perfectly, and that is all that counts. My darling Randy may not be wealthy like the marquess, but he is young and handsome and a gentleman of exquisite taste. He has made it plain he admires my keen mind and my compassionate heart, and cares little for the carnal pleasures with which most men are obsessed. I knew we were soul mates the moment I read his poem in which he immortalized the purity of his love for me."

Elsie appeared unconvinced. "Poetry is all very well, but it will not buy gowns and slippers, nor pay for a fashionable town house and a box at the opera. You have very expensive tastes, Alexandra. How will Sir Randolph support you?"

"We have already discussed that. He has but a small quarterly stipend at present, but he stands to inherit an estate in Yorkshire and a sizable fortune as well once his uncle dies. Until then, we shall do very nicely, with a little help. Papa has already promised me a generous dowry; I shall simply ask him to increase it. He won't mind in the least. He is a very wealthy man."

Elsie sighed plaintively. "How I envy you, Alexandra. You have your entire future planned out, while I have not the slightest idea what the fates have in store for me."

"That is because you are too wishy-washy. Fate has nothing to do with it. It is simply a matter of attitude. I always know exactly what I want and exactly how to get it. Have you ever seen me fail to have my way once my mind was made up?"

"Never," Elsie admitted with grudging admiration.

"And you never shall." Alexandra regarded her friend with a complacent smile. "That, dear Elsie, I can safely promise you."

A recent rain had cleared the sky over London of its usual smoky haze and a sliver of moon had risen over the stately mansions of Mayfair when Liam Campbell departed the ball, which he had attended without benefit of invitation. Pausing on the steps of the Rutherford mansion, he surveyed the seemingly endless line of carriages that had transported the guests to the ball and now waited to return them to their homes.

What a silly, pretentious lot these London aristocrats were, Liam mused. He knew that most of them lived within a few blocks of the Rutherford town house. But rather than arrive on foot, they had sat for an hour or two while their carriages inched along the congested streets. Such conduct would be looked on as lunacy in Exmoor.

He'd had no problem whatsoever gaining admittance to the ball despite his lack of invitation or carriage. It was amazing what doors in London were open to a man decked out in the latest fashion. He had simply attached himself to a group of dandies, walked with them into the Rutherford town house, then sauntered into the crowded ballroom. Not a soul had challenged his right to be there.

Still, to his way of thinking, that expensive tailor who had made his fine evening clothes was highly overrated. He'd patronized the pawky fellow on the recommendation of one of the footmen at his sister's town house, where he was staying while Fiona and her duke rusticated at their farm in Exmoor. The cocky young Irishman had assured him the toffs all considered Weston the finest tailor in London. So much for listening to footmen.

Considering the prices this Weston fellow charged, one would expect him to be a little less niggardly with his cloth. Liam wriggled uncomfortably in his skin-tight, black satin evening jacket. He strongly suspected that one good sneeze would rip out every seam in the miserable garment. In truth, if the duke's butler hadn't helped him, he'd never have managed to pour himself into it. No wonder every nobleman had a valet.

Still and all, he couldn't complain too much about the information the young footman was supplying him—so long as he kept crossing the lad's palm with silver. Some of it had been exceedingly helpful.

No sooner had he mentioned his interest in Lady Alexandra Henning than Colin O'Riley declared he had a cousin who was a footman in Viscount Hardin's household. It was from this cousin that O'Riley had learned Lady Alexandra planned to attend the Rutherfords' ball. Then with another exchange of coins, the Irishman arranged to have a cousin, who was a footman in the Earl of Rutherford's household, discreetly point her out to Liam.

To hear O'Riley tell it, he had a cousin employed in every noble house in Mayfair, and for all Liam knew, he did. He'd heard the Irish papists were as prolific as field mice.

Liam chuckled. The enterprising young footman reminded him of himself ten years earlier—always scrambling for a bit of the ready, always looking for the main chance. Now miraculously, the main chance was his and all he had to do to nail it hard and fast was take an uppity little beauty to wife.

For a beauty she was, this spirited young aristocrat he must wed—with her golden curls and her eyes as green as the moors in spring. What did it matter that she was clumsy as a newborn lamb on the dance floor? He wasn't much of a dancer himself, except for rollicking country dances, which seemed more her style than the waltz and minuet.

Now that he'd seen her, he wondered why he had tarried so long in Exmoor, dreading the inevitable. Taking on the necessary leg shackles might not be so painful after all.

Engrossed in his musings, he turned a corner and walked down the quiet street that led to the Duke of Bellmont's town house. Here not a carriage was in sight nor a link boy to light the night with his flaming torch. It seemed everyone in Mayfair was crowded into the Earl of Rutherford's ballroom.

But habits formed in his years as one of Cornwall's notorious "gentlemen" of the smuggling trade stayed with him. Even here in the seemingly safe environs of fashionable London Liam was keenly aware of his surroundings, and out of the corner of his eye he glimpsed a furtive movement in the shadows.

Instantly alert, he withdrew the knife he always kept strapped to his boot and braced himself for his stalker's attack. It came a moment later, but not from the source he expected. Strong arms encircled him from behind, pinning his own arms to his sides. "Your money or your life," his attacker demanded in a heavy Irish brogue. At the same moment, the stalker leapt from the shadows. With a curse, Liam slashed downward and felt his knife rip through cloth and flesh.

"Aghh," his captor grunted and loosed his hold to grasp his bleeding thigh. "Watch yerself, Paddy, the bloomin' toff's packin' a skean," he warned as his legs collapsed beneath him and he sat down heavily on the cobblestone curb.

"The divil you say!" The fellow called Paddy stopped just out of Liam's reach. "Is it wounded you are then, Sean?"

"That I am and me best pair o' breeches ruined to boot. A fine night's work this is."

Still clutching his now bloody knife, Liam backed away to get a better look at the two most inept footpads he'd ever encountered. Both wore black face masks and black seamen's caps pulled low on their foreheads, but there the resemblance ended. The one clutching his leg and moaning pathetically was a great hulk of a man; the other, hovering over him like a mother bird guarding her young, was a scrawny fellow half his size. Both had apparently forgotten their intended victim.

A cursory examination of his fine new jacket showed every seam intact, and Liam instantly revised his opinion of Mr. Weston's tailoring. Since he was in far better shape than at least one of his would-be assailants, it occurred to him he'd best take charge of the situation before the two bumbling idiots got themselves into serious trouble. "Hell and damnation, man, bind your leg to stem the bleeding and stop your blasted whimpering," he ordered.

"I've nothing to bind it with, your worship," the fellow whined.

With a curse, Liam whipped off his cravat and tossed it to the robber he'd stabbed just as a third man came running down the street. "Never fear, milord. I'll rescue you from these evil brigands," the fellow cried, brandishing a stout stick Liam recognized as one of the blackthorn shillelaghs he'd seen the streetfighters in Dublin wield with such deadly effect.

"O'Riley? What the devil are you doing here? And what part have you in this sorry business?"

But O'Riley had stopped in his tracks at the sight of the downed footpad and paid Liam no more heed than the others. "Holy Mother of God, what have you done to yourself, boyo?" he demanded. "'Tis bleedin' like a stuck pig you are."

"Aye and I've this fancy jackeen o' yourn to thank for it," the man called Sean declared, jerking a thumb toward Liam. "Carved up me leg like a piece of mutton, he did."

"And his best breeches too," the smaller footpad added sourly. "I'm thinking 'tis a sad day when the London toffs takes to carrying skeans same as bully boys."

Liam had heard enough. "I want an explanation from you, O'Riley, and I want it now. Why do I have the feeling these two miscreants are friends of yours?"

"Cousins, actually," Colin O'Riley admitted. "Me Aunt Mary's lads, on me mother's side o' the family, and 'tis sorry I am I went against me own better judgment and trusted the blatherskulls to do a simple piece o' work."

Liam's fingers tightened on his knife. "You call robbing your employer's relative a 'simple piece of work'?"

" 'Twas not me plan to rob you, milord, and it saddens me to learn you think I'd do so," O'Riley declared with what sounded amazingly like indignation. " 'Twas only to impress you I convinced the lads to pose as footpads."

"Ah, I see," Liam said, remembering O'Riley's battle cry. "The fearless footman to the rescue."

"Aye, milord. I see now 'twas the foolishest of schemes, but 'twas all me doing, so if 'tis charges you'll be making to the watch, 'tis against me alone they should be made."

Liam was tempted to let O'Riley squirm a while, but it was obvious the young Irishman had learned his lesson. "I'll not press charges," he said and heard three heartfelt sighs of relief.

"Then can I be taking off me mask?" the one called Paddy asked. "For 'tis an itchy thing to be sure and I'm that desperate to scratch."

"Aye, take it off and you too, Sean," O'Riley answered. "The earl is an honorable man and 'tis lucky we are he has a good heart as well." Squaring his narrow shoulders, he looked Liam in the eye. "If you've no objections, milord, I'll be sending the lads on their way, for me Aunt Mary will be that anxious to tend to Sean's wound once she hears of the fracas."

Liam waved the two cousins off and watched them slink away like the thieves in the night they'd pretended to be. Carefully, he wiped off his bloody knife with his handkerchief and returned it to his boot before walking the rest of the way to the duke's town house. The penitent young footman trotted along beside him, taking two steps to every one of his lengthy strides.

"There is one thing that still puzzles me," Liam said after a long silence. "Just why did you feel the need to impress me? You were already being paid handsomely for any information you supplied."

" 'Twas that very information that set me to thinking, milord," O'Riley panted. "For I've no desire to be a footman all me life, which most likely I'll be if I stay in the duke's employ."

Liam's scowl deepened. "I fail to see how impressing me would solve your problem."

" 'Tis plain you've courting in mind, milord, and you'll be after setting up your own household once you've won your bride. If 'tis the Lady Alexandra you have in mind, you'll be needing a clever valet—what with her such a fashionable London lady and you a country kind of gentleman. 'Tis a post I'm thinking I could fill quite nicely."

Liam had to laugh at the young Irishman's less than subtle hint he was sadly lacking in town bronze. "Your reasoning is flawed on two counts, O'Riley," he said, stopping to allow the smaller man to catch his breath. "In the first place, I am no gentleman. I'm a base-born ex-smuggler and always will be, despite coming into a title and fortune. Ergo, I see little need for a valet except when I'm moved to try to wriggle into one of Mr. Weston's tortuous jackets.

"In the second place, even I can see you're no proper gentleman's gentleman, if John Bittner, the duke's man, is an example of the breed. The truth is you're naught but a cocky young Irishman scarcely dry behind the ears."

O'Riley hung his head. " 'Tis all too true, milord."

"Still, I have to admire your enterprising spirit. That scheme you hatched had definite possibilities. I'd have been very impressed if it had appeared you'd saved my life—and felt beholden to you as well. In truth, I'd probably have granted you almost anything you requested."

"Me very thought, milord."

"For all your faults, you've a clever turn of mind," Liam continued after a moment of careful thought. "And you've guessed correctly. I do plan to wed Lady Alexandra Henning, and all things considered, I'm likely to have to do some scheming of my own to bring it about. For I doubt a 'fashionable London lady' will be too anxious to become wife to a man with my background."

"Never say so, milord." O'Riley regarded Liam through narrowed eyes. "You're as handsome a fellow as ever I've seen, and you've a grand, care-for-nothing way about you that sets you apart from the ordinary. 'Tis plain to me you can have any woman you want once you set your mind to it—Lady Alexandra included."

Liam sincerely hoped O'Riley was right. He would rather the lady went to the altar willingly, but one way or another he would marry her within the proscribed time to secure his title and wealth. For it had been driven home to him this past winter that life as a rich man was a great deal more pleasant than it had been as a poor one.

Deep in thought, Liam strode the last block to the town

house with O'Riley close behind him. "If I'm to win the lady's heart, I must spend time with her," he declared before mounting the shallow steps to the elegant carved door. "I'll make you a proposition, O'Riley. I'll hire you as my valet if you persuade your cousin, the footman in Viscount Hardin's household, to keep me informed of Lady Alexandra's activities."

"Done, milord." Grinning from ear to ear, O'Riley accepted Liam's hand and shook it enthusiastically. "And as a pledge of me faith, I'll tell you a bit of interesting news me cousin just recently passed to me."

"News?"

"Aye, milord. The lady has a young brother she fair dotes on—a sickly lad of sixteen years, with lungs still weak from a bout of the fever this past winter. Come nine each morning, if 'tis a fair day, the two of them walk the lad's dog in Hyde Park."

"Well done, O'Riley." Liam gave the little Irishman an exuberant slap on the back. "That is just the sort of information I need."

Lifting the brass door knocker to alert the night footman of his return, he silently congratulated himself on a bargain well made. It was but the first step in his campaign to win the bride he needed, but it was a fortuitous one. With the O'Riley clan as his informants, Lady Alexandra Henning's life would henceforth be an open book . . . and he had always been an avid reader.

Chapter Two

Alexandra was normally an early riser, but she could easily have stayed in bed until noon the day after Lady Rutherford's ball. She'd slept fitfully, when she'd slept at all. The night had been unusually warm and sultry for the first week of March—and it hadn't helped matters that a tawny, golden-eyed wolf had prowled her restless dreams.

With the first sign of morning light, she pulled her quilt over her head and prayed for rain—to no avail. The clock on her fireplace mantel had just struck the hour of eight when Jamie pounded on her chamber door, declaring the sun was out and Fergus and he were ready and waiting for their morning walk.

Had her tormenter been anyone else, she would have flatly refused to leave her bed. But she couldn't bring herself to disappoint Jamie. She loved her frail young brother with all her heart—doubly so since she had come so close to losing him to lung fever during the past winter.

Since his serious illness, these morning walks were the only times he was allowed outdoors, and then only because her mother was still abed and the servants sworn to secrecy. If the viscountess had her way, the poor boy would still be an invalid confined to his sickroom.

Bleary-eyed and nursing a beastly headache, Alexandra crawled from her bed, made the necessary ablutions, and steeled herself to face the day ahead. Promptly at the hour of nine, Jamie and she set out for Hyde Park with only the Scotch terrier, Fergus, accompanying them. Since she was already disobedient, she had made yet another decision and dispensed with the services of Bridget, her gossipy abigail, on these morning excursions.

She gave a brief thought to her mother's warning to always have a footman attend her, but quickly discarded the idea. She treasured this time alone with Jamie. The studious youngster was wise beyond his years and far better company than most of the Corinthians who formed her court of admirers.

Furthermore, she felt certain she would be in no danger from the infamous Earl of Stratham at such an early hour. One of her more daring admirers had given her a rather lurid description of the dens of iniquity such libertines frequented. The earl was undoubtedly, at that very moment, sleeping off the effects of his night's debauchery.

A vision of his flame-colored hair against a white pillow, his long, lean body stretched out on a feather bed, flashed before her eyes, and a flush of embarrassment flooded her cheeks at such a decadent turn of mind. She shuddered, wondering if the disturbing fellow's very gaze had somehow contaminated her.

"Didn't I tell you it was a beautiful morning?" Jamie crowed as they entered the gates of the park. Lifting his pale young face to the cloudless sky, he drank in the warm spring sunshine like a newly budded flower. Alexandra's heart gladdened, and she instantly thrust all thought of the earl from her, determined he should not spoil this precious time she shared with her brother.

As usual, they had the park much to themselves. Few of the *ton* rose from their beds before noon. Fewer yet came to the park before the fashionable hour of five o'clock to see and be seen. Except for an occasional nanny and her young charges, the beautiful expanse of man-made wilderness might have been created solely for Jamie's and her enjoyment.

Once they reached their favorite spot by the Serpentine, she released the excited terrier from his leash to chase the squirrels that scrambled up nearby trees. Then settling herself on a bench at the base of a giant oak, she removed her bonnet, leaned back against the broad trunk, and, with drowsy contentment, watched Jamie feed the flock of ducks that awaited his appearance each morning.

She had no recollection of falling asleep, but she realized she must have. For why else would Jamie be urging her to "Wake up, sleepy-head"?

The sound of rich, melodic laughter crept into her consciousness, along with the rumble of a male voice. "Let your sister sleep, lad. She looks so peaceful."

Jamie had somebody with him. Probably one of her admirers who had happened upon them while she slept. *How humili-*

ating! Alexandra stayed perfectly still, wondering how to make whoever it was aware she was awake without embarrassing herself even further.

"Alex is only ever peaceful when she's asleep. Most of the time she's stirring things up something fierce," Jamie said, and she heard him chuckle. Her brother must know this person very well. He was always shy, almost tongue-tied, around strangers.

"A temperamental female, is she?"

Alexandra bristled. How dare this jackanapes, whoever he might be, leap to such a conclusion.

"Not really. She's actually a good sort, for a girl. I think I'd like her even if she wasn't my sister. She just has very strong opinions . . . about everything."

Without further ado, Alexandra opened her eyes before her brother told the inquisitive fellow more of her secrets. The first thing she saw was a pair of spindly, trouser-clad legs she knew to be Jamie's. Beside them were two long, powerful-looking legs encased in buckskins. She took another look, and her breath caught in her throat. No man she knew filled a pair of buckskins in such a manner.

She sat up straighter, raised her head, and found herself staring into the same wicked, gold-flecked eyes that had turned her into a stumbling idiot some twelve hours earlier. "You!" she gasped before she could stop herself, and quickly scrambled to her feet.

Jamie grinned happily. "I say, Alex, I'd no idea you knew my friend, Mr. Campbell."

"Your friend?" Alexandra choked out past lips rigid with shock.

"Well, my new friend then. Mr. Campbell came to feed the ducks, but he forgot his bag of bread so I shared mine." Jamie's voice vibrated with excitement. "We've had the grandest talk while you slept. You wouldn't believe the wondrous things he's done—the wondrous places he's seen. And he's invited us to Gunter's for strawberry ices because he likes them every bit as much as I do."

"Mr. Campbell?" Alexandra echoed chillingly. "I believe it would be more appropriate to address the Earl of Stratham as my lord."

Jamie stared at his new friend, his face bleak. "Is it true? Are you someone other than you said you were?"

"I didn't purposely mislead you, lad," Stratham answered, "and I am flattered that your sister knows who I am, since we have never been introduced."

Alexandra flushed hotly, wishing the cheeky fellow to perdition.

"The truth of it is," the earl continued, "I have been Liam Campbell all my life and the Earl of Stratham but four months. I've not yet grown accustomed to my change of status."

"I knew it was something like that. I knew you wouldn't lie to me." The boy's relief was painful to behold. He had obviously developed an instant hero worship for his "new friend."

Alexandra felt consumed with rage that the insensitive clod would use a gullible young boy to promote his ugly seduction scheme. For she was certain now it was seduction he had in mind. Her mother had warned her about the clever ploys unscrupulous rakes used to trap innocent young women, and this "accidental" meeting in the park simply did not fly as a coincidence.

Cautiously, she backed a step or two away from her would-be seducer and, once out from under the shady tree, realized the sun was directly overhead. She must have slept a good two hours or more, and Jamie and she would be in the suds for certain unless they made it back to the town house before their mother was up and about.

"Where is Fergus?" she asked, searching the nearby area for a ball of brindled black fur. The animal was nowhere to be seen. "Find your dog, Jamie. We must return home at once," she ordered more sharply than she intended.

"But what about Gunter's?"

"Now, Jamie, if you please." Sick at heart, she watched the boy's narrow shoulders slump dejectedly as he disappeared beyond a massive clump of hawthorne.

Instantly, she wheeled around to face the earl, too angry to be frightened at finding herself alone with him. "What is it you want of me, my lord?"

"Want?" He was innocence personified. "At the moment, I need nothing more than to have you direct me to this Gunter's pastry shop of which your brother speaks so highly," he said in refined, but oddly accented English. "From the boy's description of his daily activities, I deduced he is allowed few treats. I thought to give him one."

"Save your stories for someone gullible enough to believe them. I am appalled that you would make my innocent young brother a pawn in this silly game you are playing," Alexandra said stiffly. "For your information, my parents have good reason to restrict Jamie's activities. He has been very ill."

Anger momentarily darkened the earl's eyes. "I was not aware that eating a strawberry ice could be life-threatening."

Alexandra could see the boorish fellow was being intentionally dense. She cast him a fulminating look meant to put him in his place. "Jamie's health is not the only reason I must decline your invitation, my lord. Surely even you can see my reputation would be in shreds should I be seen in public with a man of your ilk."

"Ah! You have been listening to scurrilous gossip about me. What is being said? Am I accused of murder?"

"Don't be ridiculous."

"Then I suppose it is that old saw about my being baseborn." He shrugged. "Well, it is true. But it seems a bit unfair to judge me for something over which I had no control."

Much as she hated to admit it, there was some truth in what he said. Nor could she, in good conscience, fault him for being born with such outrageous hair or with eyes that seemed to pierce her very soul. She gritted her teeth, at a loss for words until she was struck by a sudden thought. "You were in control of your actions last evening," she declared triumphantly.

He looked genuinely perplexed. "What did I do last evening that was so reprehensible?"

"You know very well. You made me the subject of gossip—something I do not appreciate in the least."

"I did? How so?"

"You . . . you looked at me the entire time you were at Lady Rutherford's ball."

"By George, I did. My humble apologies, ma'am. I fear we are a tad behind in the West Country. Looking at a beautiful woman has not yet been declared a hanging offense in Exmoor." He grinned. "Now if I were to steal a kiss, that might be another matter."

Alexandra's heart pounded wildly at the very thought of his lips touching hers. How dare he suggest such an outrageous thing! She gave an angry toss of her head. "Your bizarre humor escapes me, my lord, and your company sorely offends me. Be good enough to maintain your distance in the future."

Out of the corner of her eye, she saw Jamie approaching with the terrier puppy in his arms. "And stay away from my brother, as well."

Fergus usually growled at strangers. To her amazement, he leapt from Jamie's arms and barking joyfully, slobbered all over the earl's boots and made a frantic effort to crawl up his leg. It was obvious Stratham had the same mesmerizing effect on the dog as he did on her brother.

"Down, Fergus," Jamie demanded, dragging the love-struck animal from the earl's boot. "I don't know what has gotten into him, my lord. He is not acting at all himself."

"I suspect he recognizes me as a fellow Scotsman," Stratham said, giving the dog a pat on the head. "My mother was a member of Clan Campbell."

"Maybe so, my lord," Jamie said with a chuckle. He straightened up, the squirming animal clasped to his chest. "Please, Alex, say we may go to Gunter's with his lordship. It has been such a long time since I've done anything that was fun."

"I'm afraid not," Alexandra said, though it broke her heart to disappoint him. "We have been away from home much too long already. I don't have to tell you what serious trouble we shall both be in if Mama learns of your daily trips to the park.

"Furthermore, *you* have had a proper upbringing," she added, steadfastly ignoring the ill-mannered earl. "And you are old enough to know it would not be at all the thing for an unmarried lady to accept such an invitation from a strange man."

Jamie scowled. "Gadzooks, Alex, the earl is not half as strange as that silly poet you think so wonderful." Securing the dog's leash, he turned the excited animal over to Alexandra. "You can see Fergus likes his lordship, and everyone knows dogs are a lot smarter about people than people are. Fergus always tries to bite Sir Randolph."

"I think you must do as your sister says, my lad." Stratham smiled. "We shall have plenty of opportunities to visit Gunter's, providing she continues to bring you to the park each morning. For I often walk here at this time of day." His voice was solemn, but the wicked twinkle in his eyes told Alexandra he was enjoying himself immensely at her expense.

The blasted libertine could see Jamie was her weak spot. With that in mind, he had outmaneuvered her as neatly as if she were a featherbrained young miss fresh from the schoolroom.

Alexandra was not accustomed to being outsmarted and found the experience extremely unpleasant. "Come, Jamie, it is time to go home," she snapped, and dragging a protesting Fergus behind her, quit the company of the annoying earl without so much as a nod of her head.

With grudging admiration, Liam watched Lady Alexandra flounce off in a huff, hips swinging and nose in the air. She flounced very prettily to his way of thinking. He had always been a fool for women with fiery tempers. He'd found they were usually as passionate in their lovemaking as they were in their convictions. But then he had to admit his experience was limited to women of the lower classes. Who could tell if the equation held true for aristocrats as well?

Deep in thought, he wandered back to the edge of the Serpentine, removed the packet of meat he'd thought to put in his pocket when O'Riley mentioned Jamie's dog, and tossed it into the water. One thing was certain—this perfect English rose he must take to wife had a mind of her own, and a mouth to go with it. Life with her would be anything but peaceful.

Still, to his surprise, he found himself envying her brother the affection she lavished on him. His half sister, Fiona, and he had never been particularly close, probably because they had nothing in common except the unscrupulous rogue who had sired them both. In truth, though he'd known many women, Liam had always been aware that only one had ever truly cared about him, and he had buried her in a pauper's grave a month before his twelfth birthday.

A memory of his mother running her fingers through his hair as Lady Alexandra had run hers through Jamie's rose to haunt him, and pain, long buried, sliced through his heart. He wondered if the lovely aristocrat would ever feel inclined to touch him with such tenderness.

And who was this Sir Randolph young Jamie had claimed she thought so wonderful? A poet, for God's sake. Liam groaned. If the only way he could win her heart was by wooing her with sonnets, he could forget about inspiring any passion in his bride-to-be.

He assumed this poet would be Alexandra's escort to the amateur musicale and poetry reading to which O'Riley's cousin had managed to steal an invitation. It sounded exactly like the dreary sort of thing such a fellow would take in. Liam groaned at the thought of subjecting himself to such torture. He couldn't believe the tiresome ways in which the members of the *ton* entertained themselves.

For that matter, he had even more trouble believing the lengths he was willing to go in his courting of the highborn woman whom fate had thrust into his life. But then he hadn't expected to be attracted to her—and attracted he was, in spite of himself. The hidebound little spitfire reminded him of a moorland butterfly still encased in its cocoon. One knew instinctively it would be a glorious thing to behold once it broke free.

It went against his grain to trap her into marrying him. He supposed it was a matter of pride. He had never failed to win any woman he wanted once he set his mind to it. Why should Lady Alexandra be any different?

But thanks to his frittering the winter away enjoying his newfound wealth, time was running out. He could devote only so many weeks to winning her, and he would tolerate no rivals. He would simply have to take this poet's measure, then determine how best to discourage the troublesome fellow's pursuit of the lady who was destined to be the next Countess of Stratham.

Alexandra raised her fan to cover the yawn she could no longer stifle. There was, in her opinion, nothing more boring than an amateur musicale and poetry reading. If it were not that the second half of the program was devoted to Sir Randolph's recitation of one of his epic poems, she would never have talked Elsie's mama into chaperoning Elsie and her at tonight's affair.

She'd attended any number of these dismal soirees in support of Sir Randolph during the six months she'd known him, for poetry was his abiding passion. To hear him tell it, the highlight of his life had been the day he'd met William Wordsworth on a street in the town of Hawkshead and received a tip of the great man's hat.

She yawned again, wondering if the soprano soloist would ever cease her caterwauling. Apparently the rest of the audience wondered the same thing. A good many of the gentlemen and a few of the ladies, including Elsie's mama, had already disappeared into the card room. If Rowena Humphrey hit one more sour note, there would be no one left to hear Sir Randolph read his verses.

Lowering her fan, Alexandra glanced nervously around the circle of chairs to see who was left. This recital was so important to dear Randy, she couldn't bear the thought of his reading to an empty room.

Elsie sat four chairs away from her. "Look who's here," she mouthed, making frantic signals toward the end of the row. Alexandra leaned forward to get a better look and found herself staring into a pair of all too familiar gold-flecked eyes. Abruptly, she straightened up and raised her fan to cover her burning face. What was *he* doing here? As if she didn't know. The brazen fellow was stalking her like the wolf he resembled might stalk its prey.

And despite all she'd said to him this morning, he was staring at her with the same unwavering intensity he'd employed at the ball. He'd even had the gall to grin at her in that brief moment when their eyes met.

But how had he known she would be here? For that matter, how had he known she would be at the park earlier? Beset by a bewildering combination of anger and fascination, she lowered her fan again and took another peek.

Good heavens, the man wasn't even decently dressed. There was not a smidgeon of starch in his shirt points and instead of a proper cravat, he had something that looked very much like a silk scarf knotted loosely around his deeply tanned throat. Considering his state of undress, it was a wonder he hadn't been asked to leave. As it was, every eye in the room seemed riveted on him—with the exception of those riveted on her.

She could feel a fine film of nervous perspiration forming on her forehead. Horrified, she fanned herself briskly. How many times had her mother told her a lady never perspired in public.

Her mother! She could imagine what Mama would say if she knew the earl had attended the musicale. Thank heavens the viscountess had stayed at home with the megrims.

"I say, Alexandra, could you be a trifle less vigorous with that fan. You're causing a veritable hurricane." Sir Randolph regarded her with limpid brown eyes. "My throat, you know. Must be in top form for my reading."

Alexandra instantly stopped waving her fan and fixed her gaze on the singer, aware that Sir Randolph was frowning thoughtfully. "That outlandish-looking red-haired fellow at the end of the row is staring at you," he whispered in her ear. "Do you know him?"

"No," Alexandra lied. "But I believe I heard someone say he's the Earl of Stratham."

"An earl who looks like a pirate? How unique. I may make him the subject of my next epic poem." Sir Randolph's pale, aesthetic face assumed the dreamy expression Alexandra had come to think of as his "creative look." She settled back in her chair, knowing he would say no more while the muse was on him.

Moments later, Rowena Humphrey finally came to the end of her recital and took her bows to a smattering of applause by the few tenacious souls left in the audience. The earl didn't bother to clap his hands. He simply rose from his chair and disappeared through the nearest door.

Alexandra breathed a sigh of relief. If he followed the pattern he'd established at the ball, he would not return this evening. But even though he was out of sight, her heart still thumped heavily against her ribs.

Her woman's intuition warned her she had not seen the last of the Earl of Stratham. Like his father before him, he was a dangerous man with a frightening obsession and she must do everything in her power to protect herself.

"I must speak with you . . . privately," she said, clutching Sir Randolph's arm and literally dragging him from his chair.

"Now? This very minute?" He frowned. "You know how I hate to be disturbed when I am composing my verse."

"Now!" Without further ado, Alexandra hustled him out the door and down the hall until she found what looked like an empty salon. A single candle on a pie-shaped table near the entry was the only light in the deeply shadowed room.

"When are you going to speak to my father?" she asked, getting straight to the point.

"Why I . . . that is . . . It was my understanding that we would make our announcement at the end of the season."

"I've changed my mind. We need not marry right away. But

for my own protection, I want it known I am a betrothed woman." Alexandra crossed her fingers behind her back. "I am being besieged by men determined to press their suits and I find it most annoying."

"Good heavens, I should think you would." Sir Randolph's candle-lit eyes reflected his horror. "It pains me to say such a thing about my own sex, but the truth is most men are beasts at heart."

"So I've recently discovered. But not you, dear Randy, which is why I look forward to spending the rest of my life as your wife."

"Thank you, my dear. I am deeply touched, and be assured I will speak with your father first thing tomorrow morning." He hesitated. "You do think he will agree to increase your dowry sufficiently to see us through until my uncle goes to his final reward?"

"I am certain of it. Papa will never miss the money, and he loves me dearly. He will do anything to ensure my happiness. If any objections are raised to our union, they will come from my mother. But it is Papa who will make the final decision."

Alexandra smiled triumphantly at her soon-to-be betrothed. Once again she had proved that by knowing exactly what she wanted and exactly how to go about getting it, she could avoid the ugly pitfalls that beset most people—and if ever she'd seen a pitfall, the Earl of Stratham was surely it. Every time she closed her eyes, she saw his provocative mouth and remembered what he had threatened to do with it.

"Kiss me, Randy," she said, stepping closer and slipping her arms around his neck. "I have never been kissed. A number of men have tried, but I am my mother's daughter and have never believed in indulging in casual intimacy. Now I suddenly find I am curious about this business of kissing."

Sir Randolph fell back as if scalded by her touch. "Control yourself, my dear. I thought we agreed we were above such animalistic behavior—and you have quite ruined my cravat."

Alexandra's face burned with humiliation. She couldn't imagine what had gotten into her, but whatever it was, she felt certain she could lay the blame at the earl's feet. "Forgive me," she murmured. "I've had a trying day and I am not myself." So saying, she hurried from the room before she made an even greater cake of herself.

Deep in the shadows from where he'd watched the pitiful little scene, Liam cursed the pompous poet for the heartless wretch he'd proved to be. Unless he was mistaken, Lady Alexandra had been crying when she'd rushed past him—though why any woman would cry over such a ridiculous popinjay was beyond him.

Any qualms he'd had about destroying her romance were laid to rest. He could do the foolish woman no greater favor than to dispatch the frippery fellow to the farthest ends of the earth.

Stepping forward, he blocked the doorway before Sir Randolph could leave the room. "What in heaven's name . . . who are you, sir, and what business have you with me?" The smaller man's voice trembled noticeably, and Liam smiled to himself. This was going to be even easier than he'd thought.

With one hand, he grasped Sir Randolph by his precious cravat and lifted him a foot off the floor. "I've a piece of advice for you concerning the lady to whom you are not about to become betrothed," he growled. "I strongly suggest you take it."

Chapter Three

Sir Randolph's note arrived the next morning while Alexandra and Jamie were eating breakfast. Wary as she was of its contents, she welcomed the interruption, since she was having no luck whatsoever convincing Jamie she was serious about discontinuing their daily walks in Hyde Park.

The boy was desperate to see his hero again—almost as desperate as she was to avoid the same man. After her disturbing encounter with the Earl of Stratham beside the Serpentine, she had vowed to never again take the risk of finding herself alone with him. The shock of seeing him at the musicale had only reinforced that vow.

But how could she explain to Jamie that the man he idolized was a dangerous rake who was turning her life into a nightmare? Despite all the people surrounding her at the musicale, she had felt so unnerved by the earl's presence she had made a complete fool of herself with Sir Randolph. Her cheeks flamed just thinking of how she'd demanded he make his offer to her father, how she'd begged him to kiss her—how horrified she'd been when her frazzled hostess had announced there would be no poetry reading that evening because Sir Randolph had been taken ill.

Alexandra had felt ill herself—from humiliation. She'd had no doubt whatsoever that her bold attack on the sensitive poet was what had brought on his sudden malaise—and a serious malaise it must have been to cause him to miss an opportunity to read to an audience.

With a chilling premonition of disaster, she lifted the note from the footman's tray, broke the seal and read:

> My dear Lady Alexandra,
>
> After serious consideration, I have come to the conclusion that you and I are not as well suited as we first appeared

Nadine Miller

to be. I am, therefore, retiring to the Lake District to pursue my muse in the same inspiring environ as my friend and fellow-poet, William Wordsworth.

Please be assured I shall always remember you with respect and admiration.

> Your devoted servant,
> Randolph Miles Twickingham

Alexandra took a deep breath, read the note a second time, then crumpled it into a tight little ball, furious at Sir Randolph and even more furious at herself for letting the Earl of Stratham affect her so strongly she'd acted like the veriest hoyden.

She should have realized a man with Sir Randolph's aesthetic tastes would be horrified by her demands that he kiss her. But fleeing London simply because she'd asked him to press his lips to hers seemed a rather drastic reaction, even for a poet. Were all men either lust-driven libertines or emotional nincompoops? If so she would gladly embrace a life of dignified spinsterhood.

"The note is from that silly poet, isn't it? It smells like that dreadful cologne he wears." Jamie's voice shocked Alexandra to attention. She had forgotten he still sat opposite her.

"I wager you'll never catch the earl reeking of such flowery stuff," Jamie added somewhat petulantly.

"Don't extol the virtues of the Earl of Stratham to me," she snapped. "I am in no mood to hear them—nor for that matter, the virtues of any man. I despise the entire gender."

Without further ado, she rose from her chair and quit the morning room, aware her young brother stared after her with wide, startled eyes.

For the first time in her privileged young life, she had suffered a serious blow to her pride, and she needed a moment alone in her bedchamber to lick her wounds and regain her sense of balance.

With mindless preoccupation, she dropped Sir Randolph's note into the fireplace and watched the draft draw the charred fragments up the chimney. It occurred to her she should be grief-stricken over the loss of the *parti* she had convinced herself was her perfect mate. Instead, she felt nothing but anger and disgust toward a man too cowardly to end their "understanding" in person.

But whatever would she say when people asked about his sudden departure? For ask they would. She had made no effort to hide her preference for the handsome poet, and most of her other admirers had given up long ago and offered for someone else. The cats of the *ton* would be quick to sink their claws into her if they suspected she had been jilted.

The prospect was too mortifying to contemplate. She would simply have to develop a malady of some sort and stay out of the public eye until some other gossip-worthy happening caused the speculation about Sir Randolph and her to die down. If this season ran true to form, she wouldn't have long to wait.

She wondered how her parents would greet the news that she had decided to remain a single lady all her life. Chances were Papa would understand and support her; he always did. But Mama would probably be her usual difficult self. Though bitterly unhappy in her own marriage, the viscountess was a stickler about fulfilling one's obligations as a member of the aristocracy—and a woman's chief obligation was to marry and produce an heir to carry on her husband's title.

Grimly, Alexandra faced the realization that she had some difficult days ahead of her. The one consolation in the miserable bumblebroth was that she would never again have to suffer through an amateur musicale and poetry reading—nor any of the other deadly boring events Elsie and she had been forced to attend in the past two years in search of husbands.

With that cheerful bit of reasoning, she returned to the sunny morning room, ate a hearty breakfast and launched herself into a life of dedicated spinsterhood with the same enthusiasm she'd once devoted to promoting Sir Randolph's career as a poet.

A fortnight had passed since the fateful musicale, and Liam was beginning to think he had been a bit premature in congratulating himself on dispatching Lady Alexandra's suitor so easily. He hadn't expected the loss of a silly twit like Sir Randolph to turn her into a recluse.

But if O'Riley's cousin was to be believed, she'd not only abandoned her daily walks with her brother, but her social life as well since the poet disappeared. She had even gone so far as to instruct her family butler to turn away all her callers with the excuse that she was too ill to see them. Liam's frustration knew no bounds. How could he court the silly woman if he never saw her?

It helped a little that Jamie Henning, accompanied by O'Riley's cousin, had begun sneaking away to Hyde Park each morning at the very hour Liam took his daily constitutional. The boy was good company, and seemed more than happy to talk about his sister.

"There's nothing wrong with Alex except she's a girl," Jamie said when Liam asked why the two of them no longer walked together. "She's just pretending to be sick because she and Sir Randolph quarreled and people will ask her about him if she goes to her usual parties. The only person she'll see is her friend, Elsie Trumbold. I, for one, am happy Sir Randolph's not calling on her every day to recite his silly poetry. But girls are funny about things like that."

Liam was as happy as Jamie about the demise of Alexandra's romance, but his conscience pricked him nevertheless. It hadn't occurred to him that the disappearance of the poet would put her in an embarrassing position with her friends.

Another time Jamie admitted that his sister was boring him to flinders since she'd decided to remain a spinster all her life— a decision that did not suit Liam in the least. "When she isn't practicing the pianoforte, she's reading one of her silly gothic novels or making me sit while she paints my picture," Jamie complained. "And it is all so silly because Mama will never allow it. She says it is every woman's duty to marry. I'm awfully glad I'm not a girl."

But the day finally came when Jamie reported that his sister was about to go out in public again. "Mama says she has to go to the theater tonight and even Alexandra knows there is no use arguing with Mama once her mind is made up."

O'Riley had much the same news when Liam arrived back at the duke's town house. "Me cousin just popped in to say the Marquess of Nettleford will be squiring your lady and her mam to the theater this very night to see that fellow Kean in a play called *The Merchant of Venice*," O'Riley announced the minute Liam arrived home.

Liam didn't like the sound of that. Poets rarely had a feather to fly with, but he suspected a marquess might have the necessary blunt to stave off the bailiffs yapping at Viscount Hardin's heels.

He decided he might have to forget about courting the lady. Unless he made her father an offer of an exceptionally generous marriage settlement, and made it very soon, he risked the chance that someone else might steal his thunder. Then he would be forced to resort to the tactics he'd heard the old earl had employed. The idea of starting out his married life by kidnapping his bride did not sound the least bit appealing.

"Tell the footmen to prepare my bath, for I'll be off to the theater myself," Liam ordered.

O'Riley grinned. "So I figured, milord, and since I've noticed you're not so squeamish about a wash as most Englishmen, I've already had the lads set up the tub in your dressing room."

"That, I take it, is another of your backhanded compliments," Liam said, shrugging out of his jacket and shirt. "You never miss a chance to ridicule the English."

"'Tis not ridicule, milord, but plain fact. The first thing an Irishman learns when he crosses the sea is 'tis well to stay upwind of most Englishmen—especially Londoners."

Liam chuckled. "Now that I think of it, I believe I did catch a whiff of something other than horse the last time I visited Tattersalls."

"Aye. 'Tis of particular notice to me countrymen. For no matter how empty an Irishman's belly might be, he has himself a wash each morning. 'Tis a matter of pride, and Lord knows we've little else to be proud of these days."

O'Riley crossed to the armoire and withdrew a claret-colored jacket and silver-gray trousers before he followed Liam to where the tub had been set up. "Except," he continued with a mischievous grin, "for bragging 'twere a couple of Irishmen who pulled England's fat from the fire when the Corsican went on the rampage. And two finer sons of Erin never lived than General Wellington and Lord Castlereagh."

"I'll not argue with you there," Liam said, scowling at the hated garments draped over his valet's arm. "But what are you up to now, you Irish imp? I've no objection to bathing; it's a habit I learned at my mother's knee. But I do object to being trussed up in one of Mr. Weston's tortuous creations merely to watch a play. Who'll notice me with a play going on?"

"Lady Alexandra, if you're after looking like the fine man-about-town you should be, milord. But if you're that set on playin' the country bumpkin, I'll be happy to brush off that sorry-looking jacket and buckskins you've been wearing all this day."

Liam leveled a look at his valet that should have singed the cheeky fellow's ginger eyebrows. "I'll have you know that sturdy old nankeen is my favorite jacket. It has seen me through many a trip across the English Channel in my former profession."

"Me point exactly, milord. 'Tis time you gave the poor thing a decent burial."

Liam knew when he was beaten. Without further argument, he divested himself of boots and trousers and stepped into the steaming tub. From the resolute look on O'Riley's freckled face, he could see the cocky Irishman was determined to turn his employer into a nobleman worthy of his title. Another matter of Irish pride, he supposed. His new valet was the kind of fellow who'd want bragging rights over his many cousins.

With a groan, he sank deeper into the hot, soapy water. Between O'Riley's prodding and Lady Alexandra's sharp tongue, he suspected he'd have earned every blasted farthing of his inheritance by the time he got his bride to the altar.

Alexandra couldn't imagine what had possessed her mother to accept the Marquess of Nettleford's invitation to accompany him to the theater season's opening performance. Not even the great Edmund Kean was entertaining enough to make spending an evening with the insufferable old lecher worthwhile. The first act curtain had not yet risen, and he had already managed to pinch her bottom, run his hand up and down her thigh and grasp her left knee in a clawlike grip she felt certain would leave it bruised for days to come.

Frantically, she signaled her mother for help. But the usually observant viscountess merely smiled benignly, seemingly unaware of her distress. Left to defend herself as best she could, Alexandra muttered, "Keep your hands off me, my lord," and gave his wandering fingers a swat that broke the spine of her favorite silk fan.

"Prickly little chit, ain't ye." The marquess's cackle sent shivers coursing her spine. "Always did like a woman with spirit."

As if to prove his point, he once again grasped her knee.

This time Alexandra managed to divert him by stomping on his foot. But the marquess was nothing if not determined. A moment later she felt his spiderlike fingers creep up her ribs to fondle her breast.

"How dare you take such liberties with my person," she cried, and promptly gave him a shove that sent him tumbling off his chair onto the floor, a fragment of lace trim still clutched in his hand.

She had had enough. Rising to her feet, she wrapped her shawl around her shoulders. "I want to go home," she announced, close to tears.

"Sit down," her mother hissed. "You are drawing attention to yourself—something a lady must never do."

"*I* am drawing attention?" Alexandra stared at her mother in utter disbelief. "Thanks to the disgusting behavior of the miserable little worm who's our host, I feel certain every eye in the theater has been trained on me since the moment I entered this box."

"Sit down," the viscountess repeated. "We will discuss this later."

"I will not sit down, Mama, and nothing you can say will induce me to do so." Alexandra raised her chin defiantly and stared straight ahead . . . into a pair of angry, gold-flecked eyes watching her from a box directly opposite the one in which she stood—a box she knew belonged to the Duke of Bellmont. With a horrified gasp, she sat down. Having the barbarian earl witness the indignity she had just suffered made it all the more humiliating.

Gingerly, the marquess picked himself up and brushed himself off. "Hell and damnation, madam, what is wrong with this chit of yours?" he demanded. "I was given to understand she would welcome my suit."

"She is young and innocent, my lord, and I fear a bit overwhelmed by the attentions of a man of the world, such as yourself," the viscountess simpered. "Perhaps if you would be so kind as to fetch us some lemonade."

"Why the devil should I. I'm not your servant."

"It was merely a suggestion, my lord. I thought to have a moment alone with my daughter to discuss . . . her future."

"A discussion long past due, if you ask me," the marquess grumbled. "But very well, madam, I'll see to your demmed lemonade." His beady eyes raked Alexandra with an insulting stare. "You'd best be a lot more friendly when I return, missy, if you hope to snag me. You're not the only filly in this season's auction, you know."

Alexandra turned to her mother the moment their host disappeared through the curtain at the back of the box. "Did you hear what that dreadful old man just said? However could he have gained the impression I would have any interest in 'snagging' him?"

"He is an incredibly wealthy man and as such is considered a great catch as a husband."

"By whom? No decent woman would have anything to do with him."

"Calm yourself, Alexandra. I am well aware the marquess can be a trifle annoying. But you must remember—"

"Annoying does not begin to describe him. He is the most repulsive creature I have ever encountered." Alexandra shuddered. "He touched me in insufferable ways . . . and he smells positively rank. I doubt he ever bathes."

"So he is somewhat eccentric. The very rich often are. But I assure you he is harmless." The viscountess's voice dropped to a whisper. "I do not mean to shock you, dear girl, but I think you should know you have nothing to fear if you bring the marquess up to scratch. I have it on good authority the old fool is quite incapable of claiming his marital rights."

"Mama! You cannot seriously think I would consider marrying the horrid man!" But Alexandra could see from the look on her mother's face, that was exactly what the viscountess had in mind.

Never! she vowed to herself, her stomach roiling at the very thought. She pressed her fingers to her lips, afraid she might cast up her accounts, and instinctively glanced toward the box in which the earl had been sitting. He was no longer there, but the rest of the boxes were filled with elegantly dressed theatergoers, and as far as she could tell, all of them had their opera glasses trained on her. She wondered if they thought she was allowing Nettleford's insulting attention because she was attempting to "snag" him?

Did the earl think the same thing? Was that why he'd left before the play began? Had the tawdry scene he'd witnessed so disgusted him he'd lost interest in seducing her? She supposed even rakes and barbarians had their standards. Strangely enough the thought that the Earl of Stratham might find her disgusting was an even greater blow to her pride than the loss of Sir Randolph as a *parti*.

She'd barely had time to ponder the irrationality of that line of thinking when the earl returned to his seat in the Duke of Bellmont's box. Alexandra raised her opera glasses and trained them on his face. Gone was the angry scowl he'd worn earlier and in its place a self-satisfied smile that made her wonder what he could have done in the short time he'd disappeared to make him look like a cat that had just feasted on a particularly tasty mouse.

The rustling of the curtain behind her alerted her that someone had entered the box. She stiffened. But it was not the marquess—merely one of the serving boys with a tray on which sat two glasses of lemonade.

"His lordship ordered these afore 'e 'ad 'is accident," the sober-faced lad announced, setting the tray on the small table designed to hold such refreshments.

"Accident? What accident? Good heavens, is he badly hurt?" The viscountess leapt to her feet. "We must go to him, Alexandra."

"I doubt 'e would want that, milady, considerin' what's ailin' 'im. Best you leave 'im be."

"How dare you speak to me with such familiarity," the viscountess fumed. "I've a mind to see you discharged, you insolent creature."

"Beggin' yer pardon, milady. I meant no disrespect. I were just lookin' to keep you from embarrassin' yerself."

"I am quite capable of making that judgment without advice from such as you," the viscountess snapped.

Alexandra touched her mother's arm. "Please, Mama, the boy meant no harm."

"Very well. I shall overlook it this time, but make certain you never address your betters in such a manner again. Now tell me, young man, exactly where is the marquess?"

"I don't rightly know, milady. Last I seen 'im, one of the other lads was cleanin' 'im up, so to speak. But I 'eard 'im order 'is carriage brought round to the back of the theater."

The viscountess gave a sigh of relief. "Well, he must not be too badly injured then."

"No milady, more scared-like, I'd say, from the looks of 'is face."

"The marquess left the theater because he was frightened? But why? What could have occasioned such fear?"

"I don't rightly know, milady." The serving boy squirmed with obvious embarrassment. "But it must've been somethin' mighty fierce, else why would he 'ave done what I seen 'im do?"

"You are making no sense whatsoever," the viscountess complained. Grasping the boy's thin shoulders, she shook him till his teeth rattled. "Tell me this instant, exactly what was it you saw?"

"He . . . he . . ." A flush stained the boy's thin face and he stared beseechingly at Alexandra. "Does I 'ave to tell 'er?"

"I'm afraid so," Alexandra said softly. "But if you do, my mother will let you go about your work with no more trouble. Won't you, Mama?"

"Oh, I suppose so." Grudgingly, the viscountess released her grip on the lad's shoulders. "Now, spit it out, you stupid boy. What did the Marquess of Nettleford do?"

"I never seen who scared 'im, so there's no use askin' me that. All I know is when I come back with the lemonade, the old toff were standin' right where I'd left 'im, blubberin' like a babe and . . . and—"

"Yes, yes. Go on. Out with it, you idiot," the viscountess demanded.

The serving boy hung his head. "And pissin' 'is pants."

"Now that I think about it, I feel certain the mysterious person who terrorized the Marquess of Nettleford had to have been the Earl of Stratham," Alexandra declared when Elsie and she discussed the puzzling incident the next afternoon over a cup of tea. "It had to be more than mere coincidence that he disappeared from the duke's box at the exact moment the marquess was accosted—just as it has been more than mere coincidence that he managed to show up at every social event I've attended since the Rutherford ball. The scoundrel must have paid one of our servants to keep him informed of my every move."

"Are you certain it's a servant?" Elsie asked. "My brother, Thomas, rides each morning in Hyde Park, and more than once he has seen Jamie and the earl walking together."

Alexandra choked on her tea. "Good heavens. Is Thomas sure of what he saw?"

"Well, he certainly knows Jamie, and there is no mistaking the red-haired earl, is there?" Elsie sighed. "It is history repeating itself. The earl is pursuing you just as his father pursued your mother." She sighed again. "I've never heard anything so romantic."

"Romantic?" Alexandra shivered. "The very thought makes my blood run cold. Not only is the brazen fellow using my gullible young brother to further his evil plans, he seems bent on driving away any man who shows me the least attention. One of the maids came back from market this morning with the news that the marquess had fled London directly from the theater, without so much as stopping at his town house to pick up his valet. The silly old fool didn't even take time to arrange transportation for Mama and me. We were left to find our own way home. Had some kindly gentleman not provided us with a carriage, we should have had to hail a hackney cab like common cits."

"What kindly gentleman?" Elsie asked, pouring herself another cup of tea and selecting a slice of currant cake from the tea tray.

"I have no idea. Some friend of Papa's I suppose. In truth, what with the marquess disappearing and Mama having an attack of the vapors, I was too distracted to think to ask the coachman who his employer might be." She pressed her fingers to her lips and stared wide-eyed at her friend. "Good heavens, you don't suppose—"

"It was the earl," Elsie said with absolute certainty. "He was watching out for the woman he adores, as any gentleman would. I don't care what you say; it really is terribly roman—"

"I swear, if you say that word one more time, Elsie Trumbold, I will terminate our friendship here and now." Just thinking about the wicked earl "watching out for her" raised the hair up the back of Alexandra's neck. Still, though she'd never admit it, she was grateful to him for scaring off the lecherous old marquess. But that was beside the point.

"This business of interfering in my affairs has gone far enough," she declared, taking a furious bite into a vanilla biscuit. "I must put a stop to it before Papa learns of Stratham's pursuit of me. He might be moved to shoot the knave like my grandpapa shot his father—and the present earl strikes me as a dangerous man to cross."

"Too dangerous for an innocent of one-and-twenty years to handle, if you ask me." Elsie's plump face wore a worried frown. "You may be terribly clever, Alexandra, but I cannot help but feel you are beyond your depths with the earl."

"Nonsense. I have never yet encountered a problem that could not be solved with logic and firm resolve—and as far as I'm concerned, the earl is just another problem. I shall simply have to convince him that I would never in a million years consider taking a barbarian from Exmoor as my lover."

Elsie's teacup clattered in her saucer, sloshing hot tea onto the remaining slices of cake. "What a shocking thing to say, Alexandra," she sputtered.

"Well, I cannot know to what purpose the rackety fellow is pursuing me, can I? But I shall make it equally plain I will not consider marrying someone so far beneath my touch, if that is what he has in mind. It should not be too difficult. He seems relatively intelligent, and I have never had any trouble putting my point across to anyone else."

She tapped a thoughtful tattoo on the arm of her chair. But where should this meeting with the earl take place? Hyde Park was much too risky. She stared at Elsie's worried face, and a sudden thought struck her. "When are you and your mother scheduled to tour Westminster Abbey with the ladies of St. George's Altar Society?"

"Tomorrow morning."

"I shall accompany you, and I'll make certain both Jamie and the servants know where I'm going."

"Mama and I shall be glad of your company, of course, but what has a tour of Westminster to do with the earl?"

"Think, Elsie. The abbey is the ideal place for what I have in mind. There are any number of quiet alcoves where I can speak privately with Stratham and still be in a public enough place to be safe."

"But what if he should decide to kidnap you?" Elsie protested. "He could whisk you out of the abbey before anyone was the wiser."

"Not likely. I will scream the place down if he so much as touches me. Besides, I intend to carry one of Papa's pistols in my reticule just in case."

Elsie clasped a hand to her bosom. "Oh, Alexandra, you are without a doubt the most courageous woman I have ever met. I swear you could be the heroine of one of Fanny Burney's novels."

She frowned. "But how can you be so certain the earl will be at the abbey?"

"He'll be there. His spies will tell him where I am."

"I imagine you're right." Elsie sighed. "The handsome fellow does appear to have a serious *tendre* for you."

Alexandra shook her head. "What a peagoose you are, Elsie. Gentlemen have *tendres*; barbarians, like the earl, lust. But by the time I finish pinning this particular barbarian's ears back, I guarantee he will be more than ready to return to Exmoor and his own kind of woman."

Chapter Four

It was Liam's first visit to Westminster Abbey, and he found it even more impressive than he'd imagined. He had purposely arrived long before the ladies of the Altar Society were due so he could see something of the magnificent Gothic church before he set to work charming Lady Alexandra.

He had made up his mind to call on her father that very afternoon, and it seemed prudent to tell her so and gauge which way the wind blew. Haughty creature that she was, she would undoubtedly object to marrying a man of his humble background. Though why she should still be impressed with the nobility after her experience with the randy old marquess was more than he could comprehend. Nevertheless, he did not look forward to the moment when he informed the little shrew he would soon be her lord and master.

But the problems of one man seemed pitifully insignificant when compared to the centuries of English history reflected in the ancient abbey. He soon found himself caught up in that history as he progressed from the Pantheon, where so many of England's heroes were entombed, to the Confessor's Chapel to view the coronation chairs and the sword and shield of Edward III, which a docent informed him were still used in the coronation ceremony.

He stood for a long moment in the historic chapel of Henry VII, first of the Tudor kings, whose colorful history had fired his imagination as a boy, and even managed a moment of quiet reflection beside the fountain in the courtyard of the Little Cloister.

The minutes flew by, and he'd not yet managed to visit the famous Poet's Corner when he realized it was time to begin searching out the lady he'd come to see. Moments later, he spied what had to be the women of St. George's Altar Society gathering in the Children's Corner. As he watched, they clustered like chattering magpies around the magnificent urn designed by Christopher Wren for that particular section of the abbey.

To his surprise, Lady Alexandra slipped away from the others and hurried toward him. "I must speak with you," she whispered as she drew near.

"What a happy circumstance. I need to speak to you, too," he whispered back. "But why are we whispering? I believe we are out of earshot of your friends."

"In case you haven't noticed, this is a church." She frowned. "I shall get right to the point, my lord. I despise equivocation."

"As do I, my lady, and my time is limited. I have already spent two hours viewing the cathedral and I have a task I must attend to this afternoon." Liam could see he had deflated the starchy aristocrat. He struggled to keep a straight face.

She quickly recovered her poise. "Very well then. There is no way to wrap what I have to say in pretty ribbons. The plain truth is I find it beyond belief that your presence at every social event I attend is mere coincidence."

"I can see where it would appear rather odd to the casual observer," Liam agreed.

"I should like to hear your explanation for this, my lord."

Liam smiled. "Very well. But it hardly seems necessary. Surely you must have guessed by now that I am pursuing you."

Her lovely emerald eyes widened at his blunt answer. "May I ask to what purpose, my lord?"

Liam glanced briefly at the magnificent surroundings and decided that all things considered, it was probably as good a place as any to declare himself. "My intentions are honorable, Lady Alexandra," he said gravely. "I intend to make you my wife."

"You must be mad!"

Liam opened his mouth to deny the charge, but closed it again without speaking. Any man seriously considering marrying such a virago must have at least one bat loose in his belfry.

Lady Alexandra drew herself up to her full height, which brought the top of her head just even with his shoulder. "What could possibly have led you to believe I would consider marrying you, my lord?" she asked in a voice edged with ice. "Mine is a very old and respected noble family. I have my standards, and you do not meet them."

Liam couldn't help himself. He burst into a hearty laugh that

echoed throughout the nave like a note struck on a vast pipe
organ.

"Pray tell, what have I said that you find so amusing?" Lady
Alexandra asked indignantly as he struggled to contain the
laughter still choking him.

"I have seen two of your suitors," he managed at last. "One
a man-milliner who nearly fainted at the thought of kissing
you—the other a doddering old lecher who showed you less respect than the roughest sailor might show a waterfront whore. I
must say, I am greatly impressed by your standards, my lady."

Fists clenched, she took a step toward him. "So it *was* you
who frightened the wits out of the marquess. I suspected as
much. What did you do? Threaten the old man with bodily
harm? How daring! He cannot be more than twice your age."

She took another step. "And how could you know about the
kissing unless . . ." Her eyes blazed with anger. "Admit it, you
unscrupulous rogue. You were eavesdropping on Sir Randolph
and me. You threatened him, too, didn't you? It was *you* who
sent him haring off to the Lake District in such a hurry."

"I admit nothing," Liam declared. "But if, by chance, I had
done you the favor of dispatching two such contemptible spec-
imens of humanity to the hinterlands, I should expect a bit more
gratitude on your part."

"Gratitude? For what?" Lady Alexandra poked him in the
chest with her forefinger. "For turning my life into a nightmare?" Poke. "For using my gullible young brother as a pawn
in your wicked scheme?" Poke. "For making me believe I had
repulsed the man I hoped to wed?" Poke. "How dare you presume to interfere in my personal affairs." Poke. Poke.

Frankly amazed, Liam gazed down at the woman jabbing a
hole in his chest. Couldn't she see she could no more mate with
a silly fribble like Sir Randolph than a lioness could mate with
a housecat? The little termagant obviously had no sense whatsoever where men were concerned—all that rage and passion
over a man she would have tired of before the ink was dry on
the marriage lines.

She was beginning to get on his nerves. He had never known
a woman who talked so much and said so little he cared to hear.
He could think of only one way to shut her up. With lightning
speed, he pulled her into his arms, stepped back into the shadows and covered her mouth with his.

At the first touch of his lips, Alexandra felt an amazing sensation whoosh through her, gathering heat as it spread like a wildfire through a summer-dry forest. Instinctively, her eyes closed and her lips softened. Of their own accord, her fingers slid up the broad chest she'd been abusing but a moment before to twine themselves in his outrageous hair.

"Ummm," he growled deep in his throat, and raked his tongue across her lips in a way that created a new and alarming response deep in the most womanly part of her. She held her breath—wanting the shocking kiss to end—wanting it to last forever.

Then suddenly it was over. He raised his head and stared at her with enigmatic amber eyes. "Your first kiss, Alexandra," he said softly, "and neither of us will ever forget I was the man who gave it to you."

He touched a finger to her lips, tracing the path his tongue had taken. "Don't look so shocked, dear lady. It was not much of a kiss, as kisses go. But you show definite promise for a beginner. With a little proper instruction—"

"Why you . . . you bounder," she sputtered, belatedly regaining her senses. "How dare you speak to me in such a manner—and how dare you take such liberties without my permission. If I were a man, I would call you out."

"If you were a man, little hellion, I would never have kissed you," he said. "And as for my friendship with Jamie, it has nothing whatsoever to do with you. I spend time with the boy because he is one of the few genuine people I have met in London, and I enjoy his company."

He raised a hand in a gesture of dismissal. "Now return to your friends before they begin looking for you. I'd not want compromising a lady added to my already impressive list of sins."

Without further ado, the earl turned on his heel and disappeared into the shadowy recesses of the ancient abbey.

Liam ran Viscount Hardin to ground at Tattersalls a little more than an hour later, where an auction was in progress. Hardin stood apart from the crowd, looking morose and withdrawn. Understandably so, since the prime cattle up for bid in the auction all came from his stable. It was plain to see this was the beginning of the end for the proud nobleman, and Liam felt a twinge of conscience that the unhappy fellow's troubles played so conveniently into his own plans for the future.

He approached the viscount with outstretched hands. "Good afternoon, my lord. I am Liam Campbell." He hesitated before adding, "the Earl of Stratham." He doubted he would ever become accustomed to the title.

"I had heard you were in London." The viscount's handshake was cordial, if somewhat less than enthusiastic. "But I would have known you at any rate. That particular shade of flame-colored hair marks you as Stratham's offspring. No one who knew him could mistake it." His hooded green eyes searched Liam's face. "It appears you inherited the rest of your features from your mother. Dierk Wolverson was not a handsome fellow."

Liam shifted uncomfortably beneath the older man's perusal, aware that by a strange quirk of fate, Hardin and he each held the other's future in his hands. He needed the viscount's cooperation almost as much as Hardin needed his offer of a generous marriage settlement.

"I was not aware you knew the old earl," Liam said, stalling for time while he pondered how best to present his proposal.

"As young bucks, we were rivals for the hand of the same woman."

"So I understand, my lord, and you won."

"I suppose that's one way of looking at it," Hardin said, his expression bleak.

Liam cleared his throat, more uncomfortable than ever after Hardin's telling comment. Furthermore, the resemblance between the viscount and his son, Jamie, was unmistakable, and Liam felt himself instantly drawn to the slender, sad-eyed man.

He hadn't counted on liking Alexandra Henning's brother and father, any more than he had counted on being attracted to the lady herself. But attracted he was. He was still reeling from the sensations that kissing her had aroused in him. By sheer will, he'd managed to hide the unexpected jolt to his senses behind a flippant remark. But he could no longer view his marriage as a simple business arrangement, especially since he'd sensed Alexandra had instinctively responded to him as well.

"There is a matter of some importance I would like to discuss with you, my lord," he said, deciding a direct approach was the only logical one open to him. "I am aware that I should, by rights, call on you at your home to do so. But I have reason to believe I would not be welcome."

"You believe correctly, my lord," the viscount agreed. "I

spend very little time at the family town house, and my wife would have refused admittance to any relative of Dierk Wolverson's. But what is this business you have with me that should not be discussed in a public place?"

Liam lowered his voice to make certain only Hardin could hear him. "I wish to marry your daughter, Alexandra, and I would have your blessing, my lord."

A light flickered briefly in the viscount's pale eyes. "I see. You are correct then. A horse auction is not the proper place to discuss my daughter's future. I suggest we repair to my club. I believe I am still accepted there, and Tattersalls is quite capable of disposing of my cattle without my gloomy presence."

Liam had heard of Whites, but he had never been inside its hallowed walls. It was, he discovered a short time later, just as stodgy as he'd imagined. Everything about it, including the look the doorman gave him, set his teeth on edge.

A faint smile played across the viscount's distinguished features. "You have managed to shock the imperturbable Joseph, young man."

"How so?" Liam frowned. "I cannot think what I've done to give him such a sour countenance."

"I rather think it is that piece of silk you have knotted about your neck. Joseph has presided over the door of Whites for longer than anyone can remember, and I daresay he has never before opened it to a man without a properly tied cravat. It is a tribute to our long acquaintance that he has done so for a guest of mine, but I am amazed the old fellow's heart survived the shock."

"And I am amazed at the importance you Londoners attach to a man's attire," Liam grumbled, noting the odd looks he was receiving from the other club members.

A waiter appeared the instant they seated themselves at a table in a secluded corner, and the viscount ordered two glasses of brandy. "I assumed you were a brandy drinker like your father," he said a moment later, when Liam failed to raise the glass the waiter placed in front of him.

Liam was tempted to shrug off the viscount's observation without comment, but something about the man made him admit the truth. "I smuggled so much of the stuff into England during the war, I lost all taste for it. I prefer the good, dark ale for which Exmoor is famous."

Hardin blinked, but quickly recovered his poise. "I am sorry to disappoint you, but I doubt Whites keeps such a brew in stock."

He searched Liam's face with puzzled eyes. "You appear singularly unimpressed with London and its citizens. Why, then, have you set your sights on marrying Alexandra? Granted, she is a beautiful, high-spirited girl—"

"She is that," Liam agreed, remembering how she'd dressed him down that very morning.

"But with the exception of a month or two each summer at my country estate in Norfolk, she has dwelt in London all her life and happily so," Hardin continued. "Wouldn't you be better off to seek your wife in your beloved West Country?"

Liam thought of the convoluted tale he had planned to fob off on the viscount before he met him. For reasons too obscure to comprehend, he couldn't bring himself to tell it to the man who faced him across the table. Instead, he took a healthy swallow of brandy and said, "The truth is I am very much attracted to your daughter. But even if I were not, I would marry her, because unless I do I shall be forced to forfeit the fortune I inherited from the man who sired me."

Hardin blinked again. "The devil you say."

"I think it only fair to tell you, I plan to wed Lady Alexandra one way or another. I would prefer to do so with your blessing and her approval, but there is too much at stake to let anything stand in my way." Liam took another swallow of brandy, then launched into the story of how the former Earl of Stratham had plotted his revenge against the woman who'd spurned him.

"No offense intended," Hardin interjected when Liam was but a few minutes into the tale. "But Dierk Wolverson was right about one thing. He could find no better way to revenge himself on my top-lofty wife than to force her to accept his bastard as her son-in-law."

"No offense taken," Liam said, continuing his narrative. Though, in truth, it made him spitting mad to be considered the instrument of that revenge simply because of the circumstances of his birth.

Hardin's face remained impassive until the end of Liam's recitation. "So, Stratham believed me a man who would sell his daughter to solve his financial problems," he said quietly.

"The Earl of Stratham was a fool," Liam declared.

The viscount shook his head. "No, Stratham was a blackguard;

I am a fool. Why else would I have made the kind of choices that have brought me to the brink of ruin? Choices that necessitate my doing the very thing Stratham predicted I would do."

Again he studied Liam in that intense way of his. "But I think the late earl may have been so clever he outwitted himself. As I see it, if you and I cooperate with each other, we may both benefit greatly."

"My thinking exactly," Liam agreed.

The viscount's countenance brightened considerably. "And my daughter will benefit as well; for though we are but newly acquainted, I perceive you to be the kind of man I would have chosen to be Alexandra's husband—even without a generous marriage settlement. It will take a charming rascal, who has a way with women, to counteract all the nonsense my frigid wife has pounded into the poor girl's head. You are, I suspect, that rascal. That you are apparently an honorable man as well is an added bonus."

He finished his brandy and signaled the waiter for another. "But knowing my daughter as I do, I can guarantee she will hate us both if I force her to marry you against her will. Last I heard, she favored some fellow who wrote poetry."

Liam nodded. "Sir Randolph Twickingham. He has, I believe, left London."

"Has he really? And I heard today at Tattersalls that the Marquess of Nettleford has also departed the city in a great hurry. I don't suppose you played any part in those two events."

"I may have had brief conversations with both gentlemen—nothing more."

Hardin chuckled. "It would appear you have more in common with your father than the color of your hair." He cast a hopeful glance at Liam. "I don't suppose you've had occasion to converse with my daughter, as well, on the subject of marriage."

"As a matter of fact, I told her just this morning that I intended to wed her," Liam admitted. "She informed me that she had her standards, and I did not meet them."

"Just as I feared. She has been too long under her mother's influence to think otherwise. I'll just have to trust you to win her over once you have your ring on her finger."

"I shall do my best," Liam said. "Now that I know why she's so skittish, I promise I shall be both patient and gentle with her. I shall, in fact, do everything in my power to make her happy."

"I can ask no more."

"Very well then." Liam rested his arms on the table and leaned forward. "It is time we discussed the details of the marriage settlement. This is what I am prepared to offer for the privilege of wedding your daughter . . ."

A good half hour later, the viscount tossed back the last of his brandy and rose from his chair, a slip of paper in his hand and a satisfied smile on his face. "You are an exceedingly generous man, my lord. Needless to say, I feel as if a great weight has been lifted off my shoulders. My only regret is that we did not have this conversation before I put my stable of prime thoroughbreds on the auction block."

He shrugged. "Ah, well, such is life. But thanks to you, I have hopes of building another such stable in the not too distant future. In the meantime I shall have my solicitors call upon"— he checked the paper—"Waltham, Osgood and Prine this very afternoon to draw up the necessary papers, and you may feel free to publish the news of your betrothal to Alexandra in tomorrow's *Times*."

Liam breathed a sigh of relief. He would breathe another when the actual wedding had been performed and his future was secure.

"Now," Hardin said, "let us adjourn to my town house so I can inform my wife and daughter of my decision. I cannot say I look forward to telling them I have managed to lose more money in the past five years than most men see in a lifetime. But tell them I must, so Alexandra will realize I had no choice but to accept your offer. Maybe then it will be a little easier for my proud and independent daughter to understand why I could not let her make her own decision about her future."

Bidding Joseph, the doorman, a cordial good-bye, he stepped through the door of Whites, but paused before entering Liam's carriage. "By the way, young man," he said with a wry smile, "I think we should keep the bit about your having to marry Alexandra to ourselves. Women are such sensitive creatures. I believe it would be best for all concerned to let her think you are motivated solely by the desires of your heart—or some such foolishness."

"Pardon the interruption, milady. But Mr. Gibson was after sending me to fetch you. 'Tis me understandin' his lordship wishes to speak with you."

Alexandra looked up from the runner she was embroidering to find Brendan O'Riley, the young Irish footman her mother had hired some six months earlier, hovering in the doorway of her sitting room. "Papa is home? How splendid. It has been more than a fortnight since I've seen him."

"His lordship is home all right, milady, and I'm thinkin' 'tis best you make haste to the book room. Him and her nibs is havin' one of their rows—only this one's worse than usual."

With a sigh, Alexandra laid her embroidery on a nearby table and rose from her chair. Things had come to a pretty pass, when her parents' hatred of each other was so apparent, it was a source of alarm to the servants. Still, despite the footman's warning, she found it difficult to get excited over this latest altercation. She was much too busy worrying about her own problem—namely the Earl of Stratham.

It had never occurred to her that the mere touch of a man's lips could play such havoc with one's emotions. The shocking sensations the earl's kiss had evoked terrified her, particularly since he hadn't seemed the least bit affected.

He had, in fact, intimated that she needed tutoring in the art of kissing—as if it were an acquired skill she had yet to learn. She found that idea almost as bewildering as the kiss itself. Why was he pursuing her so avidly if his taste ran to the kind of women who had mastered such skills?

She heard her mother's enraged voice long before she reached the book room. "I will not have that scapegrace in this house, Osmund. I insist you remove him instantly, and yourself with him."

Her father had apparently brought home one of his friends who did not meet with her mother's approval. But then few of his friends did. She wondered in what salon Gibson, the butler, had put the poor man and if he could hear her mother's stinging condemnation of him.

She knocked, then opened the door to find her father and mother faced off like dueling combatants. Her father's angry scowl changed to a smile the minute he saw her. "Alexandra, my dear, how well you're looking."

"As are you, Papa." In truth, he appeared an entirely different man than the somber fellow he'd become in the past few months. Something had buoyed up his flagging spirits, and for that she was deeply grateful. She loved her father dearly and hated to see him so moody and depressed.

She cast an uneasy glance at her mother, who was obviously still seething with rage. This friend of her father's must be a truly disreputable fellow to upset her mother so greatly by his mere presence.

"O'Riley said you wanted to see me, Papa," she said, kissing him first on the left cheek, then the right in the continental fashion her French governess had taught her.

"I always want to see you, daughter. But especially today because I have wonderful news for you." In his usual courtly manner, he escorted her to a chair and saw her seated comfortably before he continued. "I have received a most propitious offer for your hand, Alexandra—one I could not refuse. The young man awaits your answer in the third-floor salon."

"No!" her mother shrieked at the top of her voice. "What are you thinking of, Osmund? I will not allow you to subject my gently bred daughter to the mercies of that . . . that barbarian."

Alexandra's heart hammered wildly in her breast at the word "barbarian." There was only one man she knew who fit that description. Surely her father couldn't be planning to betroth her to the Earl of Stratham.

The viscount glared at his wife. "Tell me, madam," he said in icy tones, "would you rather I turned your gently bred daughter, and you and your son as well, into the streets of London to fend for yourselves while I languish in debtors' prison? For that is what was about to happen when I received the Earl of Stratham's generous offer."

The viscountess collapsed onto a nearby chair, the high color in her cheeks quickly fading to a pasty white. "What nonsense are you prattling now, Osmund? How can a man as rich as you find himself in such desperate straits?"

"Bad decisions about investments, bad management of my estates, bad choices of friends with whom to gamble money I no longer had," the viscount said wearily. "The list is endless. Name every mistake a man can make; I have made them all and some I doubt even you could think to throw up to me."

Alexandra stared in horror at her charming, elegant father. Surely this was all a bizarre nightmare from which she would wake any minute.

"My dowry?" the viscountess asked in a voice hoarse from shock. "You swore you would put that in trust for the children, but under the circumstances—"

"Gone to pay off my most pressing debts."

"And what of the money I inherited from my grandmother?"

"Gone as well."

"To support the house in Chelsea and the tart who lives there under your protection no doubt." With an anguished moan, the viscountess covered her face with her hands and burst into tears.

The viscount didn't deign to answer his wife's charges, but from the sheepish look on his face, Alexandra could see they were true. She shivered, gripped by the chilling realization that the father she had idolized all her life had the same feet of clay as other men. Something deep within her recoiled at the thought of the fastidious viscount doing those unspeakable things with his mistress that her abigail had told her a man did with such women.

"There are many fine paintings and objets d'art in the house in Norfolk," she said in desperation. "Surely you could raise the money you need by selling them."

"I stripped the house last winter. We have been living on the proceeds ever since."

Alexandra's heart sank. "And your stable of thoroughbreds? They must be worth a fortune."

"Even as we speak they are being auctioned at Tattersalls, I regret to say." A sad little smile played at the corners of the viscount's mouth. "So you see, my darling girl, you are the only asset I have left."

Alexandra cringed at her father's thoughtless terminology. "I am neither a painting nor a racehorse, Papa. I am your daughter."

"My beloved daughter," he said gravely. "But an asset nevertheless, for which the Earl of Stratham is willing to offer a marriage settlement that far exceeds ordinary generosity. The fellow is rich as a nabob, and I drove a hard bargain with him, if I do say so. In addition to paying off all my debts, he has agreed to give your mother a quarterly stipend sufficient to maintain her place in society, as well as see Jamie through Eton and Cambridge once his health improves."

The viscountess wiped her eyes and blew her nose. "Talk is cheap, Osmund. You, of all people, should know that."

Her husband ignored her. "Because of that generosity, and other reasons as well, I strongly disagree with your mother's judgment of the earl," he said, warming to his subject. "I met him for the first time this morning when he sought me out at Tattersalls, but I instantly recognized him as a most exemplary young man. A bit eccentric, it's true. He actually had the temerity to enter Whites without a cravat. Still, I confess I am quite taken with the idea of having him as my son-in-law."

"Which is beside the point, Papa." Alexandra fought back the tears that threatened to spill from her eyes. "I am the one who must pay for your mistakes by sleeping in his bed and bearing his children, and I am not at all taken with the idea."

"Cease your silly prattle, Alexandra. There are more important issues at stake here than your sentiments on the subject." The viscountess leaned forward in her chair, her gaze riveted on her husband's face. "How can you be certain the fellow will keep his promises, Osmund? You are talking about a great deal of money. My quarterly stipend, for instance—"

"A mere pittance to one of the wealthiest men in all of England. If you ask me, Alexandra is a very lucky young lady to have caught the eye of the handsome devil."

"Balderdash!" Alexandra's mother stuffed her soggy handkerchief under the cuff of her sleeve and straightened in her chair, dry-eyed and flushed of cheek. "It is the earl who is the fortunate one. The barbaric fellow must be over the moon just thinking about gaining a *parti* with impeccable bloodlines and a reputation to match," she declared in her usual strident manner. "I see now this bastard of Dierk Wolverson's is not the same lusty beast his father was. Why do you think he is so quick to snap up Alexandra when your affairs are at low tide, Osmund?"

"I cannot say, madam, but I feel certain you will enlighten me."

"To worm his way into society by virtue of his wife's credentials, of course. To say nothing of legitimizing his bloodline." She turned her gaze on Alexandra, who had sat in stunned silence while her parents discussed her worth to them on the marriage market. "Why are you looking so down in the mouth, my girl? You need only submit to the boorish fellow long enough to produce an heir. I guarantee he will look elsewhere for his pleasure once he realizes you are repulsed by his carnal demands."

"And that, dear daughter, is your mother's formula for a successful marriage," the viscount said with undisguised bitterness. "One to which she has steadfastly adhered since the day we wed. I only hope you find greater joy in your union than I have in mine."

He caught Alexandra's chin in his long, elegant fingers. "I trust you know how deeply I regret my mistakes that have brought us to this pass. Had it been in my power, I would have allowed you to decide your own future."

Alexandra cringed at his touch. "Your noble sentiments come a little late, Papa."

The viscount regarded her sadly. "You are angry, as I knew you would be. But things will work out for the best. Most girls in your position would rejoice at the chance to be both a countess and the wife of a wealthy man of pleasing countenance."

"I am not 'most girls.' I had hoped for more than the typical marriage of convenience that is so prevalent in the *ton*. I should have known such hopes were doomed to failure for the daughter of a viscount."

"It is early days yet." The viscount's voice wavered, and he studied Alexandra with guilt-stricken eyes. "It will take a long time for your mother to arrange a proper wedding—"

"Months," his wife interjected. "If the earl hopes to impress the *ton*, he will want an elaborate ceremony. I shall, of course, be happy to make all the arrangements. You are, after all, my only daughter."

The viscount's spirits brightened noticeably. "So you see, dear girl, you will have plenty of time to get used to the idea. Perhaps by the time you stand at the altar, you will feel happier about it."

"I doubt it." Alexandra swallowed the lump in her throat. "But never fear, Papa, I am not a fool. I see that I have no choice but to marry him, for I dislike the thought of fending for myself on the streets of London even more than I dislike the idea of becoming his wife."

She dabbed at her eyes with a lace-edged handkerchief, determined to hold back her tears until she was alone in her bedchamber. "Now tell me again in which salon Gibson has placed his lordship. Since I must agree to the dreadful man's demands, I would have the humiliating ordeal over and done with as soon as possible."

Chapter Five

Liam paced back and forth in the third-floor salon to which the Henning butler had directed him. It was not that he had any doubt about the outcome of his meeting with Alexandra; between her father and him, they had left her no choice but to agree to wed him. It was, he acknowledged, that lack of choice that pricked his conscience.

He had always held to the belief that everyone should have something to say about his, or her, future. Yet he had deliberately set a trap to ensnare the proud, young aristocrat in order to ensure his possession of the old earl's fortune.

It mattered little that she would probably be better off with him than with some ambitious cit willing to marry the daughter of an impoverished nobleman to improve his social status. It still galled him to betray the tenets by which he had heretofore lived his life.

How, he wondered, would she react to the news her father was, at that very minute, imparting to her? The viscount had warned she would despise the two men who had arranged her marriage without her consent. He could scarcely blame her for that. He just wondered how she would display her feelings. If she ran true to form, she would probably pick up the first available object and hurl it at his head—and there were, he noted, any number of small art objects in the salon.

He stopped his pacing and for the first time took a good look at the lovely room in which he found himself. Embossed paper the color of rich cream covered the walls, and deep green velvet draperies trimmed with finely stitched gold embroidery framed tall, narrow windows. A number of spindly-legged chairs and an ornate loveseat that appeared much too fragile to hold a man his size sat atop a colorful Turkish carpet.

But the focal point of the room was a grouping of three magnificent watercolors depicting a part of the English countryside that was far more civilized than the lonely moors of his childhood. Even with his limited knowledge of art, he could see the remarkable detail and exciting use of color the artist had employed.

Drawn like a magnet to the glorious paintings, he stepped closer to see if they were signed. In the lower right-hand corner of each he found precise brush strokes spelling out the signature of the artist. He blinked, then looked again. But there was no mistaking it. The artist's name was "A. Henning."

He felt paralyzed with guilt and regret. Like the room in which they were hung, the paintings were as delicate and beautiful as the woman who had rendered them—the woman he had maneuvered into marrying him against her will. What in God's name did he, a bastard, ex-smuggler and general jack-of-all-trades, have in common with such a woman?

He made a mental note to never take his bride to The Aerie, the crumbling medieval castle overlooking the Bristol Channel, which had been part of his inheritance. He had loved the ancient pile of stones on sight. But he doubted anyone accustomed to such refined surroundings would feel at home in huge, drafty rooms decorated with shields and battle-axes and threadbare tapestries of grisly twelfth-century battles.

Though his back was to the door, he knew the instant Alexandra entered the room. She made no sound, but he caught a faint whiff of the spicy fragrance he had come to associate with her—a fragrance that oddly enough reminded him of moorland wildflowers.

Slowly, he turned to face her and felt his breath catch in his throat. The pale, grim-faced woman standing in the doorway of the salon bore little resemblance to the bright, self-assured young beauty he'd kissed but a few hours earlier.

"My father has just informed me he has accepted your offer for my hand in marriage," she declared, an unmistakable look of loathing in her wounded emerald eyes.

"And are you willing to accept his decision?"

"I cannot see that I have any choice but to do so."

"That, I take it, is why you look like a Christian about to be fed to the lions," Liam said with a feeble attempt at humor. "I knew, of course, I was not your first choice, nor for that matter your last, but is marriage to me that horrendous a prospect?"

"No, my lord. You are probably no worse than any other man my father might have chosen."

"Then why the tragic demeanor? Surely you expected such an arrangement to be made sooner or later. I have it on good authority that it is customary for English aristocrats to choose their daughters' husbands."

"But fool that I am, I thought my father was different. I thought he loved me and respected my right to make my own choice. After one-and-twenty years of deluding myself that I was a human being with a mind of my own, it was a shock to learn the true meaning of what it is to be a woman."

Liam searched her pale, expressionless face. "Which is?"

"I am chattel of more or less value than a thoroughbred racehorse or a prize hunting dog, depending on the whim of the man who happens to own me at the moment."

Bitterness sharpened her normally melodic voice, and Liam felt as if she had slapped him across the face. "I doubt any man will ever own you, Alexandra—not even if he has a legal right to do so. You strike me as a woman whose spirit will always be in her own keeping."

She surveyed him with eyes darkened by rage and frustration. "Nevertheless, my lord, I would know where I stand in this matter. My father freely admitted he considers me a financial asset. Perhaps you should explain what kind of asset I represent to you, so I know what you want of me. You are, after all, paying a great deal of money for me; you will need to make certain you are making a wise investment."

Liam gritted his teeth. *Damn the clever little cat for knowing exactly where to sink her claws.* "I cannot deny the injustice of British law where women are concerned, nor that it worked in my favor in obtaining the wife I desired," he said, despising the defensive note he heard in his own voice. "But as for my negotiations with your father, surely you can see I made them to save him the agony of financial ruin. I could do no less for the man who will soon be my father-in-law."

"Of course you couldn't. I would be of little use to you socially if my father was in debtors' prison."

"Socially? Good God, never say you believe I am marrying you to advance myself with the *ton*." Liam shook his head in disbelief. "Do I look like a man who cares how society views him?"

Her gaze fastened on the silk scarf knotted about his throat—the same scarf her father had ridiculed earlier. "Not at the moment, but—"

"Devil take it, Alexandra, I intend to spend as little time as possible in this blasted city. I can scarcely breathe in the foul place, accustomed as I am to open seas and lonely moors. But if it is your wish, I shall set you up in a town house of your choosing and provide you with sufficient funds to maintain the position in society you appear to prize so highly."

She stared at him in obvious bewilderment. "Why would you do that?"

"Because, contrary to what you obviously believe, I am not a monster. I would have my wife content with her lot."

Her look of skepticism told him how improbable she found that statement. "Then if not for the social position, why do you want to marry me, my lord?"

"Would you believe that I am motivated solely by the desires of my heart?" he asked, remembering the viscount's advice.

"Not likely. You have already expressed your displeasure at my lack of knowledge where kissing is concerned. I can assure you, I know even less about the other ways in which the kind of women you prefer hold a man's interest."

Liam chuckled. "Your memory differs somewhat from mine then. As I recall it, I was more interested in furthering your knowledge of kissing than displeased by your lack thereof. I shall, of course, be happy to instruct you concerning the other pleasures a man and wife might share as well."

This attempt at humor brought a vivid blush to her cheeks—a definite improvement, in his opinion, over the pallor of a moment before. Then remembering her unexpected response to his kiss, he recklessly added, "You may be surprised to find how much you enjoy the lessons."

It was obviously the wrong thing to say. The startled look in her expressive eyes warned him she was completely unaware of the passion simmering deep within her. Furthermore, he suspected the thought of intimacy terrified her—a logical reaction to her upbringing. He cursed the sexless viscountess for trying to turn her daughter into a replica of herself.

Whatever guilt he'd felt about forcing Alexandra to marry him dissolved like winter ice beneath a spring sun. He would be doing her a favor by breaking her mother's hold on her—and break it he would, no matter how difficult the task. Now that he'd had a glimpse of the gloriously sensual woman she could be, he would never be content with the sterile marriage of convenience he had originally planned. Suddenly it seemed imperative that he have his ring on her finger as soon as possible.

"I shall put the announcement of our betrothal in tomorrow's *Times* and arrange to have our banns announced at St. George's beginning Sunday next," he declared abruptly.

Alexandra had thought nothing could shock her after her father's pronouncement; the earl proved her wrong. "I expected the notice in the *Times*," she said in a voice that held an embarrassing tremor. "But why are you having the banns read so soon?"

"I have business in Exmoor and shall be away from London for the next three weeks. We can be married as soon as I return."

"Three weeks?" Alexandra gasped. "Surely you're not serious. I cannot possibly be ready to marry in such a short time."

"Why not?" Stratham frowned. "I hope you are not contemplating some grandiose affair, for it is not my style."

"But my mother will insist on—"

"Devil take your mother. It is not her wedding."

Panic engulfed Alexandra. Gripping the back of the nearest chair with white-knuckled fingers, she stared in something akin to horror at the man she had come to think of as the Barbarian Earl. She had not yet adjusted to the idea of becoming betrothed to him; wedding him in less than a month was out of the question. "You are being unreasonable, my lord," she declared indignantly. "I shall need at least five, no six, months to purchase bride clothes and prepare a proper wedding."

The earl shrugged. "On the contrary, if I were inclined to be unreasonable, I would procure a special license and demand you marry me no later than tomorrow afternoon—which would probably suit your father to a whisker. He is, I understand, desperate to meet his creditors' demands. I doubt he will want to wait any longer than necessary to have the marriage settlement funds in hand."

The veiled threat in the earl's words sent chills down Alexandra's spine. "Are you saying you will not settle with my father until you and I are actually married? That is most unusual, my lord."

Stratham's smile held no warmth. "What would you do in my shoes, dear lady? It is not as if I delude myself that my bride-to-be awaits our nuptials as eagerly as I do."

Alexandra clamped her jaw shut to still her chattering teeth. Her future with this West Country provincial looked bleaker than ever. He was obviously accustomed to getting his own way and not above using intimidation to do so. She ached to tell him what she thought of his manipulative tyranny, and so she would, once the dreaded wedding was over and her father had the necessary money to pay off his debts.

She glanced up and found the earl watching her with that same intensity he'd first displayed at Lady Rutherford's ball. "Why are you looking at me like that? What do you want of me?" she snapped, too emotionally drained to guard her tongue.

Anger flared in his golden eyes and without warning, he crossed the space between them in three long strides, to stand towering over her. Her first inclination was to turn tail and dart up the stairs to the safety of her bedchamber. Pride alone kept her slippers glued to the floor.

She raised her chin defiantly. "If you mean to terrify me, you are wasting your time. I am already well beyond terror."

"Terror is not the emotion I hope to inspire in you," he said in a dangerously quiet voice. Prying her hands from their grip on the chair, he drew her into his arms and claimed her lips in a demanding kiss that left her too shaken to do anything but stare at him in mute bewilderment.

"You asked me what I wanted of you, Alexandra," he said in a husky whisper. "Now you know. I want you to become my lawfully wedded wife in three weeks' time; I, in turn, will fulfill my part of the bargain I struck with your father within an hour of the signing of our marriage lines."

To Alexandra's utter dismay, word of the sale of her father's prize racehorses had spread through every salon in Mayfair by the time the auctioneer dropped his gavel on the last bid. The subsequent announcement of her betrothal to the Earl of Stratham was, as her mother bitterly acknowledged, manna from heaven for the gossipmongers.

Rumors abounded about the prospective bridegroom. One

elderly dowager recalled the uproar his barbaric father had raised some twenty years earlier when he'd come to London seeking a bride; another declared she had it on good authority the present earl was a legitimized bastard—product of the old earl's liaison with a French whore. One imaginative fellow even went so far as to claim he had seen the eccentric earl from Exmoor admitted to Whites sans cravat, but that particular rumor was promptly discarded as too improbable to warrant passing on.

The speculation about Viscount Hardin's financial woes did not die so quickly. Alexandra suspected too many of the *ton's* matrons had suffered the lash of her mother's sharp tongue to let such a delectable bit of gossip die an early death. Henrietta Henning's chickens had come home to roost, and Alexandra offered up a brief prayer of thanks that the Earl of Stratham had insisted on a small, private wedding. With all the rumors flying about, the lavish affair she had always envisioned for herself would undoubtedly have turned into a circus.

"Is it true? Are you really going to wed the red-haired earl from Exmoor?" Wide-eyed and flushed of face, Elsie presented herself at the door of Alexandra's sitting room the morning after the announcement appeared in the *Times*. "I thought you said you despised him."

Alexandra looked up from the watercolor still life she was attempting to finish. Though, in truth, her eyes ached so much from a night of weeping into her pillow, she could scarcely tell one color from another. "I changed my mind once I knew him better," she lied. Not even to Elsie would she admit the humiliating truth of why she had made such a turnaround.

By tacit agreement, the Hennings had closed ranks in an effort to put the best possible face on the sorry situation in which they found themselves—all except Jamie, that is. He was honestly delighted with the idea that the earl would soon be his brother-in-law.

"I distinctly remember your saying you would never marry someone so far beneath your touch," Elsie persisted, perching herself on a chair opposite Alexandra.

Alexandra racked her brain for a rebuttal to the charge. "That was before he kissed me," she said, because nothing else came to mind.

Elsie regarded her with obvious skepticism. "That must

have been quite a kiss. But why are your eyes so red and puffy if you are happy about this betrothal?"

"My eyes are red from lack of sleep, nothing more. I was much too excited to do anything but lie awake and contemplate my future with the earl."

"Well, that is certainly understandable. It is not every day one becomes betrothed to a handsome barbarian who is rumored to be rich enough to buy half of England." Elsie sighed. "Oh, Alexandra, how I envy you. You do everything with such panache."

"Panache had nothing to do with it. The plain truth is the wicked charmer swept me off my feet," Alexandra declared, certain her gullible friend would spread the tale that the marriage between the Earl of Stratham and the daughter of Viscount Hardin was a love match. Better that than the ugly truth that the viscount had made colossal errors in judgment and his daughter was paying the price of his folly.

Elsie frowned. "Then the rumor Mama heard is false?"

"What rumor was that?"

"That you were forced to marry the earl because your papa had lost all his money."

"Good heavens! Wherever did Mrs. Trumbold come by such flummery?" Alexandra managed a laugh that almost sounded genuine. "Have you ever known me to do anything I didn't want to do?"

Elsie shook her head slowly. "No, I have not, now that I think about it."

"And you never shall." Alexandra laughed again. She was becoming quite adept at mimicking the self-confident young girl she had been until yesterday afternoon.

"As for Papa's losing all his money, I don't see how that is possible," she continued in the same lighthearted tone of voice. "Just this morning I was told I might buy all the bride clothes I wished." In reality, she had received a note from the earl suggesting she present the bills for her bride clothes to his solicitors. She had instantly rejected the idea, but she could see now she might have to rethink her position if she hoped to salvage what little dignity her family had left.

A look of immense relief brightened Elsie's plump face. "Well, I am certainly glad to hear that." She smiled fondly at

Alexandra. "You are like a sister to me; I couldn't bear to think you were marrying against your will."

Alexandra smiled back. "Not to worry, dear friend. I cannot imagine how such a silly rumor got started."

Elsie rose from her chair and gathered up her reticule and pelisse. "Well, I promise you I shall do my best to correct it before it goes any further," she said firmly. "You can count on me to tell the truth of the matter to everyone I know."

Alexandra stood up and caught her friend in a fierce hug. "I was certain I could," she murmured, fighting back a new flood of tears. With Elsie as her "town crier" she would soon have the quidnuncs of the *ton* so befuddled both she and her mother could once again walk among them with heads held high.

Larkspur Farm had never looked as welcoming as it did on the cloudy spring evening when Liam dismounted at its gate. He had ridden hard, stopping only long enough to partake of a meal and a few hours of sleep at one or another of the wayside inns between London and the West Country moors. Both he and his mount were close to exhaustion.

"Liam! Whatever are you doing in Exmoor? Last I heard you were bent on making an impression on London society." His half sister, Fiona, stepped through the door of the cottage and hurried toward him, her face wreathed in a warm smile that made his detour to the out-of-the-way farm well worthwhile.

Like him, Fiona was one of the old earl's bastards, but there the similarity ended. She was surprisingly straitlaced, considering her scandalous background, and had never approved of his smuggling, nor for that matter of anything else about his free-wheeling lifestyle. Still, there had always been an indefinable bond between them that both felt, but neither could explain.

"I had to visit The Aerie to arrange for some badly needed repairs," he lied. The embarrassing truth was he found it too difficult to keep his hands off Alexandra to trust he would remain a gentleman during the three weeks before their wedding—and a gentleman he must be if he hoped to persuade her to willingly share his bed once they were man and wife.

"I think you have developed a fondness for that dreadful old castle you inherited," Fiona chided.

Liam shrugged. "I suppose I have. It is, after all, the first thing I have ever owned."

He took a closer look at his beautiful sister. There was something different about her—a kind of glow that made her appear as if she were bathed in sunlight despite the ominous clouds overhead.

"Marriage to your duke agrees with you, Fiona," he declared. "I have never seen you look so well." His gaze dropped to the newly rounded contours of her slender body, which even her simple gown of coarse drugget failed to hide. "Almost too well, I'd say. You are turning into a plump little pigeon."

Roses bloomed in Fiona's cheeks. "I am not getting plump, you silly thing. I am with child." She surveyed him with shining eyes. "Can you believe it? This is the miracle for which I dared not hope. Adam is in the boughs. You would think he was the only man who had ever sired a babe."

"Where is the duke?" Liam asked. "I should congratulate him."

"Chopping firewood—his favorite occupation. He'll have enough chopped to carry my grandmother through the winter by the time Adam and I return to London."

"I shall seek him out once I've seen to my horse." Liam lifted the reins from the fencepost around which he'd looped them. "You can, I hope, put me up for the night. Both Thunder and I are on our last legs, and we have another long ride ahead of us tomorrow before we reach The Aerie."

"Of course. There is a plentiful supply of oats in the barn and an empty stall as well. In the meantime, I'll have Molly interrupt her housecleaning to make up your bed in the attic."

Liam stopped in his tracks. "You have hired Molly Blodgett as your maid?"

"Heavens, no. I have no need of a maid here at the farm. But Adam insists upon having her come in once a week to do the heavy cleaning." She hesitated. "And she is no longer Molly Blodgett; she is Molly Pinchert now, wife to Simon Pinchert, who manages Larkspur Farm while Adam and I are in London. You must have noticed the pretty little cottage Simon built for his bride when you rode past the south pasture."

"I did, as a matter of fact, and wondered whose it was." Liam had last seen his former mistress shortly after he'd acquired his title. He'd had little to say to the buxom innkeeper's daughter then; he'd have even less to say to her now. But it had never been Molly's talent for conversation that had led him to keep company with her. Even now, remembering her lush body and her insatiable appetite for sexual gratification, he felt his blood run hot through his veins.

Fiona laid her hand on his arm. "Simon is not a handsome charmer like you, but he is a good man and deeply devoted to Molly. I wouldn't want to see him hurt."

Liam scowled at Fiona's less than subtle hint that he control his lust while under her roof. "Your faith in me warms my heart, little sister," he grumbled. "I admit to having had my way with many a comely tavern wench and farmer's daughter. But I draw the line at other men's wives. There is no toss in the hay worth a bullet in the back."

"What a scoundrel you are, Liam Campbell." Fiona shook her head. "I prophesy that someday you will meet a woman who will break your fickle heart, and when you do, I shall not waste one moment of sympathy on you. For you shall deserve every minute of the misery you'll suffer."

Liam chuckled. "Be assured, little sister, if ever such a phenomenon should occur, you shall be the first to know, for I know how much you would enjoy saying 'I told you so.' But pray do not hold your breath. I should not want to be the cause of your suffering apoplexy in your delicate condition."

Fiona waited while Liam fed his horse and rubbed it down, then walked with him to where the duke was hard at work splitting firewood. Tall, black-haired, with a thin saber scar slicing his left cheek from eyebrow to chin, Adam Creswell looked every inch a nobleman, even in the faded farmer's garb he chose to wear when at his commoner wife's moorland farm.

"It is a good thing your aristocratic London friends cannot see you now, Your Grace," Liam declared when the duke laid down his ax to offer his hand. "I fear the shock would be too much for them. You wouldn't believe the scandal I created by simply removing my cravat."

Fiona moved to stand beside her husband. "Adam has few friends left to shock; he lost all but the most loyal of them the day he married me. Luckily he doesn't seem to mind."

Her eyes clouded. "But I fear he will mind very much if his misalliance robs him of the influence he needs to bring aid to the thousands of homeless veterans of the Peninsular Army—to say nothing of those returning from the Americas."

"You worry too much, my love. I shall prevail because my

cause is just." The duke slipped an arm around his wife's thickening waist, and Liam caught the look of love that passed between them—a look that made him feel as isolated as if they had suddenly drawn a drape over a window through which he viewed them. He had never thought to envy any man, but at that moment he envied the Duke of Bellmont, and not for his prestigious title.

"I would offer to stand with you when you make your next plea in the House of Lords," he said quickly to dispel the wave of loneliness that had washed over him, "but I fear a bastard earl from Exmoor would do your cause more harm than good. You can, however, count on me for generous financial support. My father's solicitors tell me I might well be the wealthiest man in all of England once the dust settles."

The duke raised a finely arched black eyebrow. "I take it then your inheritance has been validated."

"It will be in three weeks." Liam cleared his throat. "At which time I plan to marry Lady Alexandra Henning, the daughter of Viscount Hardin."

The duke's brow shot even higher and his wife's eyes fairly popped from her head. "*You* are going to marry a nobleman's daughter." Fiona's usually husky voice came out a high-pitched squeak. "I cannot believe it. You have always preferred—"

"Tavern wenches and farmers' daughters." Liam managed a halfhearted grin. "But that was before I became an earl and felt the need to marry to secure the title." Pride kept him from telling the truth of how his betrothal had come about. A marriage of convenience for monetary reasons would seem a tawdry thing to a man like Adam Creswell, who had willingly accepted social ostracism to marry the woman he loved.

"What is she like—this Alexandra Henning who has won your heart?" Fiona asked.

Liam thought for a moment. He needed to choose his words carefully so as not to give too much away. "She is highly intelligent, strong-willed, unfailingly proper. Oh, yes, and beautiful as well."

The duke gave a brief nod—whether of approval or disapproval, Liam couldn't tell. "In other words, the lady has all the attributes a man of wealth and title, such as you now are, looks for in a wife."

Fiona laid a hand on Liam's arm. "But do you love her?"

Liam avoided her inquisitive gaze. "I'll not lie to you, little sister. I am not certain I know the meaning of the word. But I admire Alexandra . . . and I want her more than I can remember wanting any woman in a very long time. Is that close enough?"

"It is probably the most I could expect from a rogue like you." Fiona frowned. "I assume the poor girl is madly in love with you. I've yet to meet a woman who didn't fall under your spell the moment you smiled at her."

Liam laughed in spite of himself, for what Fiona said had been very close to the truth until he met Alexandra. "I fear the lady is much too practical to be swept off her feet by any man," he said, "myself included."

"Then why did she agree to marry you?"

"I have to assume she had her reasons."

"But, Liam, this simply will not do. I know I said you deserved to have your heart broken, but I didn't really mean it." To Liam's surprise, tears welled in Fiona's eyes.

"Enough, wife." The duke placed a gentle finger on his wife's trembling lips. "Your brother knows what he is doing." Over his wife's head, he rolled his eyes at Liam. "Fiona cries at the drop of a feather nowadays."

Fiona frowned. "Stop patronizing me, Adam. You know I cannot abide it." She searched her husband's face. "Will you be too unhappy if we cut our time in Exmoor short? I may not entirely approve of Liam's reasons for marrying, but I should very much like to attend his wedding and meet this paragon of practicality he is taking to wife. I am, after all, the only relative he has—at least the only one he acknowledges—and I am certain his bride will have all her family at the wedding."

The duke planted a kiss on the tip of his wife's pert nose. "Then, my love, you and I shall be the bridegroom's family at the momentous occasion. It will fit in perfectly with my plans, for I have been thinking we should not delay the trip back to London much longer."

Liam felt stunned. It had never occurred to him that Fiona and Adam would travel all the way from Exmoor to attend his wedding—much less represent themselves as his family. Before he could gather his wits sufficiently to express his gratitude, Fiona announced that she planned to make a special supper in honor of his visit and brushing past him, headed for the cottage.

The duke watched her until she disappeared around the corner of the barn, then turned to Liam. "I assume Fiona told you we are soon to make you an uncle."

"She did, and I heartily congratulate you. As for myself, I think I shall enjoy that title a great deal more than the one I inherited last November. In truth, I find the idea of relatives in general strangely appealing. I have been a man alone so long, I grow tired of my own company."

The duke nodded. "I know the feeling well, but you may find you have more relatives than you want now that you are in possession of your father's title and wealth. One of them stopped at Larkspur Farm but a se'enight ago looking for you— a big, ugly fellow with shifty eyes and a head of flaming red hair that branded him another of the old earl's bastards."

"Did he say what he wanted of me?" Liam asked uneasily, suspecting he knew who it had been.

"Not really. He claimed he was seeking you out because the two of you had once been in the smuggling trade together, but I sensed there was more to it than that."

"Stegin Hobart," Liam said, certain now of the fellow's identity. "True, we did sail together, but not for long; I never felt certain I could trust him. Still, I am in his debt, for it was Stegin who told me about the solicitor's offer of fifty pounds to any of the old earl's male bastards."

"Then I predict he will try to collect on that debt, but for now I sent him on his way, believing you were in London." The duke propped his ax against the pile of firewood and brushed away the chips clinging to his homespun shirt. "I have another bit of disturbing news I'd prefer Fiona didn't hear. That old rumor recently surfaced again about your smuggling French spies into England, as well as brandy, during the war. Perhaps you should pay a call on Dooley Twig, the farmer Molly accused of starting it last time. As I recall, she claimed he was insanely jealous of you because you stole her from him."

"Molly is too impressed with her own charms," Liam said as anger sliced through him. "As a matter of fact, I stopped at the Twig farm when first I returned from Ireland and had a long talk with Dooley. He swore he had nothing to do with the rumor, and I believe him. He is much too superstitious to lie with his hand pressed to his mother's Bible. In truth it was

Fiona, and her farm, he wanted, not Molly. He would have far more reason to be jealous of you than of me."

"Then who started the rumor and why?" The duke's raven brows drew together in a scowl. "You have an enemy, Liam—a dangerous one who seeks to destroy your good name by vicious innuendo."

"I am well aware of that. I combed Exmoor and Cornwall for information about him last winter, but to no avail." Liam swore softly but explicitly. "Sooner or later I will find him and I guarantee before I've finished with the cowardly devil, he'll regret he lived to leave his mother's womb. But enough of my problems. I am keeping you from what Fiona says is your favorite occupation."

The duke shrugged. "Not to worry. It will soon be too dark to safely swing an ax. Ergo, shall we adjourn to the cottage for some fine, dark Exmoor ale before we partake of Fiona's 'special supper'?"

Liam shook his head. "Thank you for the offer, but I believe I'll take the air a bit longer. The smoke of London still lingers in my lungs."

"A wise choice. The clean moorland air can cure a man of many a townee ailment." The duke chuckled. "But if perchance it is our farm manager's hot-blooded young wife you seek to avoid, I fear you are foregoing a pint to no avail. Unless my eyes deceive me, that is the fair Molly heading your way this very minute."

Chapter Six

Liam's first thought, as he faced his former mistress, was that Molly was as seductive as ever. He'd almost forgotten the bold look in her dark eyes, the provocative pout of her full, red lips. He cursed the duke for abandoning him with the admonition that he was now a betrothed man and should act accordingly.

"So, Liam, ye've come back to Exmoor," Molly purred. "Or must I call ye milord now that ye're a high-and-mighty earl?"

"Liam will do, and my stay in Exmoor will be a short one," he said more curtly than he'd intended.

Molly didn't seem to notice his brusque manner. "Aye, Fiona told me ye intend to wed a fine London lady in three weeks' time. A shame I say, for ye'll find no pleasure in a stiff-necked blueblood, and I doubt the sons she bears ye will be as sturdy as the ones I'd have given ye."

She moved a step closer. "But I'll not think on that, for what's done is done—and what's to be will be. Ye're here now, and a little time with ye be better than no time a'tall, for I've missed ye something fierce, love."

Liam tensed. Molly had never been shy, but he didn't remember her playing the role of the pursuer in the past. She had always left that up to him. What had gotten into the fool woman? She was, as Fiona had reminded him, married to a decent man who adored her.

He retreated a step and found himself backed up against Adam's pile of firewood. "I find it hard to believe you've been grieving over me, Molly. I was told you married Simon Pinchert less than a month after I fled to Ireland—and he built you that pretty cottage I saw when I rode in."

"Simon Pinchert be nay a man, but a green lad as wet behind the ears as the newborn colt in your sister's barn when it comes to pleasurin' a woman. 'Twere a mistake to wed such as him after being lover to ye, and that's a fact."

Liam had never been one to judge another's morals—especially when he owed that person his life, as he did Molly. But he found himself strangely offended by her criticism of her husband's performance in the marriage bed. When had he become so sensitive? Moll had always been crude; it had never bothered him before. Her earthy vulgarity had been part of her charm.

Even now, despite his disgust of her runaway tongue, his body automatically responded to the invitation he read in her sultry gaze. He had been too long without a woman, and his unexpected desire for Alexandra had only heightened his frustration. Molly offered a temptation he found difficult to resist.

Desperation made him introduce a topic he hadn't planned to discuss with her. "I understand that rumor about the French spy has sprung up again."

Molly twisted a lock of her black hair around her finger. "Aye, Dooley Twig still holds it against ye that I preferred ye to him. But who's going to listen to him now that ye've a title and fortune?"

Liam shook his head. "You're wrong, Moll. It was not Dooley who lied about me. He swore his innocence on his mother's Bible, and he's not one to lie with his hand on the good book."

"And I say ye're a fool if ye believed him," Molly scoffed. "Who else hated ye enough to accuse ye of a hanging crime? It were his bed I crawled out of when I crawled into yourn."

"I've no idea who the culprit was, but I intend to find out," Liam said, then couldn't resist adding, "It would appear I have an enemy whose hatred of me has nothing to do with you."

As he knew she would, Molly took offense at his suggestion. Vain as a peacock, she could not conceive of anything happening within the confines of her small world that did not directly relate to her. She tossed her head defiantly. " 'Twere because ye was walking out with me ye was lied about, and that's the truth of it. Why else did the bloomin' excise men come lookin' to me to find ye that dark, rainy night last autumn?"

"Who knows?" Liam shrugged, already bored with this woman for whom he had once seriously lusted. Unlike Alexandra, Molly presented no mental challenge, and he realized he missed the verbal sparring he'd come to expect each time he encountered the stubborn aristocrat. It was not a revelation he welcomed. In more ways than one, his prickly bride-to-be was complicating his life.

He took Molly's hand in his and raised it to his lips in the gesture he'd observed many a London toff perform. "I'll bid you good evening then, Mistress Pinchert," he said in an effort to take his leave of her without any hard feelings between them.

Molly shivered with obvious delight and sidled up against him. It was a move calculated to turn his blood to liquid fire, and his traitorous body responded. Still, reason prevailed and he stepped aside, explaining, "My sister will be expecting me for the 'special supper' she's cooking."

"'Tis naught but a side of pork and the season's first peas and potatoes—a meal ye've had a hundred times over." Molly shaded her eyes against the setting sun and smiled up at him. "Before ye take your supper, ye'll want to see the sturdy little colt Fiona's pony birthed this very morn," she said coyly.

"I doubt it. What sets this creature apart from the dozens like it I've seen in the past?"

Molly chuckled. "'Tis not the critter hisself ye'll find interesting, ye numskull, but the barn where he were birthed. There be a loft full of sweet-smelling hay right above the stall, and ye can look all ye wish with no one the wiser."

The implicit suggestion in her whispered words was unmistakable, and Liam's temperature rose another degree or two. He couldn't begin to count the times he'd tumbled Molly in just such a hayloft or in the back room of her father's inn. She was as lusty a woman as ever he'd met, with none of the inhibitions suffered by his future bride. The thought of once again burying himself in Molly's lush body magnified the ache in his groin tenfold.

He felt her fingers tug on his, and in spite of his better judgment, followed her toward the barn. One more tumble for old times' sake he rationalized. He owed her that for saving his life. But the closer he came to the open door, the more he dragged his feet. His body was willing, but his mind rebelled.

"What is it, love?" Molly asked when he dug in his heels. "I cannot credit ye've turned shy on me." She trailed a provocative finger from the hollow of his throat to his midsection, and instantly he knew what it was that bothered him. The last time a woman had touched his chest with her finger, she had nearly poked a hole in it.

A picture of Alexandra berating him for his many sins flashed through his mind. How had he described her to Fiona? Intelligent, strong-willed, unfailingly proper? Molly was none of those things. She was not even the good-natured trollop he remembered. There was something cold and predatory about this woman who betrayed her young husband without a second thought, and he had lost his taste for meaningless rutting.

He laughed in spite of himself. The irony of the situation was reminiscent of the Shakespearian comedies Vicar Edelson had insisted he read as a boy. He had managed, by devious means, to trap Alexandra into marrying him—but unwittingly he'd trapped himself as well. For now no woman would satisfy him except the one woman who wanted no part of him.

It had been three weeks and four days since the announcement of Alexandra's betrothal to the Earl of Stratham appeared in the *London Times*. With her mother's help—and the promise of immediate payment by the earl's solicitors—she had persuaded her dressmaker to produce her wedding dress and bride clothes within the allotted time. Invitations had been delivered to a small but select group of wedding guests; Elsie had joyfully agreed to be her only bridesmaid; and her father had made the necessary arrangements for the wedding to take place in St. George's main chapel.

All that was missing was the bridegroom. The earl had failed to return to London on the date he'd promised, and where she had once lived in dread of facing the horrid fellow at the altar, she now lived in terror she might end up standing there alone.

Her mother was certain that was what would happen. The viscountess had said as much at least a dozen times in the past four days and laid the blame for the fiasco squarely at the feet of the viscount. "What a fool you were to take the word of a barbarian from the hinterlands," she wailed. "Dierk Wolverson proved such men are without honor or scruples; why should his bastard be any different? It is all a monstrous plot to publicly humiliate me."

Jamie, of course, staunchly defended the earl, as did Alexandra's father, who declared Stratham a sterling fellow in whom he had complete faith. But Alexandra couldn't help but notice the viscount looked increasingly gray and haggard with each passing day.

It was no surprise when he took her aside to warn her to maintain a confident demeanor whenever she appeared in public. "My creditors ceased badgering me once I revealed the terms of my agreement with the earl," he confided, "but if they so much as sniff a hint of trouble, they will swoop down on me like a pack of vultures."

Alexandra did her best to do as he asked—until with St. George's chapel bespoken for but three days hence, her mother taken to her bed with the megrims and her father hiding out at the house in Chelsea, she finally cracked under the strain.

"Please don't weep, Alexandra," Elsie begged as the two of them shared a pot of tea in the third-floor salon of the Henning town house. "Some women look beautiful when they weep; you look rather like a boiled owl, and it is only a case of prewedding jitters. I know for a fact every woman has them because both my sisters turned into watering pots the week before their weddings."

"I am certain you're right." Alexandra mopped her streaming eyes, blew her nose and hiccupped noisily. "I just wish it was all behind me."

"Of course you do," Elsie murmured sympathetically. "And it doesn't help a bit that your betrothed isn't here to reassure you." At which comforting words, Alexandra sobbed anew.

Elsie was in the process of plying her with hot tea and lemon biscuits when the ever stoic Gibson appeared in the doorway to announce, "The Earl of Stratham and the—"

Before he could finish what he had to say, the earl pushed him aside and strode into the room. "What the devil have you done to make Alexandra cry?" he demanded of Elsie, instantly reducing her to a blob of quivering jelly.

Alexandra scarcely noticed her friend's deterioration, so relieved was she to see the man she had vowed but an hour earlier to despise forever. With Jamie's favorite curse word on her lips, she leapt to her feet and hurried toward him. "My lord," she gasped, "where have you been? The wedding is but three days away."

He caught her upper arms in his strong fingers and searched her face with narrowed eyes. "Never say those tears are because you thought me such a fly-by-night fellow I would humiliate you by being late to my own wedding?"

"Of . . . of course not," she stammered, aware that Elsie was listening to every word they said. Her garrulous friend had done a remarkable job of convincing the *ton* that the marriage between Lady Alexandra Henning and the Earl of Stratham was a love match. This was no time to disabuse her of that belief. "I . . . I just missed you," she finished lamely.

"You did?" Liam couldn't believe his ears, until he caught the furtive glance Alexandra cast toward the other young woman in the room and realized she was putting on an act for her friend's benefit. Apparently she had spent the past three weeks doing her best to make the *ton* believe she was marrying a man for whom she cared deeply—which would explain the suggestive comments slyly cast his way when the duke and he had lunched at Boodles. Whatever her reasons, he applauded her efforts; it would save him the embarrassing task of admitting the truth to Adam and Fiona.

"I am sorry to be so late in arriving," he said, pressing a tender kiss to her forehead. "But my return trip from Exmoor was slower than I'd planned—"

"For which I take full blame." The husky feminine voice behind him made him realize the sight of Alexandra in tears had so discomposed him, he'd completely forgotten he'd left Fiona standing in the hall.

She stepped up beside him. "My apologies, Lady Alexandra. Had Liam not been escorting my carriage, he would have been here when promised. But my husband insisted on limiting the number of miles I traveled each day."

She stared at Liam, an expectant look on her face, but before he could gather his wits enough to realize what she wanted of him, she extended her hand to Alexandra and declared, "I am Fiona Creswell. If I wait for my ill-mannered brother to introduce us, I shall never meet the miracle woman who has won the heart of the care-for-nothing rogue."

Fiona's words startled Liam. He distinctly remembered telling the annoying female he did not know the meaning of this "love" he'd heard other men profess for their wives. True, he admired Alexandra—and his desire for her grew stronger with every passing day. He even admitted to feeling a certain tenderness toward her—when she wasn't tearing strips off his hide with her sharp tongue. But as for losing his heart to the virago . . . *Never!* He breathed a fervent prayer of thanks that his was not a heart so easily lost.

"Well, my lord, are you or are you not going to present me to your sister?" Alexandra's eyes sparked with anger over what she apparently considered his lack of social grace.

He smiled, pleased to see her in a temper again. He had hated it when she'd looked so vulnerable. "Of course, sweeting," he drawled, and watched the sparks fly anew as he made the necessary introductions and was introduced in turn to the plump young woman with the slightly bulging eyes, whom Alexandra declared was Miss Elsie Trumbold, her "dearest friend in all the world." Liam gallantly raised the chit's fingers to his lips, and she rewarded him with a series of giggles and sighs that quite unnerved him.

He moved to stand by the window while the ladies perched on three of the spindly-legged chairs he was afraid to sit on and settled in for a friendly coze.

The next half hour was an edifying one. Liam was accustomed to dealing with men—namely the moorland farmers he'd known as a lad and the rough-and-ready seamen with whom he'd plied the smuggling trade in later years. Though he had known a great many women in the biblical sense, he had rarely had occasion to speak with them at great length.

Nor had he ever before watched two strong-minded females size each other up as Alexandra and Fiona were doing. The experience raised the hair up the back of his neck. In truth, by the time Fiona announced it was time to take her leave, he wondered if there was any fortune great enough to make it worthwhile leg-shackling himself to one of the mind-boggling creatures.

Then, just when he thought the worst was over, Fiona leaned forward in her chair, clasped Alexandra's hand in hers, and declared with obvious sincerity, "I am so glad I persuaded Liam I should accompany him today. Now that I've met you, my mind is at ease. You are exactly the kind of woman the scapegrace needs to keep him in line."

Liam groaned.

"And I feel much more at ease with the idea of wedding the bar—the earl now that I know I have a sister on whom I can count for guidance, Your Grace," Alexandra returned with equal sincerity.

Liam groaned again. It was obvious he would have to stay on his toes around these two formidable females who discussed him as if he were a pet pug they planned to jointly train.

Fiona rose from her chair and turned to him, eyes twinkling with mischief. "I shall wait for you in the carriage, Liam. I am certain you will want a moment alone with your betrothed after so long an absence."

Miss "Giggles and Sighs" promptly declared that she would depart as well to allow the "lovebirds" a little privacy.

Liam pasted a smile on his face, but in truth, the last thing he wanted was a moment alone with Alexandra; he might be tempted to wring the annoying chit's lovely neck before they made it to the altar, and he had no desire to see the old earl's fortune revert to the crown.

He cursed himself for his stupidity. He should have known better than to introduce Fiona to Alexandra. How had he failed to notice the remarkable similarities between the two women? Reformers, both of them, and he was not a man to be made over to suit any woman.

"Your sister is charming, my lord," Alexandra said in an obvious effort to make conversation once they were alone.

Liam scowled. "My sister is a meddlesome busybody. We have nothing in common except the evil old man who sired us. I am sorry I encouraged her to come to London for my wedding."

Alexandra's eyes widened. "Surely you do not mean that, my lord."

"No, I don't suppose I do. Chalk it up to the fact that I am in a foul mood."

"So I noticed, my lord."

Liam scowled. "Devil take it, Alexandra, my name is Liam. I would that you use it in the future. I have no use for the title I inherited and I grow weary of your everlasting 'my lording' me."

"Yes, my lord . . . Liam. I shall endeavor to remember to use your given name from now on." Two angry white lines bracketed Alexandra's mouth. "Have you any other orders for me before you take your leave . . . Liam?"

"None I can think of." Liam ground his teeth—a habit he'd

acquired shortly after his first encounter with Lady Alexandra Henning. Granted she had reason to resent him, but must the touchy female take offense at something as reasonable as requesting her to use his name instead of his title? There was nothing for it but to take his leave of her before he said something he would regret.

"I bid you farewell then, Alexandra," he said quietly. "But I shall live in anticipation of our wedding day."

Alexandra looked dumbfounded. "Surely you're not leaving London again with the wedding but three days away."

"Oh, but I am. My brother-in-law has offered us White Oaks, his estate in Kent, for the fortnight following our wedding. I want to make certain everything is in readiness for our arrival."

"But why must you see to something you could just as well send a servant to accomplish?"

If he didn't know better, Liam would swear she was loath to see him leave. "I was not aware you were so anxious for my company," he said, and watched her cheeks turn crimson.

"I am merely thinking of appearances. We have never been seen together in public. People will begin to wonder why we are marrying."

"Let them wonder. I care nothing for the opinions of strangers," he snapped, inexplicably disappointed with her practical reason for wanting him to stay in London. "I know why I am marrying you, and we both know why you are marrying me."

"Why *are* you marrying me, Liam? You avoided answering my question the last time I asked it."

Liam ignored the persistent voice of his conscience. "I have a number of reasons," he said a little too glibly to sound entirely candid. "This is just one of them."

Quickly, before she could realize what he was about to do, he pulled her to him and kissed her. He had silenced her before with a kiss; he could only hope this one would effectively forestall any more questions on the dangerous subject of his reasons for marrying her.

He meant the act to be a simple pressing of his mouth to hers. But her lips were tantalizingly soft and the scent of moorland wildflowers in her hair stirred his senses to fever pitch. With a moan of pleasure, he teased her lips apart with his tongue and proceeded to explore the sweet, warm depths of her mouth with a passion that threatened to turn him into the savage she already believed him to be.

Alexandra had known Liam was going to kiss her. She'd read his intent in the darkening of his eyes an instant before his mouth claimed hers. She just hadn't known this kiss would be so different from the other two they had shared, until his tongue slipped between her parted lips.

She tensed as a wave of heat uncoiled deep within her and spread to her fingers and toes, the very roots of her hair. She wanted to push him away, to protest his shocking violation of her person. But a strange lethargy invaded her limbs, rendering her incapable of doing anything but cling to his broad shoulders for support.

"There, little shrew," he murmured when long moments later he raised his lips from hers. "Now you have something to remember me by until the day I claim you as my bride."

Alexandra opened her eyes to stare at the handsome man who had just kissed her witless. "This is not the first time you have used your kisses to avoid answering my questions," she said, struggling to keep her balance on legs that had an alarming tendency to wobble. "I would still know why you dishonor me by refusing to be seen with me in public between now and our wedding day."

"Devil take it, Alexandra, are you so naive you cannot understand that I am far more likely to dishonor you if I stay in London?" Liam clenched his fists in obvious frustration. "Why do you think I spent the past three weeks in Exmoor? I had no business there that could not wait another six months."

Alexandra swallowed uncertainly. "I . . . I do not know."

He spat out a string of obscenities that would have curled her hair had it not been braided in a neat coronet. "Do not be misled by the fact that I speak the King's English like a gentleman," he said, turning on his heel to pace the small room like an animal in a cage. "I am as far removed from a gentleman as your Cockney maid is from a royal duchess.

"I am, in short, precisely what I once heard you call me—a barbarian. A man who has always lived by his own rules, which more often than not meant no rules at all. If you have any doubt about this, you have only to ask my sister. She will, I am certain, verify every word I've said."

He stopped his pacing long enough to search Alexandra's face. "I can see you still don't understand what I am trying to tell you."

Impatiently, he ran his fingers through his shoulder-length flame-colored hair. "I have known a great many women . . . intimately," he said in a voice devoid of all expression. "Tavern wenches, innkeepers' daughters, lusty farm girls. Some of them natural trollops, some good, honest women—but not a one of them what someone like you would term a 'lady.'

"In truth I had never thought to desire a 'lady.' The few I've observed in the past have been pale, spineless creatures who couldn't warm a man's bed half as well as a flannel-wrapped brick. But I desire you, my lovely innocent, with every fiber of my being. I want you warming my bed. I have since the first moment I saw you—and I am accustomed to taking what I want. I cannot, therefore, guarantee to keep my hands off you between now and our wedding night if I spend time in your company. Do I make myself clear?"

Alexandra took a deep, calming breath. "Perfectly clear. You are saying you are marrying me, not for social position as I was led to believe, but rather because you lust after me the same way your father lusted after my mother. It is, I presume, an inherited trait—like red hair."

Liam's hearty laughter bounced off the walls of the small salon and spilled into the hallway where a young Irish footman waited patiently to hand him his hat and gloves.

"What is so funny?" Alexandra demanded. "I cannot credit I misinterpreted what you said."

Liam extracted a handkerchief from his pocket and wiped his brimming eyes. "You misinterpreted nothing, my clever love. Indeed, you plucked the kernel of truth from my idiotic ramblings as surely as a robin might pluck a worm from a pile of dung. I am laughing because for once the devil's plans will be thwarted—and because in three days' time I shall be both the richest and the luckiest man in all of England."

Chapter Seven

Alexandra spent another in a long siege of sleepless nights on the eve of her wedding, haunted by the Earl of Stratham's words: "I want you warming my bed and I am accustomed to taking what I want."

She had so many questions about what to expect of the marriage bed and no one to whom she could pose them—certainly not her mother. The viscountess had broken her silence on the subject just long enough to state, "Men revel in the obscene act of copulation; women must endure it to produce the requisite heir."

But how could this be true if an intelligent woman like the Duchess of Bellmont was so obviously in love with the duke? Alexandra wished she knew the duchess well enough to seek her advice, but one cozy chat, however pleasant, could not be termed a close friendship.

Elsie was no help. She, too, was an innocent in a society where innocence and ignorance were considered synonymous.

In desperation she turned to Bridget. "I told you onct the shocking ways a gentleman takes his pleasure with a light-skirt," the giggling abigail replied. "My married sister says 'tis all the same—wife or whore—only the gentleman don't leave money on the bedside table for his wife."

This disturbing bit of information left Alexandra more nervous and confused than ever. In the end, she decided there was nothing for it but to face the marriage bed as she had faced every other challenge life had offered—with courage and common sense. Unfortunately, that simple homily seemed a great deal more plausible in the light of day than in the dark of night. Hence her long, sleepless travail.

She finally dozed off from sheer exhaustion shortly after she heard the rest of the household stirring, only to be awakened by her excited young brother less than an hour later. "Wake up, Alex," he demanded. "It's a beautiful day and everyone in the house is getting ready for your wedding. Even Fergus has a new collar for the occasion." He held out his terrier for her viewing.

Alexandra surveyed her brother through bleary, sleep-deprived eyes. He wore an oversized silk banyan that was a castoff of his father's, a pair of scruffy-looking house slippers, and a grin that spread from ear to ear. A squirming, elegantly collared Fergus was tucked under one arm.

"Come back later," she moaned. "I am much too tired to talk to you right now."

Jamie plopped himself down on the end of her bed. "You can't sleep late on your wedding day. Everything is at sixes and sevens downstairs and you are the only one who can put things in order."

"Someone else will have to handle it. I am too exhausted to care." Alexandra yawned and slid deeper under her quilt.

Jamie promptly tugged it off her. "There is no one else. Papa has locked himself in the book room, the butler has quit in a huff, and Mama is driving poor Cook out of her mind with last-minute orders about the wedding breakfast."

He grinned. "And you might as well forget about going back to sleep because I heard Mama order the footmen to bring up your bath."

Alexandra groaned.

"But I have something here that will perk you up." He patted the bulging pocket of his banyan. "One of the Duke of Bell-mont's footmen just delivered a gift for you from Liam. I answered the door because no one else was about."

"Liam?" Alexandra raised a disapproving eyebrow.

"The earl asked me to call him by his given name," Jamie said smugly. "*He* never treats me like I am just a stupid school-boy."

Alexandra struggled to a sitting position. "Are you implying I do?"

"Well, you do give me a lot of orders. Gadzooks. Alex, sometimes I can hardly tell the difference between you and Mama."

Alexandra glared at her young brother, wounded to the quick by the less than flattering comparison he had drawn between Stratham and her. "Where is my present from the sainted earl?" she demanded in a voice sharpened by frustration.

Jamie set Fergus on the bed beside him and withdrew a slim, black velvet jewelers' case and a neatly folded square of foolscap from his pocket.

Pearls, she surmised—the standard gift the bridegrooms of the *ton* presented their brides on their wedding day. Yawning hugely, she opened the case and to her amazement, found an exquisite necklace formed of delicate cloisonné flowers. Every flower was different from every other, yet each was perfect in itself and separated from the next by a small, sparkling diamond. She gasped, awed by the beauty of the unique piece of jewelry.

Jamie's murmur of astonishment echoed her own. "I say, Alex, that's a bit of all right if you ask me." He leaned forward to take a closer look. "What does the earl's note say?"

Reluctantly, Alexandra withdrew her gaze from the superb necklace. Unfolding the square of foolscap, she read the brief message scrawled in bold, black script.

Whenever I am near you I am reminded of the moorland wildflowers I love.

She regarded the brief note in stunned silence. It said so little, yet conveyed so much. Had she misjudged the earl? This was not the kind of gift or message she would have expected from the insensitive clod she believed him to be.

Fergus rolled onto his back and Jamie absentmindedly scratched the terrier's plump belly. "Liam must like you a lot to have had the jeweler make such a beautiful necklace especially for you," he declared in an awestruck voice. "Moorland wildflowers have a special meaning for him. He told me he picked bouquets for his mother when he was a young boy, because she said they made their dreary little cottage more cheerful. I wager he could tell you the name of every flower in the necklace."

Alexandra brushed the tip of her finger over one of the delicate creations she recognized as a cowslip. "It is incredibly beautiful," she murmured, amazed that Stratham had shared such a telling glimpse of his childhood with Jamie.

She had never thought of the earl as a child. But now she found herself picturing the sturdy little carrot-top he must have been. She wondered what his mother had been like and if she were still alive. She wondered why the woman had lain with the old earl and born a son out of wedlock.

It occurred to her that she might feel very different about the present earl if he had been as candid with her about his early life as he'd apparently been with Jamie. So far, he'd spent more time silencing her with kisses than talking to her.

"Liam sent me a gift as well," Jamie said, fishing in the same pocket and withdrawing a small, square leather case and another foolscap note. Perching cross-legged beside his sleeping dog, he lifted the lid and examined the contents. "It's a watch," he declared. "A gold watch with a gold chain like the one Papa always carries."

Carefully, he removed his treasure from its case and laid it on the coverlet while he unfolded the attached note and read aloud:

I am doubly blessed in making your sister my wife. For I gain as well the brother I have always wanted.

"What a capital fellow!" Jamie looked up from his note. "Isn't it lucky we met him by the Serpentine that day—and luckier yet he decided right off he wanted you to be his wife."

Alexandra refrained from comment. Stifling a yawn, she made a pretense of examining the watch. She turned it over, expecting to find a coat of arms like that inscribed on her father's watch. Instead, she found a miniature dragon staring at her with tiny emerald eyes. "What an odd inscription," she said, handing the watch back to its owner.

Jamie's grin spread from ear to ear. "There's nothing the least bit odd about it. Liam knew this was the sort of thing I'd like above all. He said I would have been the most honorable of knights and a true dragon-slayer had I lived in olden times."

"You've talked to the earl about . . . your stories?"

"I have," Jamie admitted. "And would you believe it—he used to make up the same kinds of stories when he was my age. He was lonely too, you see. I suspect it had something to do with his being a bastard."

Alexandra felt a stab of jealousy. She had spent many a rainy afternoon drawing pictures of the elaborate settings and the characters who inhabited them in the fantasy world her frail young brother had created to pass his long hours in a sickbed. Together they had woven tales of ancient castles and evil sorcerers, stalwart knights and the ferocious dragons they were pledged to slay.

Until recently it had been a world only she was allowed to enter. The knowledge that Jamie had invited the Earl of Stratham inside its boundaries as well came as a shock.

"Liam has promised to take me to Exmoor to see The Aerie one day before the summer is over," Jamie boasted.

"The Aerie? Surely he can't expect you to climb cliffs in search of an eagle's nest. That sounds incredibly dangerous."

Jamie laughed. "I thought you knew about The Aerie. It isn't a bird's nest, silly. It's the medieval castle he inherited from his father. It was named that because it's perched on a high cliff overlooking the sea."

Color bloomed in his gaunt young cheeks, and his green eyes sparkled with delight. "It is just like the castle in your drawing—with turrets and battlements and a drawbridge over a moat. And inside there are suits of rusty armor and battle-axes and a fireplace big enough to roast a whole ox."

He paused to catch his breath. "It's the place Liam loves most in all the world, and he's promised to share it with me because he knows I'll love it, too. But you needn't worry he'll expect you to come with us. He said it's not the sort of place he'd ever take a girl."

Jamie's innocent parroting of his hero's words hit Alexandra like a splash of ice water. Gone was the brief moment of hope she'd felt for her marriage when she'd opened the earl's unusual gift. Now she realized the unique necklace bore a striking resemblance to the jeweled collar fastened around Fergus's neck. Each in its own way was a symbol of ownership.

Apparently, like most men of title, the Earl of Stratham considered a wife nothing more than a brood mare designed to perpetuate his bloodline. He had already told her he planned to set her up in a London town house—probably after he'd gotten her with child.

"Why should the earl share his precious castle with me when he's shared nothing else of himself?" she snapped. "I am, after all, only the woman he has trapped into marrying him so he won't have to resort to flannel-wrapped bricks to warm his bed."

Too angry to care what she said, she had let the bitter words pour from her mouth unheeded—until she saw the shock registered on Jamie's face. Then she could have cut out her tongue. Until that moment, she had been careful to conceal her resentment about her marriage from her starry-eyed young brother.

"That's not true," Jamie sputtered, leaping off the bed to stand glowering over her. "Liam would never do such a thing, and if you say he did, you're a liar, Alexandra Henning." Choking back a sob, he snatched up his watch and his dog and ran from her chamber.

Alexandra couldn't remember when she had felt so ashamed or so desperately angry—with herself and with the despotic earl whose presence in her life had once again made her lose her hard-won control. Only this time her runaway tongue may have cost her something far more precious than Sir Randolph's regard.

Liam knew something was wrong the minute Jamie Henning burst through the door of the anteroom where he and his best man, the Duke of Bellmont, waited to be escorted into the wedding chapel. He stopped his restless pacing and approached the boy with an outstretched hand.

Jamie ignored his gesture of friendship and fixed him with a look so intense, Liam felt as if the green eyes searching his could see into his very soul—a soul far too black to be fit for the perusal of an innocent lad of tender years.

"Is it true?" Jamie asked in a small voice. "Did you trap my sister into marrying you against her will?"

Liam felt as if the blood flowing through his veins had suddenly turned to ice. "Where did you hear such a thing?" he demanded.

Jamie's gaze never wavered. "From Alexandra herself. I didn't believe her at first, but now . . ."

"Now you have to wonder why your sister would say such a hurtful thing if there were no truth in it." Liam cursed the vicious little shrew he was about to marry. Granted she had been ill used, but she should have vented her spleen on him and her father—not on her young brother.

"Alex has a terrible temper. Sometimes she says things she doesn't really mean when she's angry." The hopeful note in Jamie's voice made Liam's heart ache. For one brief moment he was tempted to lie to this boy he had already begun to think of as his brother. He couldn't do it—not when the lie would drive a wedge between Jamie and his sister.

"I'm afraid that what Alexandra said is true," he admitted, and heard the duke's sharp intake of breath.

Jamie looked close to tears. He was obviously having difficulty coping with the idea that he had given his trust and friendship to a man not worthy of the honor.

"But why would you do such a dishonorable thing?" His voice sounded heartbreakingly young.

Liam had all he could do to keep from confessing that honor was a virtue he had never been able to afford. He settled for a terse, "I had my reasons," and cringed at the disillusionment reflected on the boy's face.

"I fear it is my honor the earl seeks to protect, Jamie." Liam glanced up to find Viscount Hardin standing in the doorway, dressed to the nines and looking decidedly grim. He cast a warning glance at Liam, then turned his full attention on his young son. "Think about it. The earl could not force your sister to marry him. Only I, as her father, could do so."

Jamie's eyes grew wide with shock. "But why would *you* do such a thing, Papa?" he asked, repeating the question with which he'd charged Liam a moment earlier.

The viscount shrugged. "A man is driven to desperate measures when he faces the prospect of debtors' prison."

"Debtors' prison?" Jamie's voice came out a thin, high squeak.

"Exactly," the viscount said, and calmly proceeded to explain how and why he had convinced his proud young daughter she must marry the Earl of Stratham to secure the generous marriage settlement he offered.

Twice Liam tried to interrupt when he realized Hardin was taking all the blame for the agreement into which the two of them had entered. But each time, the viscount silenced him with a telling look. The man appeared determined to paint himself the sole culprit in the affair, and, from the look of horror Jamie turned on him, he was succeeding at the task.

A sad little smile twisted Hardin's lips when he finished his expurgated tale. "I can see you realize you were laying the blame for your sister's resentment at the wrong feet," he said quietly. "The earl has been all that is honorable in this sorry business."

Liam opened his mouth to object to that blatant untruth, but again the viscount stopped him with a warning look.

"I knew it all along." Jamie was pale as a ghost, but he faced Liam with shining eyes. "I might not like the way Papa treated Alex, but I am glad he picked you to be her husband. I know Alex will be, too, once she gets over being mad about not having anything to say about it. She likes getting her own way, you see."

He brightened noticeably. "She already likes the gift you gave her, so that should help. But I think it might help even more if you tell her you were only joking about marrying her because you don't like warming your bed with a flannel-wrapped brick."

Liam groaned, remembering his unfortunate comment, and behind him, the duke made a strangled sound as if he were struggling to choke back a laugh.

"Excellent advice, Jamie," the viscount declared solemnly, "and on that note I suggest you join your mother in the chapel, since the carriage bearing Alexandra should arrive momentarily."

Liam faced Hardin the minute the boy was out of earshot. "Why did you lead Jamie to believe you and you alone were to blame for arranging Alexandra's marriage without her consent? I was as much a part of it as you were—and every bit as desperate to pull it off for reasons of my own."

The viscount raised an expressive brow. "Had I not been such a poor excuse for a father, my son would not have had to look elsewhere for a man he could trust and admire. You are obviously that man, and it is important you remain so."

"Not at the expense of disillusioning him in his father."

Hardin shrugged. "Jamie is a bright youngster. It was only a matter of time until he saw me for what I am—a man whose shallow nature is suited only for the most frivolous of lifestyles. The sad truth is I have neither the temperament nor the wisdom to provide my son with the guidance he so desperately needs."

A brief flicker of pain twisted the viscount's handsome face. "I do, however, care for my children in my own haphazard way and wish the best for them. Odd as it may seem, considering your unfortunate background, you strike me as a man capable of providing the affection and stability that has always been lacking in both their lives."

"I fear you are imagining virtues in me that do not exist," Liam said, decidedly uncomfortable with the strange turn the conversation had taken.

"I think not." The viscount smiled. "I have great hopes for you as my headstrong daughter's husband . . . and as my son's mentor. In short, unless you have serious objections, I intend putting both of my children in your capable hands from this day forward."

Liam stared at Hardin in stunned amazement. "Are you saying you wish me to act as Jamie's guardian?"

"I am, unless for some reason you object to taking on the responsibility."

"I do not," Liam said without a second thought. "I've grown very fond of the boy. But what of your wife? Surely she will be opposed to such an arrangement."

"Henrietta will, of course, raise a token objection to prove to herself she is a caring mother. But in truth, she is as shallow in her way as I am in mine. I marvel that the two of us managed to produce such remarkable offspring."

Hardin brushed an invisible speck of lint off his elegant sleeve. "With the handsome quarterly stipend you have promised her, the Viscountess Hardin will be able to take her proper place in London society—something she has always longed to do. Jamie would only be in her way."

The thought of the sensitive youngster being "in the way" of his parents' superficial lifestyles sickened Liam. It was easy to see that Alexandra and her young brother had never known the kind of caring relationship he had shared with his mother in the few short years before she'd died.

"Jamie may join Alexandra and me once we are settled in our own home," he said with quiet resolve. "Be assured the boy will be a welcome addition to our household. When he is well enough, I will see him enrolled in Eton. Until then, I'll provide him with the finest tutor available."

"I could ask no more." Executing a graceful bow, the viscount bid a cordial good day to both Liam and Adam, then withdrew from the anteroom.

An embarrassing silence descended on the small room once the viscount had taken his leave. Adam was the first to break it.

"Fiona said there was more to the story of you and your lady than met the eye—but I doubt even she could have guessed how much more."

He surveyed Liam with dark, hooded eyes. "I take it your marriage to Lady Alexandra is somehow connected with the validation of your inheritance."

"It is," Liam said tersely, dreading the questions his brother-in-law was certain to ask.

Adam nodded. "I thought as much. But I'd as soon not hear the fascinating details. I tend to talk in my sleep, and as a result I have no secrets from my wife. This is one secret I think she would be better off not knowing."

Laughter tilted the corners of the duke's mouth. "But I seriously doubt I can resist the urge to inform her how her charming brother has blotted his copy book with his new bride."

He searched Liam's face with his perceptive dark eyes. "Did you really give Lady Alexandra to understand she was replacing 'a flannel-wrapped brick' in your bed? One would hope a man with your legendary prowess with the opposite sex would show a bit more finesse than that."

Liam's temper flared. "Devil take it, Adam, this is not a humorous matter. Alexandra has a fiery enough temper as it is. She does not need added provocation."

The duke chuckled. "What you say may be true, my friend. All the same, you had best pray your lady-bride has a sense of humor as well. That may be all that can save you after a comment like that."

With her father by her side, Alexandra took the first step down the central aisle of St. George's chapel. This was the moment she had been dreading for the past four weeks. But now that it was here, she was too exhausted to feel anything except an odd detachment from the scene around her. It was almost as if she were a spectator at the wedding rather than one of the major participants.

She wished she had refused the glass of wine her abigail had claimed would relax her. Between that and the multitude of sleepless nights she'd recently suffered, she could barely keep her eyes open.

With dismay, she surveyed the aisle ahead of her. The fifty carefully selected guests who had gathered to witness her marriage to the Earl of Stratham filled only the first few pews of the vast nave, and the distance she must cover to reach the altar seemed interminable.

Elsie walked ahead of her, looking plumper than ever in a pink bridesmaid gown lavishly trimmed with ruffles and bows and satin rosebuds. For once in her life, the Honorable Miss Trumbold was too nervous to giggle.

Alexandra's hand lay lightly on her father's arm, and her feet moved in measured cadence with his, but she felt strangely alienated from him. In truth, the aging dandy in an elegant burgandy cutaway coat, starched cravat and white knee breeches seemed as much a stranger as the man who waited at the altar to claim her as his bride.

"Smile for God's sake, Alexandra," the viscount muttered through clenched teeth. "This is your wedding, not a funeral."

Stifling a yawn, she managed a wooden smile. Though she doubted a mere twisting of her lips would add much to her lackluster appearance. She was too blonde and fair of skin to look anything but washed out in the virginal white her mother had insisted she wear "to silence the gossips' speculation about the hurried affair." As a result, with her pale cheeks and the dark smudges beneath her eyes, Alexandra felt certain she looked more like a wraith than a bride.

The only color on her entire person was in the cloisonné flowers circling her neck. She hadn't planned to wear the earl's gift; the comparison she'd drawn between it and Fergus's collar was still too vivid in her memory. But at the last minute, she'd changed her mind.

She was glad now that she had added that one touch of color to her drab appearance. For as she drew closer to the altar, her first glimpse of the earl confirmed that he was breathtakingly handsome in a smartly tailored coat of russet satin and a gold brocade waistcoat, both of which complemented his flame-colored hair and gold-flecked eyes. He had even abandoned his usual scarf for an elegant white stock.

Beside him, the Duke of Bellmont was equally impressive in stark black, relieved only by a snowy cravat tied in the fashionable mathematical style. It was, she decided sleepily, the crowning touch to this farce of a wedding that both the groom and best man looked more spectacular than the bride.

With an undeniable twinge of conscience, Liam watched his

bride-to-be approach the altar on the arm of his future father-in-law. She was dressed in white from head to toe and carried the bouquet of white roses he had sent her. With her somber face and downcast eyes, she looked impossibly young and vulnerable, and a fiercely protective feeling swept over him. In truth, it was all he could do to keep from stepping forward to take her in his arms and reassure her she had nothing to fear from him.

He even felt a passing urge to call a halt to the solemn proceedings, until he reminded himself that the vast fortune he coveted was not all that was at stake. Much as she resented his hold over her, Alexandra would be far better off as his wife than as the penniless daughter of a nobleman dispatched to debtors' prison.

Furthermore, if the truth be known, she did not find him as offensive as she pretended. She was much too honest and forthright to return his kisses with such passion if she did.

He smiled to himself, remembering Jamie's warning that she was enraged over his stupid comment about the flannel-wrapped brick. He had no doubt but that slip of the tongue would come back to haunt him on his wedding night. Alexandra in a temper was a sight to behold.

But one kiss and he'd wager her anger would turn to passion—passion that would send the two of them up in flames. Shocked by his body's instant, and embarrassing, reaction to the erotic daydream, he forced himself to think of something other than his long awaited wedding night. Like a drowning man spying a raft, he fixed his gaze on the necklace circling Alexandra's throat. The fragile blossoms nestling against her milk white skin reminded him of the first brave flowers of spring unfolding on a moor still dusted with snow.

He smiled, pleased with his imaginative analogy—pleased that his reluctant bride had worn the gift he'd designed for her. It was, he told himself with a certain smugness, a propitious omen.

Silently, he took his place beside her facing the vicar, and found himself shocked by the telltale signs of exhaustion so apparent on his bride's face. Had he asked too much of her—demanding she prepare for a wedding in three weeks? For all her fiery temper and sharp tongue, Alexandra was a fragile little thing.

He drew a deep breath and prayed the ceremony would be a

short one for both their sakes. To his disgust, the pompous vicar promptly launched into a lengthy discourse on the holy state of matrimony. Another twist of the knife as far as Liam was concerned; he found it difficult to delude himself that there was anything holy about a marriage based on desperation and greed. Turning a deaf ear to the pious sermon, he concentrated on counting the panes of glass in the ornate window over the chancel.

"Do you, Liam Francis Campbell, Earl of Stratham, take Lady Alexandra Henning to be your lawfully wedded wife?"

The vicar's question shocked him back to the reality of the moment. "I do," he said loudly and clearly, turning his head to gaze down at the slender, golden-haired woman standing beside him. Her head was bowed; her eyes closed, and she appeared to be swaying to some silent music only she could hear.

"And do you, Lady Alexandra Henning, take Liam Francis Campbell, Earl of Stratham as your lawfully wedded husband?"

She made no response to the vicar's question. Her eyes remained closed, her lips softly parted.

Liam held his breath, waiting to hear the two words that would guarantee his future as a man of wealth and property.

And waited. And waited.

Behind him, in the first pew, Viscount Hardin nervously cleared his throat; beside him, the Duke of Bellmont did the same. Liam's pleasant euphoria vanished like steam escaping a kettle.

Another long moment passed, and still Alexandra's eyes remained closed, her lips silent. Liam struggled to control his temper, certain this tortuous waiting game she was playing was her way of getting even with him and her father for their cavalier treatment of her. As he watched, she swayed toward the vicar, released her hold on the bouquet Liam had sent, and dropped it to the floor—clearly demonstrating her disdain for him.

A look of horror crossed the vicar's heavily jowled face. "We await your answer, my lady," he declared in a voice barely audible over the startled murmurs of the guests.

"My lady?" the cleric repeated, and Liam heard a rustling like the wind dancing through dry moorland grasses as the fifty guests leaned forward, ears straining. But Alexandra doggedly maintained her stubborn silence.

A surge of white-hot anger roared through Liam's veins. He was a man accustomed to determining his own destiny. It galled him that at this moment his future lay in the hands of a vicious little termagant bent on revenge.

There was nothing for it but to resort to the only means of communication he had managed to establish with the fiery-tempered aristocrat. Catching her upper arms in a punishing grip, he yanked her to him and crushed her lips in a savage kiss.

To his surprise she responded with a mindless passion that threatened to buckle his knees. With a muttered epithet, he ended the kiss as abruptly as he'd begun it.

"Damn it, Alexandra, say the words," he demanded over the cumulative gasp of the assembled guests.

"The words?" Her eyelids fluttered open and she fixed him with the wide, startled gaze of someone waking from a dream. *Devil take it*, the vexatious woman seemed determined to carry this act of hers to the bitter end.

Liam gave her a none too gentle shake. "Say I do!" he charged, anger and frustration sharpening his voice. Abruptly, he changed to a hoarse whisper only she could hear. "Be done with this pointless game you're playing, Alexandra, or so help me God, I will wash my hands of the whole sorry business. There is not enough money in all of England to make dealing with such a shrew worthwhile."

Chapter Eight

Alexandra was well aware her new husband was so angry he could, as the saying went, "spit nails." He had even gone so far as to threaten her—at least she assumed it was a threat. The words "There is not enough money in all of England to make dealing with such a shrew worthwhile" had seemed a bit odd, considering he was paying, not receiving, the marriage settlement.

She would be the first to admit that falling asleep at her own wedding had been inexcusably rude. But it was not as if she had done it deliberately. Her unexpected catnap had shocked her as much as it had everyone else. She had never before realized that it was actually possible to fall asleep on one's feet.

But she had been so exhausted and the vicar had droned on and on about the holy state of matrimony—a term she felt certain did not apply to a marriage in which the bride was an "asset" sold to the highest bidder. Still, she probably should have made a greater effort to stay awake.

Her ears still burned from the jaw-me-dead lecture her mother had given her after the ceremony, and her father . . . well, Papa had drunk himself into oblivion at the wedding breakfast—something she had never before seen him do.

Even Jamie had given her a sour look and mumbled something about his hero being wrongfully accused. As for the raised eyebrows and behind-the-fan tittering of the wedding guests who had crowded into the Henning town house for the lavish breakfast, that had been almost enough to send her to her bedchamber in tears. Pride alone had made her see the wretched ordeal through to the bitter end, dry-eyed and defiant.

But it had been the Earl of Stratham who had appeared to suffer the most embarrassment over her unfortunate gaffe. An odd thing, since she distinctly remembered his making a point of disclaiming any interest in what the *ton* thought of him.

He hadn't spoken a word to her since the ceremony. She shivered, remembering the icy rage in his eyes every time his gaze met hers during the wedding breakfast; she cringed just thinking about the stony silence he'd maintained on the long ride to the Duke of Bellmont's Kent estate. She would sooner have ridden in the carriage bearing his valet, her abigail, and the luggage.

With silent concentration, he had eaten the elaborate supper the duke's French chef had prepared for them. She hadn't been able to choke down a bite. Time and again she had attempted to explain . . . to apologize. He would have none of it.

Now, waiting for him to join her in the lavish rose-and-gold bedchamber to which the duke's housekeeper had assigned her, her head ached and her stomach roiled dangerously. The idea of sharing a marriage bed with a stranger had been unnerving enough; contemplating sharing it with an angry stranger was downright terrifying.

Warily, she eyed the bed that dominated the room. It was not the largest bed she had ever seen—in fact, no larger than the one she had slept in most of her life. But imagining what she might be expected to submit to in that bed turned it into the most imposing object she had ever viewed.

A sharp rap on the door took her by surprise. Before she could gather her wits, Liam flung it open, stormed into the room, and slammed it behind him. From his high color and glazed eyes, she concluded he'd been drinking; from the glass of brandy he carried, she concluded he intended to continue doing so.

Nervously, she noted that his flame-colored hair had a wildly disheveled look as if he'd been running his fingers through it, and a fine golden stubble on his jaw proclaimed he was in need of a shave. Her gaze dropped to his ankle-length green velvet robe and to his bare feet plainly visible beneath it. A flush crept up her neck and onto her cheeks; it didn't take much imagination to determine he had nothing on underneath the loosely belted robe.

Stopping just short of where she stood, he set his glass on the dressing table and surveyed her from head to toe with a look that chilled her to the bone. "What is that abomination you are wearing, madam?" he demanded, eyeing her prim flannel nightrail—one of the dozen her mother had provided her. "If the neckline of that incredibly ugly garment was one inch higher, it would cover your ears. Need I remind you that you are no longer a spinster, but a married woman who should dress to please her husband?"

Before Alexandra could reply to his churlish comment, he stepped forward, hooked his fingers into the top of the placket and ripped the gown open, sending buttons flying. "There, that's better. When I pay dearly for a piece of merchandise, I want to see what I have bought."

Alexandra choked back her cry of horror. Her worst nightmare had come to pass. The Earl of Stratham was every bit as crude and vulgar as she had imagined him to be. Her first instinct was to clutch the gaping edges of her nightrail and cover her nakedness. Instead, she raised her chin defiantly and clenched her fists at her sides. Nothing the crass fellow could do to her would induce her to cower in fear.

To her surprise he backed away, widened his stance and crossed his arms over his chest. "Cover yourself, madam," he ordered imperiously. "I can see I have made a bad bargain. You have nothing to offer that tempts me to exercise my marital rights."

Cheeks burning, Alexandra drew the two sides of her nightrail together and held them in place with shaking fingers. She searched his face, wondering if he could possibly mean what he'd intimated.

"I am entirely serious," he said, as if reading her mind. "For you are, as I heard you tell that idiot, Twickingham, your mother's daughter. A man would have to be insane to waste his time on a frigid blueblood when there are plenty of warmhearted, red-blooded tavern wenches willing to offer him the comfort he seeks."

Alexandra raised her chin a notch higher. "And who would know that better than you, my lord?"

Liam ignored her pointed insult. Retrieving his glass, he raised it high. "I salute you, Madame Shrew. You have played your cards very cleverly. With that ugly charade you carried on at our wedding, you managed to kill every last spark of desire I had for you—which I feel certain was what you had in mind."

Alexandra stiffened, torn between humiliation and relief.

"Rest easily in your chaste bed, wife," he said, his eyes narrowing to cold, amber slits. "I promise I will never join you there until you beg me on bended knee to do so."

Alexandra tossed her head. "Then I shall die a happy virgin, my Lord Stratham. For you shall see hell freeze over before you see me do that."

"Mayhaps I shall," he said coldly. Draining his glass of its contents, he tossed it against the stone of the fireplace, shattering it into a hundred sparkling fragments. "Or mayhaps you may one day tire of playing the spoiled brat and become the woman you were meant to be."

Liam woke to a throbbing headache, a sick stomach, and a taste in his mouth that made him think he must have been drinking swamp water. "Close to it," he muttered, remembering the vast quantity of the duke's French brandy he had consumed the previous evening.

Good, dark Exmoor ale never left him in such a miserable condition—only the evil stuff the London toffs prized so highly. He might legally be a wealthy English aristocrat now that he had danced to the old earl's vengeful tune, but at heart he would always remain a common West Country smuggler.

The clock on the fireplace mantel struck the hour of nine, a good two hours past his usual time of rising. He wondered if his bride was up and about, and what in God's name he might say to her when next they met. If his memory served him correctly, he had pretty well emptied his budget on her some twelve hours earlier. He rolled onto his back, stared at the ceiling and contemplated what he'd done.

To begin with, he'd drunk far too much brandy. That moment at the altar when he'd realized she held his future in her vindictive little hands had shaken him badly. He'd despised her for it. Yet hadn't he callously taken control of her life but a scant month earlier?

He'd accused her of acting like a child, and with good reason. But had his own behavior been any less juvenile?

He'd called her a coldhearted shrew, and so she was. But for all her vile temper and sharp tongue, she was a veritable angel compared to the greedy devil he'd become since he'd seen the chance to get his hands on the old earl's fortune.

It had been a classic case of the pot calling the kettle black.

Alexandra and he deserved each other. Maybe that was why the kisses they shared were so passionate. But passion notwithstanding, it was obvious they were totally incompatible.

He would establish her in London as he had promised and have done with the annoying chit. Only then would he be able to find peace of mind. But first he must devise a means by which they could survive the next fortnight without murdering each other.

"Are you awake, my lady?"

"I am now," Alexandra muttered in answer to her abigail's inquiry. Reluctantly, she opened her eyes. She had slept from sheer exhaustion, but it had not been a restful slumber. She was not yet ready to face the day or the humiliating memory of the previous evening.

Not that anything of consequence had happened on her wedding night. She had merely learned that she had disgusted her husband to the point that she need never again worry about his lusting after her—information which should have come as a great relief. Why it left her feeling strangely empty and depressed was something she had not yet had the urge to explore.

With a lazy yawn, she struggled free of the bedclothes and sat up.

"That's more like it, my lady. 'Tis past the hour of nine and you've no cause to lie abed when you've had such a good night's sleep all alone in this lovely big bed."

Alexandra gritted her teeth, tempted to give her nosy abigail a well-deserved set-down. But the annoying girl was undoubtedly echoing the gossip in the servants' quarters. Her mother had warned her long ago that servants always knew everything that went on in the houses in which they worked—and passed the information on to the servants in surrounding houses. By eventide, the failure of the Earl and Countess of Stratham to consummate their marriage would probably be the topic of conversation in every drawing room in Kent.

Bridget busied herself laying out Alexandra's new underclothes and stockings, obviously aware she had overstepped her bounds. "If you please, my lady, I have a message for you," she said in a subdued voice.

"Indeed? From whom?"

"From his lordship. He sent a footman to say he is waiting in the morning room to break his fast with you."

Alexandra stared at her annoying abigail in disbelief. Why should a man who couldn't stand the sight of her want to look at her across the breakfast table? Unless, of course, he, too, had learned of the gossip in the servants' quarters.

That had to be it. He probably planned to tell her he had decided to rescind his promise to stay out of her bed rather than have his manhood questioned by the duke's neighbors. It was exactly the sort of thing one could expect a rake to do.

She washed her face and hands. Then, with Bridget's help, donned one of her new morning dresses—a green sprigged muslin. Eschewing her usual neat coiffure, she tied her hair off her face with a green satin ribbon and let it hang in loose waves down her back. It was a small act of defiance, but she knew her hair was her crowning glory and Liam's claim that she held no attraction for him had been surprisingly hurtful.

"There now, I am ready to greet my lord and master," she declared and sallied forth to find the morning room and the man who was her husband in name only.

Alexandra took his breath away. Liam had admired her pale, golden hair the first time he'd seen her. But he'd had no idea how beautiful it would look cascading down her back like a heavy, silken mantle—or how it would gleam in the morning sunshine streaming through a window. Heart thudding like a triphammer, he stumbled to his feet as a goggle-eyed footman seated her in a chair on the opposite side of the table.

"Good morning, my lord," she said softly, and something in her melodic voice put him in mind of waves lapping gently against the hull of a ship moored in a calm Exmoor bay. *Good God*, he was waxing poetic over the vicious little shrew.

"Good morning, Alexandra," he managed through lips strangely stiff and unwieldy. "You slept well, I trust."

"Exceedingly well," she said, though the sooty smudges beneath her eyes belied her answer. Liam felt a stab of guilt, certain his unconscionable behavior had contributed to her insomnia. Whatever her sins, she had not deserved such crudity from the man whose name she bore.

He waited until she had apprised the footman of what food she wanted from the lavish display on the sideboard, then dismissed the fellow with a wave of his hand. "I have a proposal I should like to make you," he began after clearing his throat.

Alexandra cast him a disparaging look. "I felt certain you would have after I spoke with my abigail."

Liam frowned. How, he wondered, did her abigail enter into the stormy relationship he had with his wife? Unless O'Riley had been spreading tales in the servants' quarters and the woman had passed them on to her mistress. But no, he knew his valet better than that. O'Riley was the soul of discretion. In the interest of harmony, he let the bewildering statement pass without comment.

"Here is my proposal," he began again. "I have promised to set you up in a town house of your choice once we return to London, and I fully intend to do so. But in the meantime, we are guests of the Duke of Bellmont for the next fortnight, and I refuse to insult Adam and Fiona by cutting short our stay."

Alexandra studied him closely, a wary look in her expressive eyes. "What is your point, my lord?"

"My point is we have two alternatives. We can spend the next fortnight quarreling with each other—which would be devilishly unpleasant—or we can declare a truce and spend the time exploring the beautiful Kent countryside together. I, for one, vote for the latter alternative.

"That is it? Your entire proposal? Nothing else?"

"Nothing else, Alexandra. And if you are worried that I will forget my promise to you, put your mind at ease. For I give you my word I will keep it."

"Your promise about the town house in London?"

"That and any other promise I have made you," Liam said, knowing full well which promise the little prude had in mind. He saw the doubt in her eyes and watched her worry her full bottom lip with her small, white teeth, as if trying to decide if she could trust him.

She had never looked more enticing nor more vulnerable than she did at that moment. Despite their many differences, he felt an overwhelming urge to protect the golden-haired hellion from anyone who could harm her, including himself.

"A truce for a fortnight, Alexandra?" he asked softly, holding out his hand.

Alexandra hesitated but a moment before placing her fingers in his. "A truce, Liam," she said, wondering if this man she had married thought her so naive she believed his proposal was as innocent as it seemed. But she, too, was weary of their squabbling, and, in the final analysis, the choice she made was of little consequence. For nothing could 'change the fact that under English law he was henceforth her lord and master.

Liam rose from the table, a congenial smile on his face. "What is your pleasure then, my lady? We will take turns choosing our daily pastimes, and yours is the first choice."

Alexandra thought for a moment. "If we are to see the Kent countryside, I should like to do so on horseback. It has been a long time since I've ridden anywhere but on the bridle paths of Hyde Park—a frustrating experience at best for an avid horsewoman. I should like to feel the wind on my face again."

"Then a ride it shall be. I am told Adam keeps a fine stable, but I shall leave you to determine that. I am no judge of horseflesh."

Alexandra rose to stand beside him, amazed at his frank admission. There was not another man she knew who would dare make such a statement. In the circles in which she traveled, it would be considered unmanly. She frowned. "You didn't ride in Exmoor? How then did you get about?"

"I rode when on shore, of course, but mostly astride Exmoor ponies, which are the only logical mounts on the moors. One pony looks pretty much like another."

Liam offered his arm and walked with her to the foot of the magnificent stairway leading to the upper floors. Strangely enough, not a servant was in sight. Alexandra glanced about her, wondering how many eyes were peering through the keyholes in the dozen or so doors lining the vast entryway.

"I'll wait here while you change into your riding habit," Liam said, glancing down at his own rather shabby nankeen jacket and buckskins. "These are the only clothes I own that are suitable for riding, so you will have to take me as I am."

Alexandra felt a twinge of annoyance. The man was an earl, for heaven's sake. Yet he offered no apology for looking like a stable hand—merely informed her she would have to take him as he was.

"I suppose that fierce scowl on your face indicates you find it strange that I am not more interested in fashionable attire," he said, and to her surprise he sounded a bit sheepish. "The thing is Mr. Weston's jackets and the starched cravats Beau Brummell advocates are so blasted uncomfortable, and since I couldn't care less if I impress a gaggle of London aristocrats I shall probably never see again . . ."

Alexandra shook her head. This man to whom she was married was a puzzling fellow. One time he maintained he cared nothing for the opinion of the *ton*; another time he flew into a towering rage because she had embarrassed him before fifty of its members. Such behavior was erratic even for a male of the species.

He favored her with a boyish grin. "But take heart, Madam Wife. We do have one thing in common."

"And what is that, my lord?"

"I, too, like the wind on my face, but I am more at home on the deck of a ship than astride a horse."

"You have a yacht?" Alexandra wondered if that, like his medieval castle, was forbidden to women.

"I have only recently acquired a yacht. It was part of the inheritance I received when the Earl of Stratham died last autumn. But I have yet to captain it." He hesitated a long moment. "The truth is all my experience at sea has been on a fishing smack."

Alexandra stopped on the first step and turned to find her eyes nearly even with Liam's. "You were a fisherman then before you inherited your title. It is, I believe, an honest profession. Did you think me so high in the instep I would belittle it?"

Liam's mouth curved in a wicked grin. "There may have been fish caught aboard *The Wayward Lady*, but not while I captained her. A fishing smack was my vessel of choice because such a ship was as little noticed on the French coast as on the English—and the deep well in her hold meant to transport sole and flounder was just as handy for storing kegs of brandy."

"Brandy?" Alexandra blinked. "Good heavens, never say you were a smuggler!"

"Ah, but I was. And it was an excellent way to make a living while the war lasted." Liam laughed. "Don't look so shocked. Smuggling is considered an honorable profession in Exmoor and Cornwall—by everyone except the excise men."

He leaned against the banister, one long buckskin-clad leg crossed over the other. "It was either that or become a farmer. Tell me truthfully, can you picture me behind a plow?"

Alexandra smiled in spite of herself. "No, but it is not too difficult to picture you as an outlaw. It is a wonder you survived long enough to inherit your title."

Liam shrugged. "There were only two occasions when I was in any real danger. But I shall save those stories for another day."

She had climbed two more stairs when a thought struck her. "Did my father know of your former profession when he arranged my marriage to you?"

"He did. But don't judge him too harshly. Even a nobleman tends to become more democratic when desperate for money."

"And Jamie. Does he know you were once a smuggler?" she asked, frowning at the man who watched her from the foot of the stairwell.

"Of course. But it makes no difference in our friendship. Your young brother is one of those rare individuals devoid of prejudice. I've spent many a pleasant morning at Hyde Park recounting my adventures at sea to the lad."

Alexandra shook her head. "The young scamp never said a word to me."

"He probably thought you would refuse to marry me if you knew about my past. I take it he didn't realize you had no choice . . . until you apprised him of that fact yesterday morning, that is."

A guilty flush heated Alexandra's cheeks. "He goaded me into it. I fear my tongue has a tendency to run away with itself when I am angry."

Liam chuckled. "I shall remember that in the future."

Alexandra had reached the first landing when she heard him call out, "One thing more, Madam Wife."

She turned to stare down at him. "Yes, my lord."

"Leave your glorious hair unbound . . . if you please. I would enjoy seeing it soar on the wind as you ride."

Liam might be an indifferent judge of horseflesh, but he was a bruising rider. Once they reached a stretch of open meadow, Alexandra gave her mount its head, and Liam easily stayed with her until she slowed her lively mare to a trot and then a slow walk.

Her heart pounded from the exhilaration of her reckless ride, and she laughed aloud from the sheer joy of feeling the wind on

her face and in her hair. "That was wonderful," she declared.
"I don't know when I have enjoyed anything so much."

"Nor I." Liam slowed his gelding to match the mare's pace.
"You are a superb horsewoman, Alexandra. I have never before
appreciated the phrase 'the lady has an excellent seat.' I do
now."

His gaze swept the part of her anatomy for which a sidesad-
dle was designed, and the devilish twinkle in his eyes brought
the usual flush of heat to her face. She raised a questioning
brow. "I thought it was my hair that interested you."

"That too," he purred, leaning forward in the saddle to brush
a stray lock off her cheek. "There are many things about you
that I find interesting, Alexandra."

She frowned. "I was not aware that the truce you proposed
included flirtation."

"But of course it did. I always flirt with beautiful women. It
is one of life's greatest pleasures."

"Which undoubtedly explains all those red-blooded tavern
wenches waiting for you with open arms."

Liam grinned. "If I didn't know better, Madam Wife, I
would think you were jealous."

Alexandra tossed her head. "Dream on, my Lord Stratham."

He laughed aloud, and she felt the ice that had encased her
heart for the past month thaw a fraction. It was fun to tease and
be teased. It was even more fun to have a handsome man flirt
with her—and it had been a long time since she had enjoyed
such a pastime.

But what was she thinking of? Liam had made it all too clear
what he really thought of her last evening. If he was flirting
with her now, it was merely to gain his own ends. With a sharp
command, she urged her mount forward onto a narrow lane
bordering the hawthorne hedgerow at the edge of the meadow.

For the next few minutes they rode in silence until the grassy
swale gave way to an orchard of ancient apple trees, the gnarled
branches of which bore a sparse crop of tiny green apples.
"We're in luck," Liam said, picking two of the apples from a
low-hanging branch. "I know this variety. It is one that thrives
in Exmoor. We call it Spring Transparent because it bears fruit
in early May, sometimes even late April if we have a warm
spring."

Alexandra watched him withdraw a neatly folded handkerchief from his pocket and lovingly polish both apples. "Granted, these are still pretty green," he said, handing one to her, "but that is how I ate them when I was a boy, because I could never wait for them to ripen. My mother and I started looking forward to a special treat as soon as we spied the first pink blossom on our tree in early spring."

Gingerly, Alexandra bit into her apple and found it so tart it made her mouth pucker. "It is an unusual flavor," she said, wondering how she could dispose of it without offending him.

Liam took a healthy bite of his, wiped the juice from his chin and scowled at what was left of the apple. "Strangely enough, it isn't as delicious as I remember. It is just an under-ripe apple, and a rather inferior one at that compared to those grown in the duke's orangery."

He shook his head. "Is that what affluence does to one? Or do we always remember our childhood treasures as more perfect than they were?"

Something told her it was not just his memory of an apple that he questioned. A certain bleakness in his expression prompted her to say, "Jamie told me you and your mother lived in a small cottage on the moors."

"We did, until I was twelve years old."

"And then?"

"And then she died." The chill in his voice invited no further questions about his past. But with the few words they had exchanged on the subject, Alexandra had gained a brief, illuminating glimpse into the heart of the man she had been forced to marry.

Once she thought about it, she realized that until that moment it had never occurred to her that the Earl of Stratham had a heart.

Chapter Nine

The first day of the truce had been surprisingly pleasant, despite the new Countess of Stratham's discovery that her husband, the earl, was not only a bastard, but an ex-smuggler as well. Oddly enough, she did not find this unduly shocking—perhaps because for once in her life she was not subjected to her mother's interpretation of the news.

Furthermore, Liam had proved he could be a perfect gentleman when he put his mind to it. He was also a charming companion, both on their morning ride and on their leisurely afternoon tour of the thirty odd rooms in the Duke of Bellmont's gracious brick and timber manor house.

So charming, in fact, she had decided to celebrate their newfound amity by wearing her favorite dinner dress that evening. It was an elegant green silk with a skirt that rustled nicely when she moved and a neckline two inches lower than any she had ever before worn.

She had been aching to show off the gown ever since she'd purchased it over her mother's objections, and tonight seemed as good a time as any. It was, in fact, the first time she had been free to wear such a vivid color. Young, unmarried women were restricted to virginal white or the palest of pastels—insipid colors she had always despised.

A glance in the cheval glass confirmed that the classic lines of the gown complemented her slender figure, and the deep lustrous green brought a glow to her pale skin and turned her eyes a sparkling emerald. Her wedding necklace of jeweled wildflowers was the perfect crowning touch, and she turned this way and that, admiring her reflection. If nothing else, marriage had given her the freedom to dress as she pleased.

Bridget spent a good half hour arranging her mistress's heavy flaxen hair in a simple but elegant coronet, then sent her on her way with the parting words, "I'll wager me yearly earnings you'll not be sleeping alone this night, my lady."

For once, Alexandra was too pleased with herself to take offense at the audacious maid. "You would be working for nothing if by some miracle my Lord Stratham turns out to be a man of his word," she murmured under her breath.

He was waiting for her in the salon adjacent to the formal dining room, lounging in his usual indolent fashion against the sash of the French windows. He appeared to be staring through the glass at the chilly, moonlit garden.

He, too, had dressed for dinner in a rich brown serge frock coat with matching drill trousers and another of the silk scarves he favored knotted loosely around his neck—as formal attire as she was ever likely to see on her nonconformist husband. He really was a handsome man—so handsome, in fact, he quite took her breath away.

He turned from the window as she entered the room, and the ready smile on his face slowly changed to a look bordering on awe. "You have outdone yourself, Madam Wife," he said as she walked toward him. He murmured something about the provocative whisper of her silken skirt. But she noticed his gaze lingered on the necklace circling her throat and the expanse of bosom exposed by her daring décolletage.

"You are not, I hope, planning to wear that gown in public," he said with a frown.

"It is entirely proper now that I am a married woman."

"On the contrary, Alexandra, a gown that fires a man's imagination the way that one does will never, under any circumstances, be proper."

He raised a finely arched brow. "Is this some fiendish plot you've devised to become a wealthy widow at an early age?"

"My lord?"

"Surely you realize that as your husband, I shall be forced to call out any noble lecher who loses his head over you. I might make a creditable showing with a pistol. But if the blackguard chooses swords, I shall be run through before I can take a deep breath. A smuggler has little call to perfect the gentlemanly arts."

Alexandra laughed. "How is it I have never before realized you are a wicked tease?"

"Probably for the same reason I have never before realized

you are a dangerous siren. We are strangers to each other, Madam Wife."

"Perhaps if our truce holds, we may become friends in the next two weeks."

"I think not."

Alexandra stared at him, shocked by his terse words and the bitter disappointment that unexpectedly gripped her.

"I cannot be your friend, Alexandra. Fool that I am, I lied when, in the heat of anger, I claimed I no longer desired you. We can be lovers . . . or we can be strangers, possibly even enemies. But you and I can never be just friends."

Liam saw the startled look in her eyes and the brief flash of pain. He had to ask. "Why did you do what you did at our wedding? Do you truly hate me that much?"

"Hate is probably too strong a word to express how I feel toward you. I resent your power over me—your ability to control my life. Can you blame me for that?"

"No. I would feel the same. But your behavior at the altar expressed more than resentment."

Her cheeks flamed. "Yes, well I've been trying to talk to you about that, but you refused to listen to me. It wasn't as if I did it on purpose. I hadn't slept for ever so long, you see, and the vicar kept rattling on about 'holy matrimony' which I felt certain didn't apply to our . . . arrangement."

She stared at the floor, as if unable to meet his gaze. "Was what I did so horribly embarrassing to you? I thought you didn't care what others thought of you."

"I don't."

"Then why did it make you so angry? I dozed off for only a few seconds. It is not as if I fell across the altar, or anything dreadful like that. Though I suppose dropping my bouquet was bad enough. My mother certainly let me know what she thought of it."

Liam stared at her, dumbfounded, as a picture flashed before his eyes of her bowed head and closed eyes, her swaying body and limp arms after the bouquet had dropped to the floor. How could he have failed to see she had succumbed to exhaustion?

He cupped her chin in his fingers and forced her to look him in the eyes. "I called myself a fool a moment ago. I am worse than that. I am a complete idiot. I didn't realize you had fallen asleep. I thought you were purposely refusing to speak your vows, and when you tossed—no, dropped your bouquet to the floor, I thought—well never mind what I thought. I fear it is I who should be apologizing to you, Alexandra."

"Well, I should hope so!" Her eyes flashed with anger. "No matter how much I might resent your high-handed ways, I would never purposely make a public spectacle of myself. I am, after all—"

"I know, you're your mother's daughter. But I am going to kiss you anyway." Drawing her into his arms, he did just that—deeply, passionately and with a profound tenderness that welled up from the very depths of his being

Her response, as always, was instant and instinctive. Gold-tipped lashes brushed her heated cheeks; lips that had been tight with indignation curved softly beneath his, and her slender body melded against him in unconscious surrender. A strange mixture of triumph and terror engulfed him and he realized that sometime in the last two turbulent months, his jaded, care-for-nothing heart had begun to soften toward this troublesome minx whom a bitter old man had decreed he take to wife.

Ending the kiss, he studied her innocent young face with an intensity that made her blink. She was as different from him as noonday is to midnight. Yet he was beginning to think a future without her in it would be unbearably dull.

He wanted her in a way he had never wanted any other woman—not just her body, which he knew he could seduce if he employed a little of the expertise he'd gained over the years. He wanted her clever mind, fierce loyalty and caring heart as well.

His painful early morning soul-searching had brought him face-to-face with a startling truth. It was a case of all or nothing where Alexandra was concerned—and to gain one, he must be willing to risk the other.

"Lovers or strangers," he said softly. "The choice is yours, Alexandra—and I swear I will abide by it."

Gently he pulled the pins from her hair, tossed them aside, and combed his fingers through the heavy silken strands he'd set free. "When our fortnight in Kent is over, I will purchase that town house in London I promised you. Then it is up to you to say if you want me to share it with you."

Lovers or strangers. Alexandra had fallen asleep with Liam's words ringing in her ears. She woke to the same litany. All her life she had clamored for the right to determine how she

would live her life. Now the most unlikely of men had given
her that right, and strangely enough, she felt more bewildered
than liberated.

If he truly meant what he said, then the day would come
when she must make the decision he demanded of her. But that
day was a fortnight off—ample time to learn why a man who
admitted he desired her and had paid a fortune to claim her as
his wife, would be willing to leave it to her to decide if she
would share his bed and bear his children.

She sighed. Nothing was the simple black or white she had
once believed it to be. Everything was, in fact, a muddled gray.
Her astonishing response to Liam's kisses proved she was not
the ideal candidate for sedate spinsterhood she had believed
herself to be; his remarkable offer proved he was not the insensitive barbarian she had believed him to be. In truth, she no
longer knew what she believed about anything.

Now fate, in the form of the weather, had seen fit to add yet
another complication to her perplexing life. For there would be
no jaunting about the Kent countryside for Liam and her today.
Rain splattered against the windows and coursed in crystal
rivulets down the glass in the morning room, where she ate her
solitary breakfast. The room that had looked so bright and cheerful yesterday was this morning dark enough to warrant a brace
of lighted candles on the table and another on the sideboard.

She wondered if Liam had gotten soaked to the skin during
his nocturnal rambling. She wouldn't ask. She refused to give
him the satisfaction of knowing she had stood at her window
and watched him ride into the night just minutes after he'd
kissed her tenderly at her chamber door.

Most likely he had been on his way to visit one of those red-
blooded tavern wenches for whom he'd expressed such a fondness. It was, she knew, the sort of thing men did—especially
men who were known rakes. There was nothing too shocking
about that.

But the fierce jab of pain she'd felt at the thought of his sharing another woman's bed had been profoundly shocking. She
wondered if he would be faithful to a wife whose bed he shared,
or if he would expect to continue his rakish ways once he took
up residence in that London town house he'd promised her.
That was one of the first things she must determine before she
made her fateful decision.

"You are up and about at an early hour, Alexandra." The cheerful-sounding male voice jolted her to attention. She glanced up to find Liam standing in the doorway, looking amazingly bright and chipper for a man who'd had but a few hours of sleep.

He was dressed in tight black trousers, a pair of well-worn boots, and a white shirt, wide of sleeve and open at the throat. A wide leather belt with an ornate gold buckle circled his narrow waist. Alexandra swallowed hard. She had never seen a man dressed in such a manner—much less one with flaming red hair and eyes that gleamed like amber gem stones.

He filled his plate, took a seat opposite her and poured himself a cup of the fragrant black coffee she'd noticed he preferred to tea. "I thought London aristocrats were supposed to be notoriously late sleepers," he remarked with a quizzical smile.

She shrugged. "I have always been an early riser." Her gaze slid to the curl of reddish-gold hair visible in the opening of his shirt. "Is that your smuggler's outfit?" she asked in a hoarse whisper to keep the ever-present footman from hearing. "You look like an illustration of a swashbuckling West Indies buccaneer I saw in one of Jamie's history books."

"Swashbuckling?" he whispered back as he waved the footman from the room. "I wish you'd tell that to my valet. O'Riley swears I am ruining his reputation by refusing to wear a starched cravat like a 'proper nobleman'."

"O'Riley? Mama recently hired a footman named O'Riley. I wonder if they are related." Liam's sudden flush of color answered her question. "So that was how you always managed to be at the same social events I attended."

She was more flattered than annoyed that Liam had pursued her so avidly. If the truth be known, she found it rather exciting to have him lust for her. But this latest discovery reminded her that she knew little about him except that he would go to any lengths to get his own way. She needed to know a great deal more than that before she made her decision.

"We cannot go out and about on a day like this," she said, angling for a way to force him to answer some of her questions. "And since it is not fair that it should be your day to choose what we should do to entertain ourselves—"

"Indeed it is not," Liam interjected. "I shall need a sunny day for what I have in mind."

"Which is?"

"I want to see Canterbury Cathedral, which I understand is no more than a two hour ride from here. We can take a picnic and make a day of it."

Alexandra was frankly astonished. She would never have guessed a man like Liam would have an abiding interest in cathedrals. Yet he'd admitted to spending hours exploring Westminster Abbey, and now there was no mistaking his enthusiasm over Canterbury. She wondered how many more surprises he would afford her before the fortnight was over.

He finished the last of his coffee, pushed back his chair, and stood up. "Since it looks as if we shall be housebound all day, I suggest we stoke up the fire in the duke's book room and settle down in comfortable chairs with a couple of good books."

She rose to stand beside him. "Or better yet, you can tell me the stories you told Jamie about your days as a smuggler."

Liam looked surprised. "I didn't know women were interested in such things."

"I don't imagine most women are, but then I am not most women."

"So I am finding out." He caught her hand in his. "Very well, Madam Wife, if that is what you wish, come with me. I shall tell you all I know about smuggling. But don't hold it against me if you find yourself dead bored. I doubt the reality is anything like what is portrayed in the gothic novels you've read."

A fire was already burning merrily in the book room fireplace. Alexandra settled into one of the upholstered armchairs placed before it; Liam stretched out in the other and propped his boots on the raised hearth. "Now tell me what it is you wish to know about my former profession?"

In actuality, it was not smuggling that interested her, but Liam himself. But since it had been so much a part of his life, it was a good place to start. "How did you become a smuggler?" she asked, remembering stories she'd heard of the ruthless men who risked their lives transporting contraband between England and the Continent. She couldn't bring herself to ask, but she had to wonder if he had ever killed anyone.

"As I told you, it is an accepted way of life, albeit not a legal one, in Exmoor and Cornwall. It is, in fact, the only way a man can make a decent living. Those of us who ply the trade call ourselves 'Free Traders' in protest against the exorbitant taxes

levied on imported goods. The citizens call us 'The Gentlemen,' and in case you're wondering, today's West Country
smugglers bear little resemblance to the murderous lot whose
ships put into Kent and Sussex fifty years ago. We prefer to live
by our wits, not our weapons."

"You speak as if you are still a smuggler, not an earl."

Liam laughed. "At heart I probably always shall be. It was
great fun outwitting the excise men. Everyone in the West
Country is involved in the dangerous game. Fishermen, farmers, innkeepers—even magistrates and vicars."

"You cannot be serious. Magistrates I can understand. We
have our share of dishonest officials in London also. But surely
not vicars."

"I first sailed as one of the crew on a smugglers' rig when I
was a lad of thirteen," Liam said. "The vicar in my village
taught me to read and write and cipher during the day and
served as first mate on the smugglers' rig at night. It was the
only way he could keep body and soul together. A vicar's living
in Exmoor is a sorry thing."

He grinned. "Vicar Edelson, incidentally, is why I want to
go to Canterbury Cathedral. He was born and raised in Kent
and spent many an hour at sea telling me about the Trinity
Chapel where Thomas Becket was murdered some seven hundred years ago. He claimed miracles still happen to the pilgrims
who visit it." He gave her a sidelong glance. "All things considered, I could use a miracle right about now."

Alexandra felt her cheeks flame at his less than subtle reminder of the decision she must make in two weeks' time. She
had blushed more in the past two months than in her previous
one-and-twenty years, and she had Liam to thank for it. If the
old wives' tale about blushes being good for one's complexion
was true, she would soon put every other woman in London to
shame. "Tell me about the two times the excise officers nearly
caught you," she said to hide her momentary confusion.

He sobered instantly. "The first time was on the coast of
France, and the English excise men had nothing to do with it.
We were just pushing off in the lighter we used to convey the
brandy to *The Wayward Lady* when a company of French dra-
goons fired on us from the cliffs above the beach. I can only suppose the fools mistook us for English spies, as the Bonapartist

government had never discouraged smuggling. At any rate, I took a bullet in the back and was left for dead by my crew."

Alexandra sucked in her breath, shocked at how calmly he related his frightening tale.

"Had it not been for the Frenchman who found me, carried me to a hidden cave, and tended my wounds," he continued, "I would have proved my crew's assumption correct. All he asked in payment for saving my life was that I locate his sister, who was married to an English nobleman, and assure her that he was alive and well. Which I did."

He stared into the dancing flames of the cozy fire, a pensive expression on his finely sculpted face. "Yves Durand and I became good friends during the six weeks we hid out in that cave, but I never saw him again."

"And what happened the second time you encountered trouble?" she asked.

"An enemy, whose identity I do not know, informed the excise men I had provided transportation for an Englishman who spied for Bonaparte during the war."

Alexandra felt as if her heart had dropped to her toes. "But that would make you a . . . a traitor."

"Of course it would—if it were true, which it wasn't. But I'd have hanged just the same. Thanks to Fiona and Adam . . . and a friend of mine, I escaped to Ireland until Bellmont could clear my name. I owe the three of them my life."

Something in his tone of voice when he mentioned his "friend" told Alexandra it had been a woman who had helped save him. One of his tavern wenches, no doubt, she decided sourly.

It was all too apparent that Liam was a man who drew women to him like honey drew flies—something she must take into consideration before she risked losing her heart to the charming rogue. But not today. Not when the fire was so warm and the chair so comfortable—and the man who sat across from her had so many fascinating stories to tell. There would be plenty of time in the next fortnight for such serious contemplation.

The unexpected summer rainstorm lasted four days. Nearly half their time in Kent was over, and they'd not yet visited Canterbury Cathedral. Still, to Liam's way of thinking, the time had been well spent. He had learned a great deal more about

Alexandra than he could have while exploring an ancient edi-fice, including the revelation that she was as formidable a card player as he ever hoped to meet.

She was also a sympathetic listener. He'd told her stories of his childhood he'd never told another soul. He'd even found himself waxing enthusiastically about The Aerie, and discov-ered she was as thrilled as young Jamie with the idea of explor-ing a medieval castle.

He'd quoted her passages from the works of John Donne, Vicar Edelson's favorite Metaphysical poet. Then he'd sent her into whoops of laughter when he'd related how he'd come upon the vicar secretly reading one of Donne's more erotic poems not an hour after he'd forbidden his students to do so.

She'd confessed to being addicted to the novels of Fanny Bur-ney and the poetry of Robert Burns, despite her mother's condem-nation of one as a "purveyor of lascivious trash" and the other a "vulgar Scotsman." All of which made him think his aristocratic wife might not be as stiff-rumped as he'd originally believed.

Each hour they spent together seemed to fly by faster than the last; each good night kiss he gave her at the door of her bed-chamber was more deeply passionate than the one before. For, as he explained when she made a weak protest, kisses had never been mentioned when he'd promised to wait for an invitation to share her bed.

After four days of being housebound with her, Liam had come to the conclusion that Alexandra was not only a beautiful, desirable, woman—she was also a remarkably interesting one. He could never remember being so happily entertained . . . or so miserably frustrated.

Now, with midnight approaching, they ended their fourth day as prisoners of the rain in the duke's book room—she with a glass of sherry, he with a tankard of the good, dark ale O'Ri-ley had found at a nearby tavern. It was, he decided, too warm to light a fire. He chose instead to throw open the French win-dows and breathe in the moist night air.

"The storm is over at last. We should be able to ride to Can-terbury tomorrow," he said, catching his first glimpse of a twin-kling star. He expected a sigh of relief from Alexandra; instead he heard a small whimper of distress.

He turned from the window to find her staring at him with

stricken eyes. "We do not have to go there," he said quickly. "It was only a thought. I am open to any suggestion."

"I have nothing against Canterbury. It is just that these past four days have been so . . . so wonderful." She gulped. "I almost wish they would never end."

Liam went very still, afraid to believe the implication in her halting words. "As do I, Madam Wife," he said in a voice hoarse with emotion. "But I promise you we will have other days . . . and nights that will be even more wonderful."

Alexandra knew he alluded to the marital intimacies that had once made her blood run cold. Tonight it surged hotly through her veins. She had changed in the past four days and she had only Liam to blame.

Time and again he had inspired her to think more profoundly than she'd ever done before—then promptly kissed her witless.

Time and again he had reiterated his promise to never enter her bed without invitation—then touched her in provocative ways that left her aching with needs she'd never known she had.

In short, he had teased her and challenged her and stirred her senses until she felt consumed with the same raw desire she read in his eyes. She no longer questioned that she would give herself to the charming rogue. She was too busy feeling wonderfully wicked and wanton to fear the consequences of that daring decision.

He watched her now with eyes brilliant with desire, and the air between them seemed charged with an energy like summer lightning. As if in a dream, she heard herself say, "Kiss me, Liam," in a breathless, throaty voice she scarcely recognized as her own.

"Do not tempt me, love. I am only human."

"Kiss me . . . please," she said again. "For I need to bolster my courage to say what I want to say."

Liam inhaled deeply. "My God, Alexandra, do you mean what I think you do?"

"Are you going to insist that I fall to my knees and beg you?" she asked softly.

His answer was to lunge forward, sweep her into his arms, and capture her sweetly parted lips in a hot, hungry kiss. Instantly, he was awash in her fragrance, in the soft, womanly contours that fitted in his arms as if the Creator had designed her especially for him.

"Ummmm," she murmured as he lifted his head to gaze

down at her flushed face. Her eyes were closed, her beautiful mouth curved in a satisfied cat-in-the-cream smile. It was all he could do to keep from picking her up and making a headlong dash for the stairs that led to her bedchamber—or his. He couldn't for the life of him remember which was closest.

She opened her eyes. Even in the dim light of a single candle he could see the passion in their emerald depths—until, without warning, the passion changed to horror and she stiffened in his arms. "There is someone on the terrace," she whispered, staring over his shoulder.

Liam tightened his arms protectively about her. "It is only the wind, my love," he murmured and once more lowered his mouth toward hers.

She pushed frantically against his chest. "It is not the wind. I saw his face at the open window." Her voice rose in a frightened wail. "Dear God, there he is again."

Liam instantly emerged from his erotic daze—his senses fully alert despite his aching groin. "Get behind the desk and stay there," he ordered. Reaching for the knife strapped to his boot, he wheeled around to face the window. The intruder, if there had been one, was nowhere in sight.

"More than likely it was one of the footmen returning from a tryst with a girl in the village," he said, praying they could recapture the romantic mood of a few moments ago.

"I don't think so. I am almost certain he was wearing a soldier's uniform."

"The devil you say. Maybe I'd best take a look around before I close and lock the window. If it was one of Adam's poor, homeless devils, he'll be in need of a meal and a place to sleep."

"Be careful, Liam." Alexandra's voice broke in what sounded suspiciously like a sob. "He could be dangerous."

Liam liked the idea that she was worried about him. It bode well for his chances of improving his sleeping arrangements in the near future, if not this very night.

He stepped through the window, surveyed the darkened terrace, and immediately spied a mysterious shadow moving toward him. "Stop where you are or you'll find a knife in your gullet," he snarled.

"I beg your pardon, my lord." The voice was too cultured to

be that of a servant or an ordinary foot soldier. Liam took a tighter grip on his knife.

A slender, gray-haired man in a soldier's uniform stepped forward. Liam recognized him as the Duke of Bellmont's former batman, who presently served as his valet. "I didn't mean to intrude at an inopportune moment, but it was imperative I find you as soon as possible."

"John Bittner? What the devil are you doing in Kent? And why are you in uniform and creeping about on the terrace in this furtive manner? The duke's doors are always open to you."

"I am in uniform because it seemed the safest way to travel the highways. As for my 'creeping about,' I bring an urgent message from His Grace, and the fewer people who know I've been here, the better."

Liam frowned. Something told him this "urgent message" would drastically alter his plans for the balance of the night. "You've had a long ride," he said. "Give me Bellmont's note. I'll read it and, if needs be, pen my reply while you have a bite to eat."

"Thank you, my lord, but I have eaten. His Grace insisted I fill my saddlebag with food before I left."

"Very well then, John. But you'll want a few hours of sleep before you return to London. I counted more than twenty bedchambers on our tour of the manor house. I'm certain we can sneak you into one and out again in the morning with no one the wiser."

"Thank you again, my lord, but I'll not need a place to sleep. I will, however, need a fresh horse from the duke's stable."

"Never say you are planning to return to London tonight."

"I am, and hopefully you will accompany me. For that is His Grace's message, which I carry in my head since he didn't wish to put it on paper. He begs your forgiveness for interrupting your honeymoon, but a matter of life or death requires you join him at his town house as soon as possible."

Liam's heart thudded painfully in his chest. "My sister?"

"She is well, my lord. I am not at liberty to divulge the nature of the matter to which the duke's message refers, but I can tell you it does not involve the duchess."

Liam breathed a sigh of relief. "Of course I'll come with you if that is what Bellmont wants. But first I must escort my lady to her chamber."

"Natually, my lord. I understand. I shall wait here on the terrace while you do so." He paused. "But a word of caution. It would be best for all concerned if you say nothing to the countess about this."

"How could I do otherwise?" Liam grumbled, "since nothing is the sum total of what I know about the murky business."

When, he wondered, had Adam become involved in what appeared to be some sort of espionage—and why now, of all times, with the war over and Bonaparte safely imprisoned on Elba?

He groaned. And how was he supposed to explain to Alexandra that just when she had decided to invite him into her bed, he had discovered he had commitments that required him to be elsewhere?

Chapter Ten

"Trust me," Liam had said when he'd returned from the terrace and hustled her up the stairs to her bedchamber. "I must leave you for a little while, but promise me you will trust me until I return," he'd said again when he'd left her at her door with only a chaste kiss on the forehead and not a word of explanation for his strange behavior.

Oddly enough, Alexandra had never doubted that he would deal with the fellow in the soldier's uniform, then promptly return to her chamber. But she had waited in vain throughout most of the long night, growing more angry and humiliated with each passing hour.

It made no sense. Liam had to have understood her invitation, even though she'd not put it in so many words. Then why had he so cavalierly rejected it when he had done everything he could in the four days they had spent together to entice her into making it? Furthermore, he had been the most amorous of men right up until she'd convinced him there was an intruder on the terrace.

Surely then that must be the answer. Whoever he was, the soldier on the terrace had to have presented a great deal more serious problem than Liam had anticipated. With that comforting thought she had finally fallen asleep.

But now that the morning sun was streaming through her window, that simple explanation had seemed a paltry one indeed. She wondered what had possessed her to act in such a wanton manner in the first place. She wondered even more why she had succumbed to Liam's plea to trust him, when everything that had happened to her in the past month had proved she could trust no one but herself.

"Good morning, my lady. I can see you slept well ... again." The smug expression on Bridget's face left no doubt that she was gloating over the obvious fact that Alexandra was still a virgin bride. The annoying girl looked particularly complacent today. It was plain to see she was eager to race back to the servants' quarters and make her daily report.

Alexandra gritted her teeth. If she had been able to manage without an abigail, she'd have sent Bridget packing days ago. She wondered how smug the cheeky maid would feel when she was given her walking papers once they returned to London.

"Will you be wanting to wear your riding habit on this fine sunny day, my lady?" Bridget asked, throwing open the armoire.

"I am not certain what my plans for the day will be. Until I am, I shall require one of my morning dresses," Alexandra snapped, making no effort to hide her annoyance.

But Bridget wasn't the only person whose neck she'd cheerfully wring this morning. She had no idea if her husband intended to ride on horseback to Canterbury or take a carriage. Indeed, she was not yet certain she would agree to accompany him. It would all depend on how she felt after she'd gotten past the embarrassing business of seeing him again at the breakfast table.

As it turned out, she was saved both the embarrassment and the necessity of making a decision about Canterbury. Liam was not in the morning room. Nor, so the Irish footman on duty in the morning room informed her, was he anywhere else in the manor house. He had, in fact, ordered up his mare, and one of the duke's as well, shortly after midnight and ridden off without a word to anyone as to where he was going.

Instantly, Alexandra's peeve was forgotten. Liam's odd behavior had to have something to do with the stranger on the terrace— and the entire affair had a sinister feel to it that made her skin crawl. Had that rumor about Liam's smuggling a spy into England raised its ugly head again? The very thought filled her with terror.

Shivering, she reached for the teapot to pour herself a cup of soothing hot tea, and that was when she saw it—a fold of foolscap tucked beneath her teacup. The message in Liam's bold script was brief and to the point:

I shall return as soon as humanly possible. Until then, please hold the thought we shared when last we were together.

He had left her alone! In Kent! On their honeymoon! And just when they had been about to . . . She blushed, remembering what it was they had been about to do.

She read the note again; the words were different, but the thought was the same as his parting entreaty at her chamber door. Once again he was asking her to trust him. All things considered, that was a great deal to ask of a relationship as tenuous as the one they had begun to establish in the past four days.

But he had challenged her to grow up and act like a woman. So she made an effort to curb her rising temper and stem her childish tears. "I will trust him," she muttered to herself, "but only so far and only so long."

"Beg pardon, my lady?" The young auburn-haired footman left his post by the sideboard to approach her, an anxious look on his face. "If 'tis something you'd be wanting me to do, you've just to say the word and 'tis done."

"It was nothing important," Alexandra murmured, loath to admit she'd been talking to herself. "But thank you . . ."

"O'Riley, my lady. Timothy O'Riley."

"Another O'Riley? Good heavens is there one employed in every noble house in England?"

"I'd not be surprised, my lady. For I've seven brothers and more cousins than I can count, and all of them in service. 'Tis me second brother, Colin, who's valet to the Earl of Stratham hisself and me cousin, Brendan, a footman in the Viscount Hardin's grand house in London." Timothy O'Riley's chest swelled with pride. "The streets of Belfast was near emptied the day the O'Rileys took ship to England."

Alexandra had never made a habit of chatting with footmen; her mother had always stressed the importance of keeping servants in their place. But this particular footman had a winning smile and a quick wit that she found rather appealing. In fact, the handsome young Irishman reminded her a little of Liam. He, too, was a cock-of-the-walk rather than a little bantam rooster like his brother. She had no doubt that every upstairs maid in the duke's household had eyes for Timothy O'Riley.

"Seven brothers. You do have a large family," she said as she rose from her chair to quit the morning room.

"I've a sister as well, but there's none will be hiring poor Emmy." He paused. "Unless, by chance, some fine lady should tire of having her personal business blathered about by a gossipy abigail."

Alexandra stopped in her tracks. Scowling, she turned to face the talkative footman. Timothy O'Riley was the picture of innocence, except for the knowing twinkle in his blue eyes. "Our Emmy's bright as a pin, she is. She has but fifteen years on her plate, but she can read and write and cipher better than me or any of me brothers. Nor does the lass have the least bit o' trouble making herself understood when she has something to say—only not with words same as the rest of us. For she's ne'er made a sound since she fell on a hay rake when she was a wee scrap and tore a hole in her throat."

Alexandra gasped and instinctively pressed her hand to her throat.

"'Tis not that her speaking parts is damaged, for there's times at night when she cries out in her sleep," the footman continued. "'Tis her head that don't believe she can talk—so the old duke's fine London doctor explained. But unless a miracle happens, the poor little thing will go through life silent as death."

Alexandra cringed at the thought of what the girl must have suffered. But after three years with Bridget, she had to admit a mute abigail sounded amazingly appealing—especially since Timothy O'Riley had intimated that gossip in the servants' quarters was even more rampant than she'd suspected.

"Where does this sister of yours live?" she asked.

"Emmy bides right here in Bellmont Village, my lady, in a cottage behind my da's forge."

"Your father is the village blacksmith?"

"Aye, he is that, and me mam and young Annie the finest seamstresses in all of Kent. 'Tis sitting together with their sewing and a cup of tea you'll find them any morning of the week but Sunday."

"A seamstress you say?" Among her other failings, Bridget couldn't sew a straight seam if her life depended on it.

Alexandra made an instantaneous decision—her first as the Countess of Stratham. The very act of doing so raised her spirits immeasurably. "Please send word to the duke's head groom that I shall require a mare saddled in half an hour, and a groom to accompany me on a ride . . . to the village."

"I'll see to it right away, my lady." The footman's grin spread from ear to ear. "Fot 'tis a ride you'll ne'er regret."

The skies over the capital had turned the smoky mauve of a London dawn by the time Liam and John Bittner stabled their horses in the mews behind the Duke of Bellmont's town house.

Liam expected to find Adam fast asleep, but Bittner led him directly to the book room, where he found Adam, and three other people as well, waiting for him.

"May I introduce Robert Londonderry, Lord Castlereagh," Adam said as he and a distinguished-looking gentleman rose from their chairs. Liam had heard enough about England's powerful foreign secretary to know that Adam must be involved in something vitally important to the welfare of the nation to have roused such a man from his bed at this ungodly hour.

"I believe you have already met Baron and Baroness Ogilthorpe," Adam continued, indicating the couple standing on the opposite side of the fireplace. To Liam's surprise, he found himself staring into the pale, drawn faces of the sister and brother-in-law of the man who had tended his wounds in France.

"Does this life-or-death matter John Bittner mentioned concern Yves Durand?" Liam asked. "And if so, what may I do to help? I owe Yves my life."

Adam smiled for the first time. "I felt certain that was how you would respond." He drew another chair into the circle around the fireplace and poured Liam a glass of brandy. "Please sit down. We have much to discuss and the baron and his wife seem to feel you might be able to contribute something of particular importance. I should tell you first off, Durand is an assumed name. The man who rescued you was in reality Yves St. Armand, the Comte de Rochemont and one of Whitehall's most valued agents."

"I knew, of course, he was not the simple French farmer he first appeared to be," Liam said. In truth, he and Yves Whatever-His-Name had exchanged enough stories in the six weeks they were together to determine they were two of a kind—men who courted danger and beautiful women with equal passion. He had sensed his French savior was an ardent royalist, but it had never occurred to him the charming rogue was a British agent as well.

"He and his sister, Ghislaine"—Adam nodded toward the baroness—"were the only members of the St. Armand family to escape the guillotine during the terrible days of the Reign of Terror."

"I was four years old, Yves six, when the Canaille came to my father's estate in Bourgogne for our parents and grandparents," the baroness said in her beautifully accented English. "But I remember it well. My nurse hid us under the hay in the stable until they were gone."

She drew a shaky breath. "We lived for the next ten years at her brother's farm in Normandy, posing as his children. Yves swore he would one day make the butchers pay for the slaughter of our family."

"And so he did," Lord Castlereagh interjected. "For without the continuous information he supplied Lord Wellington about French strategy and troop movements, the greatest butcher of all, Napoleon Bonaparte, might be residing in Buckingham Palace today. Every citizen of Britain owes the count a debt of gratitude—a debt we are hoping you might be able to help us pay, my Lord Stratham."

Liam frowned. "I fail to see how."

"The answer is somewhat complicated." Lord Castlereagh exchanged a speaking look with Adam. "To begin with, though it is not yet generally known, Napoleon Bonaparte has escaped from Elba and landed with one thousand men in the Gulf of Juan near Cannes."

"The devil you say. How in God's name did *that* happen?"

A dull flush spread across Castlereagh's face. "The officer I assigned to guard him turned out to be something of a disappointment. I set a mouse to guard a snake, and the result was disastrous. Bonaparte is, as we speak, marching northward through France, gathering support as he goes. He has boasted he will crown himself emperor again once he enters Paris, and he may well do it."

"And Yves is somewhere in France and in terrible danger," the baroness cried. "His identity, and his part in the victory of England and her allies, was made known to the Corsican by an Englishman in the pay of the French."

Adam turned to Liam. "The traitor, incidentally, whom you were once accused of aiding."

"The Bonapartists will hunt Yves down like a mad dog," the baroness continued, "and they will . . ." She covered her face with her hands and sobbed openly.

"Your brother is too clever to let such jackals trap him, my darling." The baron drew his petite black-haired wife into his arms and pressed a tender kiss on her forehead. Over her head, his gaze met Liam's. "We persuaded Lord Castlereagh and the

duke to call on you because you were the only person we could
think of who might have some idea where Yves could be hiding. We remembered your telling us he had carried you to a
place he called 'the safest spot in all of France'."

"The cave where we hid out until my wounds healed," Liam
exclaimed, struck by a sudden inspiration. "Now that I think of
it, I feel certain if Yves could find a way to get there, that is
where he would be."

As if it were yesterday, he remembered parting from the
Frenchman when the time came for him to work his way down
the coast to an inlet the English smugglers put into regularly. He
had shaken Yves' hand and tried desperately to think of some
way to express his gratitude. Of course he couldn't, so he had
made a somewhat ridiculous offer to keep from turning maudlin.

He paused to search his memory. "As I recall, my exact
words to Yves when last I saw him were, 'If you ever need rescuing, my friend, you can count on me.' And his response was,
'If that time should come, you will know where to find me,
Englishman.' Meaning, of course, the cave where he nursed me
back to health."

Adam shook his head. "That is not much to go on—a
promise neither of you could possibly have taken seriously.
How many years ago?"

"Five, almost six," Liam admitted. "I have never been back
to the inlet, but I feel certain I can find it again."

"And you believe Yves will be there?" The baroness's dark
eyes were suddenly alive with hope.

"I cannot know. But if I remember the words we exchanged,
so might he. It is worth investigating."

"Such an investigation could be very dangerous," Adam
protested. "We know that even while on Elba, the Corsican has
had his spies in England—at least one of whom we suspect is
an English traitor in a high place in Whitehall. These black-
guards will expect us to try to rescue the man on whom Bonaparte has sworn to take revenge. Every port will be watched;
every yacht that sets sail suspect."

"But not every fishing smack that leaves an out-of-the-way
harbor like Lynmouth." Even as he spoke, a plan was beginning
to form in Liam's mind. "My new wife has expressed an interest in medieval castles, as has her young brother. I believe I

shall take the two of them to visit the ancient edifice on the cliffs of Exmoor that I have recently inherited."

"Are you saying you plan to go to France to find Yves, my lord?" Ghislaine Ogilthorpe asked.

"But of course. I am the only person who knows where to find the secret cave—as well as the only one who would recognize Yves on sight."

"How can I ever thank you?" The baroness threw herself into Liam's arms with a Gallic fervor that nearly knocked him off his feet.

The baron calmly peeled his wife off Liam's chest. "The French are very demonstrative people," he remarked with a smile that led Liam to believe it was a trait he found most endearing.

Half an hour later, after the baron, the baroness, and Lord Castlereagh had taken their leave, Liam and Adam sat facing each other before the dying embers in the book room fireplace. Adam frowned thoughtfully. "I am not at all comfortable with this reckless venture of yours, but I see I cannot hope to dissuade you. So, tell me what I may do to help."

"Two things only," Liam said. "First, I should appreciate the loan of your heavy traveling coach. The one I purchased before my wedding was sufficient for the short journey to Kent, but it would not be adequate to comfortably transport Alexandra and Jamie to Exmoor."

"Consider it yours. A good idea that, taking Lady Alexandra and her brother with you to Exmoor. It will allay any suspicions that, through me, you may be involved in the Yves Durand business. For it appears you are but taking your new bride and your ward to see the demesne of the Earls of Stratham."

Adam poured two glasses of brandy and offered one to Liam. "Sorry I have none of your precious dark ale to offer you. Never did acquire a taste for the nasty stuff, myself." He took a drink, then set the glass on a handsome Sheraton library table next to his chair. "Now tell me the second way in which I may help you."

Liam stared thoughtfully into the fire. "I do not expect to encounter any difficulties on what you term my 'reckless venture.' But I want to make certain that if the unthinkable should happen, Alexandra will inherit everything I own. Since I have never before owned anything, I am not sure how to go about that."

"I take it your estate is not entailed."

"Not if my solicitors are to be believed."

Adam nodded. "Then it is a simple matter of writing out exactly what you want done. I shall witness your signature, have John Bittner do the same and keep your instructions in my safe. That should suffice until you can have your solicitors draw up the proper papers."

Adam drummed a thoughtful tattoo on the arm of the chair. "But first, you will need to name an executor to handle your estate if the need should arise. I caution you to think carefully before doing so. You are an extremely wealthy man."

Liam pondered what Adam had said. "No," he said finally. "Alexandra is an intelligent woman of legal age; she would want to handle her own affairs. The last thing she needs is yet another man with the power to decide how she should live her life or spend her fortune."

"I take it this marriage the old earl demanded is working out then."

Liam smiled to himself, remembering the invitation he had read in his wife's eyes just before John Bittner's untimely interruption. "Let us say," he said somewhat smugly, "it is beginning to show definite possibilities."

If anyone had prophesied but a se'enight earlier that Alexandra would enjoy her role of Countess of Stratham, she would have called them mad. But enjoy it she had her first day on her own at the Duke of Bellmont's Kent estate.

She had ridden to the village in the morning to call upon Emmy O'Riley and liked the shy young girl immediately. With Mrs. O'Riley's approval, she had engaged Emmy as her abigail and promised she would have a groom pick her up in the pony cart and deliver her to White Oaks later that day.

Then she had returned to the estate, ordered Liam's grays harnessed to his carriage, and promptly dispatched Bridget to the Henning town house in London. The note she sent with the indignant abigail informed her mother that she could feel free to employ Bridget in whatever capacity suited her purposes as she, Alexandra, would no longer require the maid's services.

Now with her new abigail happily settled in the servants' quarters under the watchful eyes of her two brothers, Alexandra was left with nothing to do except wonder where Liam had gone and worry that he might be in some kind of trouble. The duke's French chef prepared an excellent dinner of salmon à la

Genevoise, roasted pheasant with Madeira sauce, fresh spring vegetables, and a superb ragout of breast of veal. She managed a bite or two of each offering, more to appease the chef than her own nonexistent appetite.

A frowning Timothy O'Riley had just removed her plate and put a serving of raspberry truffle before her when she heard what sounded like a carriage rumbling up the manor house driveway. Who, she wondered, could be calling at this inappropriate hour?

Moments later, the dining room door burst open and a slight figure in muffler, cap, and oversized greatcoat flew across the threshold, arms outstretched. Alexandra leapt to her feet. "Jamie! Whatever are you doing here?"

"Liam brought me. We're going to The Aerie, and we're leaving at first light tomorrow morning. Brendan O'Riley has promised to take care of Fergus until I return."

The Aerie. The medieval castle to which Liam had told Jamie he would never take a woman. Alexandra knew her mouth had dropped open, but she seemed incapable of doing anything about it.

Jamie appeared totally unaware that his carelessly spoken words had shocked her to the core. He eyed Alexandra's helping of trifle and the plate of vanilla biscuits the footman had served with it. "Gadzooks, I'm hungry. Do you suppose I could have some dinner. Liam was in too much of a hurry to stop for anything but a change of horses."

Before she could answer him, Liam appeared in the doorway, his handsome face wreathed in a warm smile. "So there you are, Jamie. I've asked the housekeeper to show you to a bedchamber and arrange for a hot bath and a tray of dinner. Then it's off to bed for you. We have at least four long days of travel ahead of us before we reach our destination."

Alexandra had never seen Jamie move so fast. Dropping the serviette she still clutched in her hand, she followed him, too furious at this baffling turn of events to deal with the man who less than twenty-four hours earlier had begged her to trust him.

Liam caught her arm as she hurried past him. "What have I done now to turn your face into a such a thundercloud? I know it is short notice, but an unexpected problem has arisen at The Aerie that I must attend to and I thought Jamie—"

"You thought Jamie would enjoy exploring your medieval castle," Alexandra interrupted bitterly.

"I was certain he would. I am aware it is a rather odd way to spend our honeymoon—"

"To say the least."

"I refuse to quarrel with you, Alexandra. If you do not want your brother to accompany us, just say so and I will try to explain it to the boy."

Alexandra blinked. "Us? You were planning to take me as well?"

"Surely you didn't think I would leave you behind."

Alexandra studied the section of embossed wallpaper visible behind his right shoulder, avoiding his eyes. "You told Jamie you would never take any woman to The Aerie."

"That was before you convinced me you were not just 'any woman'." Liam cupped her chin in his strong fingers and forced her to look him in the face. "So that is why you're so angry! It occurs to me that most of the trouble between us stems from one of us failing to understand the other's motives. Maybe if we were a little more forthcoming with each other, Madam Wife, we could make this oddly matched marriage of ours work."

"Maybe so, my lord. But we are, as you say, oddly matched." Alexandra sighed. "You asked me to trust you. But I find that difficult to do when I cannot understand why you—" Her face flamed when she realized what she had almost said.

"You cannot understand why I left you to sleep alone last night. Believe me when I say it was the hardest thing I have ever done." Throwing caution to the winds, Liam divulged, "The man you saw on the terrace was John Bittner, the Duke of Bellmont's valet. He carried an urgent message from the duke which I dared not ignore, or I would never have left you."

Alexandra surveyed him solemnly. "Perhaps I would find it easier to accept what you do if I understood you. Just when I think I am beginning to know you, I find I don't know you at all. Why did you marry me, Liam? At least tell me that."

Liam froze, stunned into momentary silence by her probing question. "You are a beautiful, desirable woman," he said somewhat lamely when he found his voice.

"The world is full of beautiful, desirable women—and you are not some green lad to lose your head over one with whom you have little in common. Why, when you admit to having no interest in London society, would you go to so much trouble to secure a wife who has been trained from birth to take her place in that society? Surely you could have found a far more suitable woman to wed in Exmoor."

It was the same question her father had asked. But, as the viscount had reminded him, he dare not give her the same answer. "You belittle yourself needlessly, Alexandra. In the short time I've known you, I've come to realize you are much more than the shallow creature your mother raised you to be."

"But you could not have known that when first you spied me at the Rutherfords' ball. Yet you have single-mindedly pursued me ever since. It was almost as if you had purposely searched me out. Was your curiosity piqued because I was the daughter of the woman who rejected your father when he came to London seeking a bride?"

Liam squirmed uncomfortably. This was dangerous ground they were treading. "That may have entered into it initially," he admitted, staying as close to the truth as possible. "But it has nothing to do with the regard I feel for you now."

Alexandra raised her chin to a haughty angle that made her look a perfect picture of the arrogant aristocrat he had once believed her to be. "How comforting to know my husband feels 'regard' for me. It is so much more dignified an emotion than lust."

With a swish of her skirt, she flounced past him into the hall. "Now, if you will excuse me, my lord, I have a great deal of packing to supervise in the next hour if I am to have that early night you advised."

Liam stared after her with mixed feelings. On the one hand, he was relieved that she was willing to leave for Exmoor on such short notice; on the other, he feared he had just forfeited all the progress he'd made toward sharing his wife's bed.

The irony of it was he suspected that Yves Durand would have a good laugh if he knew what it had cost his English friend to save the scoundrel's neck from the guillotine.

Chapter Eleven

Alexandra was not looking forward to four or five days in a rolling carriage with her young brother. It was, as Liam had admitted, an odd way to spend a honeymoon. It was also painfully reminiscent of the miserable treks Jamie and she had made each summer in the ancient Henning travel coach to her father's estate in Norfolk—and those had been through the most civilized parts of the English countryside. She could imagine what discomforts she might have to endure traveling into the unknown West Country.

She consoled herself with the thought that a genuine medieval castle awaited her exploration at the end of the long journey, as well as a new and fascinating landscape she might capture in watercolor. To that end, she packed her paints and had one of the duke's footmen strap her easel to the side of her trunk.

What with one thing and another, she had not so much as lifted a paintbrush in weeks. But now she felt the familiar excitement at the thought of once again taking up the avocation she loved.

She had taught herself to paint by emulating in watercolor John Constable's glorious oil paintings of the Suffolk and Norfolk countryside. In Exmoor there would be no one to copy except nature herself. If nothing else, the challenge of painting the lonely moors, or mayhap the angry waves lapping at the cliff on which The Aerie perched, gave her something to think about besides her confusing relationship with Liam.

She rose at the crack of dawn, dressed with Emmy's help, and portmanteau in hand, hurried down the stairs to make certain her trunk and precious easel were properly loaded into the luggage carriage. To her surprise, there was no such carriage in sight. Instead, she found Colin and Timothy O'Riley busy tying her trunk to the roof of the Duke of Bellmont's elegant travel coach while Liam watched from below.

"What are you doing?" she demanded. "It is customary to carry the luggage in the servants' coach—or are you reserving that space for the linen box?"

Liam scowled down at her. "What linen box?"

"The one carrying the sheets, blankets and pillows the duke's housekeeper has loaned us, of course. Surely you don't expect me to sleep on the filthy linen provided by public inns. Mama never traveled without carrying the linens for the family."

As if on cue, two footmen struggled down the steps of the manor house, carrying a mammoth wooden box between them. Liam lifted an eyebrow. "Luckily your mother is not traveling with us, since there is no way we can carry a box this size."

Alexandra's temper flared. She had been routed out of bed before dawn to embark on a journey her husband had arranged behind her back. She did not intend to do so without enjoying any of the amenities a countess might normally expect—even if that countess's husband was a barbarian from the West Country.

"If it will not fit inside the servants' coach, it can surely be tied on top."

Liam's scowl darkened. "We are not taking a servants' coach. It makes no sense to subject the people who serve us to the misery of a poorly sprung carriage when there is plenty of room for all of us in this comfortable one."

"I told his lordship 'twas not how 'tis done, my lady. But he'll nay listen to me." Colin O'Riley's pixie face wore a worried frown. "I pray you can talk him into acting like a proper earl."

Liam gave Alexandra a broad wink. "Ignore O'Riley. He's a dreadful snob and a nag to boot. I am seriously thinking of sacking the unpleasant fellow."

"And who would you find to put up with your odd ways if you did, milord?" O'Riley grumbled. "Very well. 'Tis settled then. I will ride in your fine carriage. But I'll not be comfortable doing so."

Liam chuckled. "Will you be more comfortable astride the lively mare I ordered for you?"

O'Riley's eyes lit up at the sight of the three horses the head groom was leading up from the stable. "Aye, my lord, that I will. For I've not been up on a horse since I left Ireland."

Snatching the reins from the groom's hands, he quickly mounted the closest nag, a spirited chestnut, and settled into the saddle as if he had been born to it. "'Tis not that I approve of your democratic ways," he said with a happy grin, "but I'll not be turning down the chance to feel a bit of horseflesh beneath me again."

"I thought not." Liam turned to Alexandra. "Now, wife, let me hand you into the carriage so we may get under way before any more time is lost."

"Not until the linen box is stowed on top."

"Damn it, Alexandra, didn't you hear a word I said? We do not have room for your blasted linen box."

Alexandra folded her arms and planted her feet.

"We shall be stopping at reputable inns. It will not hurt you this once to make use of the linens they provide."

Alexandra stood her ground. After a tense moment or two, Colin O'Riley dismounted the chestnut and with his brother's help, lashed the linen box on top of the carriage directly behind Alexandra's trunk, thus saving face for both his stubborn master and equally stubborn mistress.

"Are you satisfied now, Madam Wife?" Liam's voice was gruff, but Alexandra glimpsed a twinkle in his eyes as he handed her into the coach, then turned to do the same for Emmy. "And who is this pretty child?" he asked, raising an eyebrow.

"My new abigail," Alexandra said.

"My sister," Colin and Timothy O'Riley answered simultaneously.

"Another O'Riley! Good God, has the entire clan taken up residence at White Oaks?" Liam surveyed Emmy with narrowed eyes, and Alexandra saw the color leach from the girl's face. "I must admit you're an improvement over that sour-faced pudding bag we conveyed from London five days ago." He raised his head and peered into the coach at Alexandra. "Where is the pudding bag, by the way?"

"I sent Bridget back to my mother. I wanted an abigail of my own choosing."

"Bravo, Madam Wife. That's the spirit." He returned his gaze to the trembling girl, whose arm he still held. "And what is your name, child?"

"Emmy," three voices declared in concert.

Liam frowned. "Let the girl speak for herself."

The two O'Riley men fell silent, leaving Alexandra to explain. "Emmy doesn't talk. She had an injury to her throat when she was a small child."

"I see," Liam said, but Alexandra wasn't certain what it was he thought he saw since his gaze was on her, not her abigail.

"Welcome to our household then, Emmy." Liam's voice softened as he returned his attention to the trembling maid. "It is plain to see that with those speaking eyes of yours, you'll need no words to express yourself." With a gentle nudge. he urged her into the carriage and onto the seat next to her new mistress just as Jamie appeared in the doorway of the manor house.

Liam stepped aside so the boy could enter the carriage. "So, lad, are you ready for your great adventure?"

"I am." Jamie held up a leather-bound volume. "I found the map and book you told me to look for in the duke's library."

"Capital! Then I hereby appoint you the official historian of our expedition. As the map will show, we'll be traveling through five counties, and I shall expect you to inform us of the most interesting historical facts pertaining to each one. That way, we shall all arrive at the end of our journey wiser than we were at the beginning."

With a final look around him, Liam mounted the second of the three horses and instructed the groom to tie the last one to the back of the carriage. "The piebald is for you, Madam Wife, should you feel the urge to ride," he said, favoring Alexandra with a tender smile that made a mishmash of her insides. "With two of the duke's grooms, as well as O'Riley and me, as outriders, it should be entirely safe for you to do so."

Alexandra mumbled her thanks for his consideration and sank back against the soft squabs of the luxurious coach as it started forward down the wide gravel driveway. They had not yet passed through the gates of White Oaks, but she could see that traveling with the Earl of Stratham would be a far cry from the Henning family journeys.

An expedition indeed! And Jamie the official historian! Her young brother's face glowed with pride as he clutched *A History of the Counties of England* by Sir Hubert Markham to his narrow chest and pretended to ignore the look of awe Emmy turned on him.

With grudging admiration, Alexandra admitted that Liam had sensed just what would make the otherwise tedious trip a memorable experience for all concerned—herself included. For knowing that she could, whenever she wished, forsake the carriage to ride the pretty little mare would take much of the pain out of the four days on the road.

Oh, her husband was a charmer all right. But once burned, she would be twice wary. Jamie and the servants might dance to his tune for a figurative pat on the head; she intended to be a great deal more cautious in the future about succumbing to his provocative words and burning looks.

Vowing to resist Liam's charm and living up to that vow turned out to be two very different things. In subtle ways that she doubted anyone else noticed, the sly rogue launched an assault on her senses obviously designed to recapture the passionate mood the duke's messenger had interrupted.

He had already managed to hold her hand a trifle longer than necessary when he'd handed her into the carriage; he held it even longer when he helped her disembark at the roadside inn where they stopped to rest the horses and break their fast. Then he promptly destroyed the effect by casually ordering the innkeeper to serve the meal to family and servants alike at a single long trestle table beneath a budding apple tree.

Alexandra's hackles rose at this latest evidence of disrespect shown her by her new husband. On the one hand, he wooed her with intimate touches and tender looks; on the other, he subjected her to his deplorably democratic manner of travel and expected her to dine *en famille* with the servants as well. She could just imagine what her mother would say should she learn of such scandalous arrangements.

Gingerly, she seated herself at the end of one of the benches flanking the table, determined to have words with Liam later on the subject of social protocol. His valet had been on the mark; this Johnny-come-lately earl had no comprehension of how a proper nobleman should conduct himself.

She watched Jamie take a seat next to her new abigail on the opposite side of the table, and grimly acknowledged she would have to do something about that budding friendship as well. The two of them had spent the entire morning with their heads together over that blasted history book, just as if he were not a future viscount and she an Irish ladies' maid. It was obvious Liam was setting a bad example for his impressionable young brother-in-law.

"Move over, Wife, if you please." Her husband's hand on

her shoulder left no doubt he expected her to obey his request. Alexandra gritted her teeth, but slid far enough along the rough-hewn bench to allow him ample room to sit beside her. A moment later, she felt his hard, muscular thigh pressed intimately against hers.

"What a pleasant place to break our fast," he declared conversationally as the innkeeper's buxom young daughter placed a platter of bread and jam and slabcake with clotted cream before him. For no apparent reason, this brought on a spate of girlish giggles. Alexandra glanced up in time to catch the brazen creature ogling Liam in the same hungry way Jamie was staring at the food.

"That, I take it, is an example of the 'red-blooded tavern wenches' you find so attractive," Alexandra muttered under her breath once the girl was out of earshot.

"That she is, Madam Wife, and from the provocative sway of the chit's hips, I'd judge her to be a prime example indeed." He reached for the platter. "There is nothing like the sight of a lusty woman to whet a man's appetite . . . for slabcake."

With a wicked grin at the flush that suffused Alexandra's cheeks, he poured himself a cup of tea, raised it to his lips and happily pronounced it "a fine stout tea, much like that brewed by the good wives of Exmoor."

Alexandra nibbled at a piece of cake, choked on a sip of the potent tea and did her best to pretend she had never met the Earl of Stratham, much less married him.

His breakfast finished, Liam glanced across the table at Jamie. "So, Master Historian, I hope you have been studying that book I recommended because I have two questions to ask you. The first of which is: What are the five counties we must pass through to reach Exmoor?"

Jamie swallowed a healthy chunk of bread, liberally spread with raspberry jam. "Surrey, Berkshire, Wiltshire, Somerset and Devon."

"Excellent! And my second question is: What can you tell us about that great stone structure on the hill above us?"

"It is Surrey's famous Farnham Castle. Emmy and I just finished reading about it." He cleared his throat and recited, "It was built in the twelfth century and was the former seat of the Bishops of Winchester and Guildford."

He glanced toward his beaming fellow reader and was rewarded with a gesture that meant nothing to Alexandra. Jamie, however, appeared to have no difficulty interpreting it. "Emmy says I should tell you the body of water that lies between the inn and the castle is not actually a lake, but a great pond damned a century ago to raise fish for the castle kitchens and to lure birds to the area for the same purpose."

He cast a look of distaste at the breeze-rippled water. "It seems a bit unfair to the fish and birds, but I suppose the people in the castle couldn't live forever on bread and jam and slabcake."

"An astute observation, lad, and a lesson worth remembering." Liam took a long, slow drink of tea. "A man does what he must to survive—even if it sometimes necessitates going against his nature." His gaze locked briefly with Alexandra's, and she gained the distinct impression his comment held a deeper meaning than was immediately apparent.

Not for the first time, she sensed that he wrestled with some dark and troublesome secret—one he had not divulged when he'd discussed his past. She wondered if she would ever know what that secret was, or if this man she had married would always remain a mystery into which she dare not probe too deeply.

He constantly amazed her. For a smuggler and bastard son of a brutish barbarian, he admittedly had a certain crude panache that at times was most impressive. She'd seen peddlers on the streets of London in less disreputable buckskins and jackets than he wore; yet the innkeeper had instinctively addressed him as "Milord" and hastened to serve him. He'd had the duke's coat of arms removed from the carriage; but the ostler had leapt to tend his cattle and polish the heavy black coach before it returned to the road.

There was a quiet authority in Liam's voice that made others automatically do his bidding—a strangely hypnotic charm in his manner that turned those he dealt with into the people he wished them to be, rather than the people they really were.

She, herself, was a good example. Much as she prided herself on her logic and self-control, she had lost both that fateful night in the Duke of Bellmont's book room and turned into a wanton creature longing to give herself to the very man she had despised but a fortnight before.

As if sensing her mental turmoil, Liam turned his head and searched her face with his golden lion's eyes. "Why the troubled frown, Madam Wife? Trust me, you have nothing to fear." His sensuous lips curved in a reassuring smile. "Had you not

fallen asleep at the altar, you would have heard me promise to
keep you safe from harm for as long as I live—and as anyone in
Exmoor will tell you, I am a man who keeps his promises."

Alexandra wanted to trust him. Like it or not, she had spoken marriage vows that included "until death do us part" and
the four glorious days they had spent together in Kent had been
the happiest of her life.

When he reached for her hand, she smiled and twined her fingers in his. Maybe if she made a concerted effort to overlook his
odd eccentricities . . . and maybe once they reached that magnificent medieval castle of his . . . but she had enough to worry about
in the present. She would let the future take care of itself.

In the meantime, she found his promise to keep her safe
from harm more comforting than she would have believed possible—until over his shoulder she spied the sign above the door
of the inn. She was not normally given to prophetic omens, but
something about the weathered piece of wood struck a note. For
the name of the inn at which Liam had chosen to stop was The
Lion and The Lamb.

They had been on the road for four long days and suffered
nary a broken wheel nor a lamed horse. In Liam's opinion, that
alone was enough to declare the trip across the breadth of England a success. But the weather had remained pleasant as well,
and the wayside inns had proved more than adequate.

Now, gathered around the table in the candlelit parlor of
Devon's famed Gray Gull Inn, the weary group of travelers
were partaking of their last evening meal on the road. He surveyed them fondly. Though he had pushed them at a relentless
pace, they had kept their spirits high and their curiosity keen
about the countryside through which they passed.

Appointing Jamie the official historian of the expedition had
been a stroke of genius. Overnight the shy, often tongue-tied
lad had changed into a confident storyteller who held his audience captive with fascinating snippets of historical data.

In Berkshire, he had relived in glowing detail the Battle of
Hastings, in which the local lords had supported Harold, the
last of the Saxon kings, and for their foolishness, been stripped
of their lands by William the Conqueror.

In Wiltshire, he'd pointed out the famous white horse cut
into the chalk cliffs by King Alfred to commemorate his defeat

of the Danes a thousand years earlier. Then spurred on by
Emmy's look of wide-eyed admiration, had gone on to explain
how four thousand years before that the Druids had determined
the dates of the summer and winter solstices by measuring the
movements of the sun and moon.

In Somerset, he'd astonished everyone by declaring that
the Romans as far back as the first century after the birth of
Christ had benefited from the medicinal waters at the site of
the modern-day city of Bath.

Liam was amazed at the way Jamie had risen to the challenge offered him. In three days this sixteen-year-old lad had
managed to impart more of England's history than Vicar Edelson had in all the years he had been Liam's tutor.

Alexandra had proved even more surprising than her
brother. Viscount Hardin had not exaggerated when he'd
claimed to have sired two amazing children. Not once had the
delicate aristocrat complained of the long days on the road or
the short nights on lumpy hostelry mattresses. After the first
trying night, she had even declared herself willing to sleep on
the linens provided by the wayside inns rather than ask the exhausted servants to unpack the ones she had brought with her.

She had risen each morning at dawn and embarked on another twelve- or fourteen-hour journey without question,
though he knew very well she had to wonder why he was so
frantic to reach Exmoor in record time.

True, their sleeping arrangements were not yet to his liking.
But he had been too tired each night to make proper love to his
wife, even if she had indicated an interest in sharing his bed—
which she had not. She had, however, ridden companionably
beside him for a few hours each day on the little piebald and returned the good night kisses he'd claimed with increasing passion. It was only a matter of time. Surely once they reached The
Aerie . . .

He glanced up to find her watching him in that solemn way
of hers. The game little trooper looked pale and drawn; dark
smudges lay beneath her lovely emerald eyes and her silver-
blonde hair was gray with dust. He had never seen her look
more beautiful or more in need of the protector he had
promised to be.

He cursed the cruel fate that had disrupted his carefully laid
plans. If all had gone as he'd hoped, Alexandra would truly be

his wife by now, and he could carry her up to his chamber, make slow, tender love to her, then let her sleep away the night wrapped in his arms. His pulse quickened at the very thought. Was it some perverse streak in his nature that made his desire for his reticent bride burn hotter than it ever had for any of the lusty wenches who had freely offered him their favors in the past?

His eyes sought hers across the table. "It is a beautiful moonlit night and I am in the mood for a walk. Are you too tired to accompany me?"

"No, I should enjoy a bit of exercise." She rose to her feet. "But first I must see Jamie to his chamber. His head is drooping in his plate."

Colin O'Riley pushed back his chair. "With your permission, my lady, I will see Master Jamie into his bed." He leveled an accusing look at Liam's faded nankeen jacket and buckskins. "For 'tis certain I've little to keep me busy as the earl's valet on this journey."

Liam ignored the Irishman's gibe. For all his nagging, O'Riley was a good man—one of the few Liam felt he could trust implicitly.

Jamie yawned and stretched. "I can put myself to bed, O'Riley. I am not a child, and like Liam I've little need of a valet. But you'd best see to Emmy." He regarded the little abigail dozing beside him with a look of tender affection. "I fear your sister has fallen asleep in her chair."

To Liam's surprise, Alexandra turned on her heel and swept from the room without a word. He smiled to himself; the little darling was as eager to be alone with him as he was with her.

He caught up with her at the door to the inn yard and taking her hand in his, led her into the warm spring night. The scent of wild honeysuckle drifted on the evening breeze and a three-quarter moon cast a silver glow over the ancient cobblestones beneath their feet. It was a night made for lovers and if Liam had his way, lovers they would be before they saw another dawn.

He slipped an arm around her waist and drew her close to his side. She felt small and fragile—nothing like the buxom wenches he was accustomed to bedding. But his heart had never beat so fast nor his blood run so hot. This delicate, aristocratic wife of his stirred his senses as no other woman ever had.

He smiled down at her, expecting to receive one of her saucy smiles in return. Instead, a frown furrowed her brow. "What is troubling you, my love?" he asked, ready to pluck the moon from the sky if that was what it would take to make her happy.

"I'm worried about Jamie."

"Jamie!" Liam couldn't have been more shocked if she'd slapped him. "You're worried about your brother at a time like this?"

"Of course I'm worried. Didn't you see how he looked—"

"He looked sleepy, but that's to be expected after a long day on the road," Liam grumbled, removing his arm from his wife's waist. "Other than that, he looked happier and healthier than he has in a long time."

"I meant how he looked at Emmy. Surely you've noticed how . . . how attached he has become to her in the past four days."

Something in her tone of voice struck Liam wrong. Without thinking, he snapped, "And, of course, you think an Irish maid an unsuitable friend for a future viscount."

"Never say *you* think it a proper friendship."

"You're asking a bastard and ex-smuggler to determine what is socially proper?" Liam's laugh held little humor.

Alexandra gave him a withering look. "I am asking the Earl of Stratham how best to keep his sensitive young brother-in-law from being hurt by an inappropriate friendship."

Liam struggled to control his rising temper. He felt consumed with anger—frustration—disappointment. Just when he'd begun to have hopes for her, his aristocratic wife was showing her true colors. What in God's name had made him think that the blood flowing in her veins would ever be anything but cold and blue.

"And what of young Emmy?" he asked in a glacial voice. "Or don't the feelings of a member of the lower classes count?"

Too late, Alexandra realized the Earl of Stratham would always take the part of the commoners because he would always consider himself to be one of them. "Of course they count. I bitterly resent your unreasonable attitude. You have managed to twist my words to where I sound as stiff-necked as . . . as—"

"The Viscountess Hardin. As you have remarked more than once, you are 'your mother's daughter'."

Alexandra gasped. Never had she been so thoroughly put in her place.

"Very well, Madam Wife. You asked my advice and you shall have it. Leave them be. Emmy is a sweet, innocent child

with no aspirations to climb the social ladder that I can see—
and Jamie is an extraordinarily sensible sixteen-year-old. He is
also a young lad on the verge of manhood, enjoying his first
taste of having a female worship at his shrine. It is a heady experience he will remember all his life. But I can assure you
nothing will ever come of it. Colin O'Riley will see to that. My
esteemed valet is, in his own way, as great a prig as you are."

"So now I'm a prig!" Alexandra bristled like an indignant
hedgehog. "If I am so repugnant to you, why were you willing
to part with a fortune to secure me as your wife?"

That question again. Would she never let it rest! "One of these
days, when the time is right, I may give you the answer you
seek," he muttered. "But tonight is not that time." With a groan of
frustration, he pulled her into his arms and kissed her soundly.

Alexandra clenched her fists and pressed her lips tightly
shut. He was doing it again—substituting kisses for answers
when the question of why he married her came up. This ploy of
his was becoming exceedingly tedious.

Pressing her hands against his chest, she shoved herself away
from him. "I have never liked mysteries, my lord. Yet you per-
sist in maintaining this baffling secrecy about why you coerced
me into marrying you in such a hurry. 'When the time is right'
you say you *may* give me the answer I seek. Very well. When
that time comes, I *may* give you the answer you seek of me."

Liam grasped her upper arms in his strong fingers and
pulled her to him. "Devil take it, Alexandra, do not push me too
far. I have been more than tolerant with you, but you are my
wife and I can make you so in deed as well as name any time I
choose."

"So you can, my lord, except for one thing—you promised
you would never do so unless I begged you to. Are you saying
now you are a man who does not keep his promises?"

Liam instantly dropped his hold on her arms and spat out a
string of curses that scorched her ears. More than ever, he reminded her of the king of beasts, and this time he made no effort
to subdue his roar.

Alexandra's knees trembled like a bowl of warm blanc-
mange, and her heart had somehow become lodged in her
throat. But she raised her chin defiantly. "I take it, from those
vulgar obscenities with which you just insulted me, you are not
going to take me for a walk after all, my lord."

Chapter Twelve

Alexandra woke to a gray dawn and a pitiless, wind-lashed rain that stung her eyes and reddened her nose when she hurried from the inn toward the safety of the travel coach. With one hand holding her bonnet, the other clutching the flapping edges of her pelisse, she scarcely registered Liam's hand beneath her elbow until he fairly lifted her into the carriage and onto her seat. A good thing, since she would have found it extremely embarrassing to face him after their ugly quarrel of the previous evening.

He appeared to suffer no such embarrassment. "Welcome to Exmoor, Madam Wife," he shouted over the roar of the elements, then tucked the lap robe around her knees and slammed the door of the carriage against the howling wind.

Jamie and Emmy were already seated side-by-side across from her, their noses in "the book" as usual. Alexandra did her best to ignore this painful reminder of the reason for the ugly quarrel. Liam had called her a prig and likened her to her mother—a judgment that had wounded her more than she cared to admit. For if she had learned nothing else in the last few traumatic weeks, she had learned that Henrietta Henning, Viscountess Hardin, was the last woman on earth she would choose as her role model.

"There are times, especially in the spring, when it rains in Exmoor for weeks on end," Jamie read from his "bible" in a nauseatingly cheerful tone of voice. "Other times dense mists descend, narrowing visibility to no more than a foot or two and eliminating all travel on the moors."

"They why would anyone in his right mind want to live in such a dreary place?" Alexandra wondered aloud.

"Liam loves Exmoor. He says a man can breathe here because the air is pure, unlike London with its everlasting smokestacks."

"Well, the air is wet today, and so is the earl, since he apparently hasn't the sense to come in out of the rain," Alexandra retorted. Though in truth, she suspected he would rather face the wind and rain than ride in the carriage with her.

"That's because he is a true nobleman who would never ask the men who serve him to endure such weather while he sat warm and dry inside the coach," Jamie stated unequivocally.

Alexandra had heard all she cared to about the Earl of Stratham's admirably democratic ways. "Papa is a nobleman as well," she said. "But I doubt he would feel it necessary to become soaked to the skin to prove it—particularly since doing so would not render his coachman or grooms one iota less miserable."

Jamie looked up from his book. "Papa has the manners of a nobleman, but he does not have a noble heart. If he did, he would never have traded his only daughter for the blunt to keep himself out of debtors' prison."

Alexandra stared, astounded, at her young brother. When and where had he learned the truth of why she had married the earl? But whatever Viscount Hardin's sins might be, he was still their father, and Jamie should not criticize him in front of a servant. "Papa had no choice in the matter," she said staunchly.

"Well, it was not a lack of choice that made him talk Liam into accepting the guardianship of his only son as well."

Alexandra gasped. "Whoever told you such a preposterous thing?" she demanded once she recovered her voice.

"Papa told me. He took me aside while you were in Kent and explained that he had asked Liam to be my guardian until I came of age because both Mama and he were going to be too busy to spend much time with me for the next few years." A bitter smile twisted Jamie's mouth. "As if they had ever done so in the past.

"Luckily, Liam wasn't too busy to care about me. He agreed to be my guardian, and he wants me to live with the two of you as well. Then when I am strong enough to go back to school, I'm to take my holidays with you." Jamie searched Alexandra's face with anxious eyes. "I hope that meets with your approval."

"Of course it does," she said automatically. But one thought tumbled over another as she strove to sort out this latest tangle in her already confused life. At every turn she was confronted with new proof that the man she had talked herself into despising was everything good and honorable—everything any woman could wish for in a husband. Why had it taken her so long to recognize this truth?

"I've said it before; I say it again," Jamie continued in a

solemn voice that made him appear ages older than his sixteen years, "we are very lucky we met Liam Campbell that day by the Serpentine, and luckier still that he wants us both in his life."

Beside him, Emmy made a series of graceful gestures with her hands, touched her fingers to her eyelids, then placed them over her heart.

Jamie nodded his agreement. "Emmy says it is easy to see that the Earl of Stratham is a man with a loving heart—just like his brother-in-law, the Duke of Bellmont. She is very observant about such things, you know. Probably because she doesn't waste her time talking as the rest of us do."

With that pronouncement, Jamie returned to his book, leaving Alexandra to wallow in shame as she recalled every nasty thing she had ever said or done to Liam, including the latest petty declaration she had made in the heat of anger. How she wished she had it all to do over again. Thanks to her shrewish ways, she had managed to drive a seemingly impenetrable wedge between her husband and herself.

She glanced out the window to find the object of her ruminations riding beside the carriage. With his wind-tossed hair and broad shoulders, his lean hips and muscular thighs, he looked more than ever like the magnificent, tawny lion to whom she had likened him in the past.

He turned his head and stared down at her. Even through the rain-washed window she could see the fire that leapt into his amber eyes. Her pulse quickened. Could it be possible that in spite of everything she had done he still desired her?

She smiled tentatively, and Liam, in turn, grinned back with such warmth, a wave of answering heat coursed through her. His grin slowly faded, but a question smoldered in his narrowed gaze—a question to which she finally had the answer.

She had never dreamed that just looking into a man's eyes could create such myriad sensations—such wanton yearnings. If this was desire, then she desired her husband with every ounce of her being. She felt dizzy with exultation. She was not her mother's daughter after all. Her blood was as warm and red as that of any of the bold-eyed tavern wenches who had ogled Liam at every stop they'd made between London and Exmoor.

At long last she knew that what she wanted more than anything else was to be Liam Campbell's wife in every sense of the word. At the first opportunity she would tell him she had made her decision. Then surely they could, as Fanny Burney's novels promised, live happily ever after.

As if to prove the author of Jamie's precious history book incorrect in her description of Exmoor, the rain stopped shortly before they arrived at the inn Liam had chosen for their midday meal. He had sent his valet ahead to alert the innkeeper to their imminent arrival, and a hearty meal of mutton stew, fresh-baked bread and fine, dark ale was waiting for them when they pulled into the inn yard.

This was not, however, one of their democratic meals. When Colin O'Riley made the arrangements, proper protocol was strictly observed. Liam, Jamie and Alexandra dined in the inn's private parlor, the servants in the taproom. Ergo, Jamie bolted down his meal, excused himself and headed for the taproom and his friend.

Liam's sober gaze followed the boy's retreating figure. "I have been thinking about our . . . discussion last night," he said quietly. "If you wish me to, I will have a talk with Jamie about the inadvisability of losing his head over a female at age sixteen."

It was the olive branch for which Alexandra had been hoping. "No, my lord. Let him be. Your judgment of the situation was correct, and I am ashamed of how I acted. I know now my fears were groundless."

She raised her head and stared directly into his eyes. "We Hennings have had so little affection in our lives, we tend to be a bit overwhelmed by uninhibited admiration. But we are reasonably intelligent people. Give us a little time, and we will learn to deal with it."

Liam blinked. Did he just imagine it, or was Alexandra alluding to her feelings toward him as well as her brother's friendship with Emmy O'Riley? He had been ready to declare his marriage a hopeless cause after last night; now for no apparent reason, his wife had done a complete turnaround. He dared not ask why. It was enough that the look in her eyes gave him hope that they might have a future together after all.

As if all nature were celebrating this amazing turn of events, a ray of sunshine slanted through the window and captured the two of them in its brilliant radiance. Alexandra raised her face to the warm, golden light. "Thank goodness! The sun at last! If you have no objection, Liam, I would like to ride with you across your beloved moors. Maybe if I see them through your eyes, I may begin to understand the man with whom I intend to spend the rest of my life."

In something of a daze, Liam escorted his wife to the stable, stopping only long enough to inform O'Riley that the two of them would ride ahead of the carriage for the next few miles. A small voice in a remote corner of his mind warned he was dancing to a woman's tune—something he'd sworn he would never do. He chose to ignore it.

A luminous glow in Alexandra's lovely eyes told him that the look they had exchanged through a rain-streaked window had miraculously kindled a spark of passion in his prim little wife. Properly tended, that tiny spark might be the tinder that awakened the sensuality he felt certain was an integral part of her nature. He smiled to himself. Who better to light that tinder than her husband?

"We are traveling along one of the oldest trackways in all of Britain—one used by the Saxons in the fifth and sixth centuries," Liam said, reining in his mount once they'd left the carriage and outriders far behind.

"The soil here has a rocky base that makes a good, solid road bed. But directly ahead is a peaty bog that can be dangerous ground for a heavy carriage. I should wait here to supervise the passage through that area."

Alexandra patted the neck of her spirited piebald to calm it down. "And to where does this ancient trackway lead?"

"Eventually to Foreland Point on the Bristol Channel, which is where The Aerie is located. But we have a good stretch of moor to travel before we reach the coast."

Raising a hand to shield her eyes from the sun, Alexandra surveyed the surrounding countryside. Flat as a tabletop, the desolate stretch of rock and sand was ringed by a dozen or more massive fingers of jagged black stone pointing sharply skyward. "Tors" Jamie had said these towering crags were called in his history book—an apt name for the sentinels that guarded this land once inhabited by the ancient Celts.

No vegetation grew here except clumps of blackened heather and a few scrub oaks gnarled and twisted by the moorland winds; no sound was heard except those winds wailing through the crevices of the tors. It was a land of stark, savage beauty that both repelled and fascinated her—a land to which Liam Campbell seemed infinitely more suited than to the drawing rooms of London.

She turned her head to study the man who rode beside her. "Jamie said you love Exmoor. I begin to see why."

Liam nodded. "I suppose I do . . . for the same reason I love the sea. A man can be free here—as free as the eagles that circle above him or the red deer that roam the grasslands. There are no hedgerows to hem him in, no smoke or refuse to foul the air he breathes and the water he drinks. The hand of man is everywhere in cities like London and Plymouth. But the gods rule what man cannot tame. On the moors, man is no more powerful than the humblest ant, and he has no more jurisdiction over the vast unconquerable sea than the tiniest minnow."

Alexandra swallowed the lump in her throat. Here in the land where he was born, she was finally beginning to understand this complex man whose name she bore. She would ask no more why he had chosen her to be his mate; she would simply take a fierce delight in knowing he had.

Suddenly, she couldn't wait to arrive at the ancient castle that was the demesne of the Earl of Stratham . . . and his lady. "How soon will we reach The Aerie?" she asked breathlessly.

Liam smiled, pleased by her eagerness. "If this good weather holds, we'll take our evening meal at the inn in Lynton. From there it is but a short ride to the castle."

"A good idea—dining at the inn, that is. We could not logically expect your staff to prepare a decent meal on such short notice."

"My . . . my staff?" Liam stammered. He'd left Henry Pippin, a former member of the crew of *The Wayward Lady*, as caretaker of The Aerie. Henry could brew a fine batch of ale, but he doubted the old fellow could cook anything Alexandra would consider a decent meal.

"But maybe we should send your valet ahead to make certain the windows are opened and the bedding properly aired," Alexandra continued. "It is my understanding that medieval castles tend to be a bit musty."

Good God! Bedding! He's never even considered such a thing. All at once, the enormity of the blunder he'd made in bringing his aristocratic wife and brother-in-law to Exmoor struck home. He had been so fascinated by The Aerie's turrets and battlements, the enormous fireplaces and rusted suits of armor, he'd never given a thought to what it would be like to actually live in a great pile of moss-covered stones atop a lonely, windswept cliff.

There was nothing for it but to confess his stupidity. "I fear I have done Jamie and you a great disservice dragging you across England to this medieval castle I inherited. I see now there is no way you can take up residence at The Aerie."

"But why? I thought you told my brother you found it absolutely fascinating."

"I did. I do. But I just realized I know nothing about the practical day-to-day living in such a place. How could I? I've lived half my life in a thatched roof cottage on the moors, the other half on a fishing smack."

He took a deep breath. "The truth of the matter is my staff at The Aerie consists of one old jack-tar who sailed with me on *The Wayward Lady*, and the castle itself is in a state of hopeless disrepair."

Liam's stomach clenched at the thought of what a fool he was making of himself, but with dogged determination he continued his painful recital. "I've spent but two nights at The Aerie since I inherited it, and on both occasions I slept, fully clothed, on the sofa in the library. Now that I think about it, I remember the books smelled so strongly of moldy leather, I attempted to open a window. The blasted thing didn't give an inch. I suspect the rest of them are in like condition.

"As for bedding, I haven't the slightest idea if such a thing as a sheet or blanket exists in this place I'd foolishly planned to spend the night. I vaguely remember coverlets of some kind on the beds when I made a cursory tour. But what was under them and how long they had been there I cannot say."

He fixed his eyes on the horizon, too embarrassed to look his wife in the face. "I shall have O'Riley arrange for rooms at the inn in Lynton for you and Jamie until I complete my business."

Alexandra registered the dull red flush that stained Liam's lean cheeks. For just a moment the proud barbarian looked as young and vulnerable as Jamie, and her heart ached for him. "I refuse to stay at the inn," she said firmly. "I have not traveled four long days to stay in a village inn. You promised I could live in a medieval castle. I demand you keep your promise."

"Hell and damnation, Alexandra, be practical. You would be miserable under such conditions."

"I have been practical all my life. It is high time I had an adventure. Surely we can hire the servants we need in a nearby village. I am very good at that sort of thing."

Liam shook his head. "No self-respecting servant would work in the place as it stands now. I can just imagine what O'Riley will say when he sees it."

A mischievous twinkle danced in Alexandra's eyes. "But what care you for the opinion of a prig, my lord? And do not worry your head over the problem of linens. Have you forgotten that box of mine that you cursed so loudly? The contents will do nicely until we determine what is under those coverlets you saw."

Liam groaned. He had known some stubborn women in his day, but not a one of them had been as pigheaded as his wife. "And how do you propose to feed this staff of servants, to say nothing of yourself and Jamie?" he demanded. "For all I know, the kitchen equipment consists of nothing more modern than a spit on which to roast an oxen."

"I shall send your man, O'Riley, to Plymouth—or London if needs be—to purchase a Robinson roasting range. It is all the thing since Prinny had one installed at Brighton Pavillion. Cook was forever badgering Mama to buy one. But, of course, Mama never did. She was annoyingly parsimonious when it came to her household budget." Alexandra gave Liam a sidelong glance. "You are, I hope, rich enough to allow for the purchase of a Robinson roasting range."

"I am rich enough to allow for the purchase of Brighton Pavillion, or so my solicitors tell me. But that is beside the point. I am responsible for you and Jamie. I cannot imagine what possessed me to consider leaving you in a decrepit medieval castle with only my cocky Irish valet to see to your welfare. I would worry about you every minute I was gone, and the nature of my business is such I dare not allow myself to be distracted."

Alexandra's eyes narrowed. "You have been planning all along to leave us once we reached The Aerie?"

A feeling deep in his gut warned Liam that his careless slip of tongue could not be passed over without some explanation. "A friend to whom I owe my life is in grave danger and I am the only one who can rescue him," he said simply, hoping she would ask no questions.

"The Frenchman, I assume, since it cannot be the Duke of

Bellmont, and I feel certain the third person to whom you are indebted is a woman."

This wife of his was too clever by half, Liam realized. "It is indeed Yves Durand," he admitted, "and in telling you this I place his life in your hands. He is actually the Comte de Rochemont, a royalist who kept Wellington supplied with vital information on Napoleon Bonaparte's troop movements during the Peninsular Wars. The Corsican learned his identity from the very spy I was once accused of smuggling into England."

He paused. "It is undoubtedly common knowledge in London by now that Bonaparte has escaped Elba and is about to crown himself emperor of France again. He would dearly love to get his hands on the man who played so great a part in his defeat. Lord Castlereagh himself informed me that every major port in England is being watched by French sympathizers hoping to prevent our going to Yves' rescue."

"Which is why you propose to sail from a little-known port in Exmoor? In what? A fishing smack?"

"Exactly. What better way to slip past any waiting French ships? In a few days' time I will be anchored off the coast of France—hopefully to transport my friend to safety in England."

Alexandra paled. "The plan sounds logical, but I cannot help but believe it is terribly dangerous."

"No more so than what I did for a living for a number of years, and I survived that unscathed." Liam spoke with careless confidence, but in truth he was deeply touched by Alexandra's concern. He slid from the saddle, raised his arms and demanded, "Dismount that horse this instant, Madam Wife."

"Why?" Alexandra asked, her eyes widening in alarm.

Liam grinned. "Because I say so, and despite the fact that you outwit me at every turn, I am still your lord and master."

With an endearingly shy smile, she slipped into his arms and slid down his body to stand molded against him. "What is it you desire, my lord?" she asked softly, nestling deeper into his embrace.

"What I have desired since I first laid eyes on you, little siren." Tipping up her chin with one finger, he fit his lips to hers in a tantalizing kiss that was like nothing he had ever before experienced. Vaguely, he heard a low, contented growl and realized it came from the depths of his own throat.

"Ummm," Alexandra purred. "Perhaps we could strike a

bargain." Slowly opening her eyes, she sent his senses reeling with a limpid emerald gaze. "I will agree to what you want if you agree to what I want."

Liam loosened his hold on her sufficiently to search her face. "We both know what I want. The question is, what do you want?"

A guileless smile tilted the corners of her mouth. "I want to sleep this night at The Aerie," she said softly.

"And if, against my better judgment, I should agree to such madness—"

"Then my wish will be fulfilled, and we can devote all our efforts to seeing that yours comes true as well . . . my lord and master."

The last scarlet glow of the setting sun had slipped beneath the western horizon when Liam rounded a bend in the road from Lynton to Foreland Point and reined in his mount at the top of the small rise overlooking The Aerie. The cliff was barren of trees here, and from far below came the sullen roar of surf breaking on rocky shingle. As he watched, a pair of gulls circled above the shore and came to rest on one of the crenellated towers of The Aerie, home to ten or more generations of his paternal forebears.

A wide-eyed Alexandra edged her mare to a halt beside him. "Oh, Liam, what a glorious old castle!" she exclaimed. "I cannot wait to explore it."

Behind them, the coachman brought the duke's carriage to a stop and Jamie leapt out with Emmy close behind him. "Gadzooks, it's even more awesome than I expected!" he declared reverently. "Those walls must be ten feet thick, and look at that incredible stone parapet. I'll wager your Saxon ancestors poured boiling oil on a few Danes from that!"

Alexandra visibly cringed. "Good heavens, Jamie, what a gruesome picture you paint."

"The boy is right. That is how wars were fought in the eleventh and twelfth centuries," Liam said. "And those slit windows in the tower were for the defending archers. I've been told the early inhabitants of The Aerie fought off a good many attackers shortly after it was first built."

Jamie stared up at the imposing structure, a worshipful expression on his thin face. "I wish I'd lived here then."

"Well, I'm glad I didn't," Alexandra declared. "Life under siege must have been dreadful."

Liam chuckled. "I fear your sister lacks the zeal of the true historic purist, Jamie. She has already proposed substituting something called a Robinson range for the spit on which my ancestors roasted oxen."

"She's a girl," Jamie said disparagingly." She'll probably have an army of maids washing and waxing everything in the castle before the week's end."

Liam feared it would take more than soap and wax to make The Aerie inhabitable, but he held his counsel. He had warned Alexandra what to expect; the next move was up to her.

"Holy Mother of God, will you look at what's before me eyes." Colin O'Riley reined in his mare beside Liam, the same awestruck expression on his face as that on Jamie's. "'Tis as like one of the old Irish chieftains' castles as two eggs laid by a sitting hen. If I didn't know better, I'd be after thinking the faery-folk had whisked Kilbourne Castle itself off the cliff overlooking Belfast Lough and carried it to this heathen land."

His gaze still locked on the mammoth structure before them, he asked, "Will we be biding here awhile then, milord?"

"It remains to be seen if Lady Alexandra and that army of maids Jamie mentioned can make the old place livable."

O'Riley's eyes lit up. "Milady will have my help for certain. I've been that keen to see the inside of an ancient castle since I was but a ragtail lad, as has many another God-fearing Irishman. For to our everlasting shame, 'tis our English landlords who sit in the great halls of the old chieftains nowadays. 'Twill be worth many a free pint in the alehouses of Belfast if I can claim to have bided a time in a genuine castle."

Liam shook his head. Leave it to O'Riley to find a way to turn every situation to his advantage. "Well, the only way into this particular castle is through that archway on the other side of what was once the moat," he said. "It leads to the bailey off which all the exterior doors of the castle open. Since darkness will soon be upon us, I suggest we get ourselves settled for the night."

With a murmur of agreement, Alexandra and the rest of the party of weary travelers followed Liam across what had obviously been a drawbridge, but was now but a series of rough timbers lying across the centuries of refuse and soil that filled the former moat. He urged his mount forward through the opening in the massive wall, and Alexandra followed close behind into the cobblestoned enclosure beyond.

Once the carriage and outriders were safely through the arch-way, Liam dismounted and raised the lion's head knocker on the iron-hinged door that was recessed in the vast stone wall. He waited a moment, then pounded the knocker again. With much creaking and squeaking, the door finally swung open to reveal a gaunt old man with silvery hair and a face as brown and wrinkled as a dried apple. He was accompanied by a large shaggy dog of indeterminate lineage. The hoary fellow's bird-bright eyes peered intently at Liam. "So, Cap'n, ye've come back at last."

"That I have, Henry Pippin," Liam said, escorting Alexandra through the wide doorway and into the great hall. Then step-ping aside, he allowed Jamie, Emmy and Colin O'Riley to enter as well.

"Well 'tis high time ye showed up if ye asks me," Pippin de-clared sourly. "Dawg and me was beginning to think ye'd had yer throat cut in some back alley of London town or worse yet, was pressed into the king's navy."

"Sorry to disappoint you, but you'll not be rid of me that easily," Liam said, and to Alexandra's surprise, laughed at his caretaker's disrespectful manner of addressing him. The fellow would have been sacked on the spot had he spoken so impu-dently in the Henning household.

Henry Pippin's gaze shifted to Alexandra. "I see ye managed to snabble yerself the London wife ye needed. Not that I doubted fer a minute ye would. Ye've always had a way with the wenches."

Liam glared at his close friend and fellow smuggler, sorry that he had entrusted the garrulous fellow with the truth about his inheritance. "And you've always had a tendency to let your tongue run away with itself, old man."

Pippin raised a bushy white eyebrow. "So that's the way the wind blows. Then belay yer fretting, for mum's the word from now on, Cap'n."

The old man raked Alexandra with a speculative gaze, then nodded as if satisfied with what he saw. "She be comely enough. I'll say that fer her," he declared and without so much as a "by your leave" he disappeared into the deeply shadowed hall. Over his shoulder he added what sounded amazingly like "Though if ye asks me, the daughter don't hold a candle to the mother."

Chapter Thirteen

"What did he say?" Alexandra asked as soon as the old man was out of earshot.

"He thinks you greatly resemble your brother." Liam crossed his fingers and made a mental note to remove the portrait of a young Henrietta Henning from the old earl's bedchamber.

To his relief, Alexandra had been so engrossed in studying the great hall, she had apparently missed Henry's telling comment regarding the "London wife" the new Earl of Stratham had needed to marry. He wasn't certain how he would have covered his tracks on that one. This was no time to broach the touchy subject—not when she had offered him an implicit invitation into her bed if he agreed to sleep this night at The Aerie.

"You have suits of armor," she said, clapping her hands in delight.

"Fourteenth- and fifteenth-century gothic," Jamie pronounced. "My last tutor was an expert on such things."

"And a musicians' gallery and a domed ceiling two stories high with a chandelier hanging from it that must be at least ten feet in circumference," Alexandra continued. "I've read about such things, but I never thought to actually see them."

"Nor did I." Jamie's eyes glowed. "Gadzooks! Look at that fireplace! It's big enough to hold a coach-and-four. Think of the Yule log we could burn in that." He turned to his sister. "I say, Alex, I wouldn't be the least bit surprised if we find an *oubliette* once we start exploring the old place."

"A what?" Liam asked when he saw the look of horror on Alexandra's face.

"An *oubliette*," Jamie intoned ominously. "A cold, dark dungeon with the only opening in the ceiling, where your ancestors tossed their enemies once they captured them." He studied the massive tapestry that covered one wall, depicting a fierce, hand-to-hand battle. "Look at those fellows; then tell me they wouldn't let their captives starve in a dungeon."

Liam laughed. "I don't know about the dungeon, but there is an ancient chapel on the west side of the castle with stained glass windows that rival anything I've ever seen in a cathedral. You might want to look into that."

So far, so good. Liam breathed a sigh of relief. These two history enthusiasts were too taken by the medieval ambiance to notice the inch of dust on the stone floor or the curtain of cobwebs hanging from the domed ceiling. Or so he thought until he glanced down and found Alexandra sniffing the air like a hound on the scent of a fox. "Just as I thought," she declared. "This old castle smells unbearably dank and musty. I shall have to do something about that first off."

Liam groaned. "But not tonight, Madam Wife."

"Of course not, silly. I can accomplish nothing tonight except arrange temporary sleeping accommodations." She smiled at Emmy. "It is a good thing you reminded me to buy a flint box and a dozen candles from the innkeeper's wife. We shall need them to find our way to the bedchambers on the upper floors."

In truth, with Jamie as interpreter, Emmy had also reminded her to purchase six loaves of fresh-baked bread, a crock of butter and a packet of black tea. Alexandra suspected that in many ways, the fifteen-year-old Irish girl was a great deal more knowledgeable about maintaining a household than she was.

But one thing she did know. Raising her head, she sniffed again. "Sugar and vinegar," she said. "That is what my mother's housekeeper used to clear the air of offensive odors. First thing in the morning, I shall have the coachman drive me to the nearest village to hire a proper staff and procure a keg of vinegar, a sack of sugar and the necessary supplies to give this place the scrubbing it needs."

"I told you so," Jamie grumbled.

Liam, however, was not disheartened by Alexandra's housewifely tendencies. In truth, he was happy she had found something to keep her busy while he was off rescuing Yves Durand. By the time he returned, she would undoubtedly have realized the task she'd set herself was a hopeless one, and they could enjoy The Aerie for what it was—a fascinating relic of history that was ill-suited to modern-day nineteenth-century living.

In the meantime, there remained the problem of finding a place for everyone to sleep this first night. Henry would be no help. He had turned two small rooms on the ground floor into his living quarters and steadfastly ignored the rest of the huge, drafty structure.

But thanks to the generosity of the Duke of Bellmont's housekeeper, they had sufficient linens so everyone could have a clean bed, if not necessarily a comfortable one. With the assistance of O'Riley and the two burly outriders, Liam unloaded the huge, unwieldy box from the roof of the carriage, dragged it into the great hall and pried it open.

Instantly, the fragrance of lavender wafted from the stacks of snowy linens, reminding him of the luxury he had enjoyed at White Oaks. There would be nothing to compare to it here at The Aerie, but with Alexandra sharing his bed, it would seem finer than the softest feather bed at the duke's elegant country home.

He appropriated two of the candles from Emmy's basket, lit one, and handed them both to Alexandra. Then he selected two sheets, two pillows and a thin blanket from the box. "These will suffice for my lady and me," he said to the group of curious onlookers surrounding him. "Now if you will excuse us, we shall find ourselves an empty bedchamber and get a few hours of much needed sleep. I suggest you do the same."

So saying, he tucked the bedding under his left arm, grasped Alexandra's elbow with his right hand, and steered her toward the staircase at the far end of the great hall.

"What in heaven's name are you doing?" she cried, frantically trying to tug free of his hold.

He tightened his grip. "Exactly what I said I was going to do. We made a bargain, Madam Wife. One you proposed," he added in a hoarse whisper. "I have lived up to my part of it; now it is your turn to live up to yours."

Alexandra tugged harder. "Have you gone mad? I cannot leave Jamie to fend for himself in this monstrous great castle. He is terrified of the dark."

"Nonsense. O'Riley will see to your brother's needs. The man is not happy unless he's playing mother hen."

Alexandra couldn't argue with that. If the truth be known, Colin O'Riley would probably do a much better job of making Jamie comfortable for the night than she could. For all her brave talk, she had never done anything more domestic than ring for a servant.

Also, though she would never admit it to a living soul, she shared Jamie's terror of the dark. Even her martinet mother had recognized that and allowed her a small night candle in her bedchamber when she was a child—a custom Alexandra had continued to this day.

"I shall need my portmanteau," she protested as Liam continued to haul her toward the staircase. "My nightrail and slippers are in it."

"You won't need them tonight."

Because she could see arguing with Liam in his present mood was a hopeless cause, she gave in and with no further complaint, accompanied him up the stairwell and down a dark, sinister-looking hallway to the first door they found standing open. The faint beam of moonlight that managed to penetrate the grimy window outlined tall posters and bed curtains, proclaiming it the bedchamber they sought. But the smell of mold was even stronger here than on the floor below.

"Phew! You are right. We shall have to do something about that blasted odor." Liam dropped his bundle of bedding on the room's only chair and crossed to the casement window. "Let's hope this thing will open," he said, and with much cursing and grunting, managed to accomplish the prodigious feat. He promptly threw both sides of the window wide open to the moonlit night.

A moment later he cheerfully announced, "We're in luck again. There is a two-pronged candle holder on the floor beside the bed." Lighting the second candle with the first, he set them both on a massive iron trunk standing against the wall nearest the bed. Then, to Alexandra's amazement, he yanked the bed curtains from their rod, tossed them out the window and heaved the dirt-encrusted coverlet and bolster after them.

"Well, that's one way of cleaning house," she said, choking on the cloud of dust he'd raised.

"The only way in The Aerie if you ask me." Liam brushed the dust off his hands. "That's that then," he added with obvious satisfaction. "The mattress on this feather bed may not compare to the one on which you slept at White Oaks, but at least it doesn't date back to medieval times. I'd estimate it is just a little over twenty years old, which I've been told is when the old earl had the castle partially renovated."

"When he planned to take a wife, no doubt."

"Probably so," Liam agreed, looking so uncomfortable, Alexandra felt certain he, too, had heard the story of the earl from Exmoor's disastrous courting of a London incomparable. She found herself feeling sorry for the man her mother had described as an "ugly brute with the manners of a jungle savage and the morals of a gypsy." The poor fellow couldn't have offered for a less suitable bride than the future Viscountess Hardin. She suspected her father wished the barbarian earl had succeeded in kidnapping the coldhearted beauty.

"Now all that needs be accomplished before we can properly celebrate our belated wedding night is the making up of the marriage bed," Liam declared. "I'll leave you to that while I hunt up some soap and water so we can both have a much needed wash before we retire."

Alexandra searched Liam's face, certain he must be jesting. To her dismay, he appeared perfectly serious. "You want *me* to make the bed?"

"It seems a simple enough request." Liam's expression remained sober, but his golden eyes held a devilish twinkle. "Unless, of course, the task is beyond your capabilities."

"A viscount's daughter is not expected to learn such menial household chores," Alexandra declared in her haughtiest tone of voice. "It would upset the natural order of things. How then would servants earn their keep?"

"What a corker! Once a nobleman's daughter becomes mistress of her own household, she is like the captain of a ship. She should know how to do every task she assigns to those who serve her. I could hoist a sail or swab a deck better and faster than any water dog who sailed with me on *The Wayward Lady*. I could also, thanks to my mother's training, keep my own house when the need arose."

Alexandra raised her chin defiantly. "I, on the other hand, received training more suitable to the life of an aristocrat."

Liam shrugged. "I am aware of that. I have seen three of your excellent paintings, and I stand in awe of your talent. But it is of little use to us at the moment."

Picking up one of the linen sheets, he unfolded it and flicked it neatly into place atop the mattress. "Now, Madam Wife," he said in a quiet voice that brooked no argument, "if you will be good enough to station yourself on the opposite side of this bed, I shall teach you the first of the many menial household chores you will need to master to be a proper Countess of Stratham."

Now what was she supposed to do? Alexandra had washed herself as best she could in the bucket of tepid water Liam had produced. Then she had removed the pins from her hair, brushed it with the brush Emmy had placed in her reticule and managed to braid the flyaway stuff for the night—despite heretofore having always relied on an abigail to perform such tasks. Her husband might not find these accomplishments very impressive, but she was rather proud of herself for showing such ingenuity.

Her ablutions completed, she seated herself on the edge of the newly made bed, barefoot and dressed in nothing but her chemise and pantalettes. A shocking state of undress, to be sure, but it seemed illogical to put her soiled carriage dress back on since she was going to bed and she had no nightrail at hand. Evidently, her eccentric husband expected her to sleep in her chemise.

Very well. Then sleep in her chemise she would. She had struck a bargain with him and she intended to see it through. She knew now that he was a kind man and a caring one, for all his barbaric ways. Furthermore, there was something to be said for a man who, for whatever reason, wanted her for herself. With the exception of Jamie, everyone else she had ever cared about had seen her as a means of acquiring money.

Hands folded in her lap, she waited to see what Liam would do next. But as usual, what he did took her completely by surprise. Mouth agape, she watched him strip to the waist and slosh the remaining water in the bucket over rippling muscles she had heretofore only imagined lay beneath the homespun shirts he was so fond of wearing.

Her gaze lingered on the wicked scar below his right shoulder and the series of red dots on either side of it where a needle and thread had sewn the jagged flesh together. She shivered, thinking how close he had come to dying on that French beach.

He turned to face her, still wiping his dripping chest with his discarded shirt, and she found herself fascinated by the patch of red-gold curls that emerged from beneath his makeshift towel.

It had never occurred to her than men might have hair on their chests.

His thoughtful gaze lingered on her flaming cheeks. "Would you prefer I blow out the candles before we undress?"

Alexandra panicked. "No! Leave one candle burning, please. I . . . I have never liked the dark."

"As you wish. I would prefer seeing your lovely face—and body—when we make love."

She hadn't considered that. Fear and modesty waged a brief skirmish inside her head, and fear won. The candle would remain lit. But she clasped her arms over her bosom. "As to undressing, I am as undressed as I intend to get, my lord."

"You have that look of the early Christian martyr about you again, love. I thought you had decided you wanted to make ours a marriage in more than name only."

"So I did, and I do want to truly be your wife," Alexandra said instantly. "I just wish I knew a little more about . . ." She took a deep breath. "I do not like mysteries. I never have."

"So you've mentioned before." Tossing his shirt aside, Liam hunkered down before her and caught both her hands in his. "Are you saying you know nothing at all about what goes on in the marriage bed, my love?" he asked softly.

Alexandra nodded. "Only what my mother said about it, and that does not bear repeating." She hesitated a moment, then added, "Bridget told me an unlikely tale about the things a man does with his mistress. She claimed it was the same between man and wife, but I cannot credit any decent husband would expect his wife to indulge in such obscene acts."

Liam silently cursed both the frigid viscountess and the stupid abigail who had done their best to confuse Alexandra. Though she bravely tried to hide it, he could see she was both frightened and bewildered at the thought of what lay ahead.

He felt a little bewildered himself. He had never before bedded a virgin, much less the woman with whom he planned to spend the rest of his life. Not since his own initiation into the mysteries of sexual intercourse at age sixteen had he felt so unsure of how to proceed. The pattern of their future life together could well depend on what transpired between them this night.

Tenderly he tucked a flyaway strand of pale hair behind her ear. "Do you trust me, Alexandra?"

"Yes," she answered without hesitation.

"Then believe me when I say that despite what your mother and your abigail may have led you to believe, there is nothing obscene or ugly about making love. It is the perfect physical expression of the feelings a man and woman have for each other. But they cannot fully employ the remarkable bodies the Creator gave them to express those feelings unless they divest themselves of their clothing."

"Oh!" Alexandra's blush deepened, but she nodded in sober agreement. "I suppose that is logical, when one thinks about it."

Liam's heart went out to his courageous little innocent. "Such intimacy may seem shocking at first," he continued in the same soft tone of voice. "But if you can but give yourself to the moment without reservation, I promise you our spirits will soar together like the gulls we watched wheeling and gliding in the coastal winds."

A shy smile crept across Alexandra's delicate features. "I should like that. It sounds very much like the wondrous freedom you have found on the moors and at sea. I envy you that feeling. I have never known such freedom."

She surveyed him with bright, trusting eyes as green as an April fern in a moorland marsh. "I put myself in your hands then, Liam. Please teach my spirit to soar like the seabirds."

"I shall do my best, love." He hadn't prayed in years. He prayed now that a kindly God would show him the way to liberate the deeply passionate woman he felt certain was imprisoned inside his starchy little blueblood wife.

He stood up and drew her to her feet as well. "Let us begin this magical flight of ours by freeing your hair from that braid. I have longed to see it unbound again, as when you wore it that way the morning after our wedding."

Strangely clumsy, he untied the ribbon at the end of her braid, separated the intertwined strands and let the heavy, silken mass flow down her back. "Beautiful," he murmured, running his fingers through it. "So beautiful."

"Am I allowed to run my fingers through your hair as well?" Alexandra asked, wishing he would spell out the rules that applied to lovemaking. She would feel more secure if she knew exactly where she stood.

"There are no rules to lovemaking," he said, somehow reading her mind. "Every time is different—every feeling unique. You may do anything you wish as long as it pleases your lover—and your fingers in my hair would please me very much."

Anything she wished. The provocative idea overwhelmed Alexandra—and excited her. Tentatively, she slipped her fingers into the flame-colored hair that brushed Liam's shoulders. It felt smooth and silky and damp from the water he had combed through it with his fingers, yet different somehow from her own hair. Impulsively, she buried her nose in the fascinating swirls of red-gold hair covering his chest. "It tickles," she said, and sneezed to prove it.

Laughter rumbled deep in Liam's chest, and the word "siren" escaped his lips even as they claimed hers. Lost in his demanding kiss, she scarcely registered that he had scooped her up in his arms until she found herself lying on the bed with Liam stretched out beside her. Nor could she say how or when he divested her of her chemise and—*good heavens*—her pantalettes as well. A magician, he waved his wand and they disappeared.

Oddly enough, she felt no embarrassment over her nakedness—or his. How could one be embarrassed by magic?

The heat of Liam's strong body enveloped her; the touch of his lips, his tongue, his wildly wicked fingers sent her soaring into the heavens as he'd promised. Higher and higher she flew on the wings of passion—until her body and soul fused into one glorious being of fire and light and joyous sensation.

Slowly, she descended to earth to lie limp and boneless in her husband's arms. His fingers were in her hair again—stroking, stroking in a gentle, soothing rhythm. "Are you all right, little love?" he asked softly. "I didn't hurt you? I meant to be so gentle—so careful on this, your first time. But I fear my good intentions went up in flames the instant I touched you."

Vaguely she recalled a brief, sharp stab of pain—instantly forgotten. "I am fine," she said, aware that even now in the aftermath of their lovemaking, her body still throbbed from his touch.

She nestled against him, just as if she had always slept with her head on his shoulder, her arm across his chest. "I just remembered something very important I meant to tell you," she murmured drowsily.

"What could that be, Madam Wife?"

"I love you, Liam."

"That pleases me very much," he said after a long moment of silence.

How amazing, she mused as sleep claimed her, that Henrietta Henning's daughter could so quickly become accustomed to loving and being loved.

Liam rose before dawn and, with aching regret, left his beautiful, passionate wife sound asleep in the tangle of bedclothes that bespoke their glorious night together. He was tempted to wake her with a lover's kiss, but how could he leave her if she returned his kiss or asked him to stay?

And leave her he must. For it was crucial that he reach the coast of France as soon as possible. Even now Yves might be waiting in the cave, and it would take the better part of a day and night to make *The Wayward Lady* seaworthy and prowl the local taverns to find a proper crew.

But he needed to leave Alexandra a note. He spied a piece of charcoal in the ashes of the fireplace with which to write it, but not a scrap of paper could he find until he fished in his pocket and discovered a neatly folded square of foolscap he couldn't remember putting there.

He didn't bother to unfold it. He couldn't have read a message if it contained one. The last remnant of the candle had guttered and died and in the predawn light, he could barely see the bold black strokes of charcoal, much less anything written by pen. He finished his brief message, laid it next to Alexandra's pillow and tiptoed from the room.

He was halfway down the staircase when he remembered the portrait hanging in the old earl's chamber. Cursing the necessary delay, he climbed back up the stairs and headed for the room at the end of the long hall. By the time he'd taken the painting down, wrapped it in a sheet from the bed and hid it at the back of the armoire, dawn was breaking over the Bristol Channel.

To his surprise, he met Colin O'Riley a few minutes later crossing the great hall. "What are you doing out of bed at this hour?" he asked the weary-looking Irishman.

O'Riley grinned foolishly. "Mayhap you noticed the dark-haired serving wench at the inn in Lynton, milord? One o' the Black Irish from Gweedore on the coast of Donegal she is, and as fair a lass as ever I've seen this side o' the Irish Sea."

"Say no more. I admire your stamina after a hard day in the saddle. I hope you saw all of our traveling companions settled for the night before you rode to Lynton."

"I did that, milord. Settled and happily so, as I see you are, yourself. And I don't mind telling you, 'tis glad I am to see it."

He raised a hand, as if swearing an oath. "Not that I doubted you for a second, but with that devilish abigail spreading her ugly tales through the servants' quarters each day, 'twas all I could do to hold up me head."

"Tales? Of what, pray tell?"

O'Riley avoided Liam's eyes. "Of how you was neglecting your husbandly duties."

"The devil you say!" It had never occurred to Liam that the duke's servants would notice whether or not he slept with his wife. But then what did he know of servants? He smiled to himself. So that was why Alexandra sacked her pudding-faced abigail.

Well, the problem was over and done with, and much of it had been of his wife's making, so he felt no need to apologize to her. But he did feel a certain guilt that his faithful valet should have suffered embarrassment on his account.

"Not that it is any of your business," he said brusquely, "but I had good reason for waiting until now to properly claim my bride. I was a near stranger to Lady Alexandra when her father arranged our marriage, and I found no joy in the thought of my wife accepting me in her bed out of duty alone. So, I waited until she invited me of her own free will."

O'Riley slapped his forehead with the palm of his hand. "Can you believe it? 'Twas the very explanation I gave me brother Timothy for this latest hitch in your gallop. For the both of us had seen the good night kisses you gave the mistress each night at her chamber door. And why else, said I, would a man just nibble at the leaves when the fruit was ripe on the tree?"

O'Riley wiped a sentimental tear from his eye. " 'Tis proud I am to serve you, milord. For 'tis plain to see that though you're an Englishman born and bred, 'tis an Irish heart that beats in your breast."

"I thank you for the compliment, O'Riley, and I hope you'll keep it in mind when I'm gone missing these next few days. For nothing short of a matter of life or death would make me leave my lady just now."

Colin O'Riley drew himself up to his full height. "If 'tis indeed such a matter, I'll be going with you, milord. For 'tis me duty to see you back safely to me mistress."

"Not so fast, O'Riley."

"Now don't be telling me I should stay here to protect milady. For we both know the duke's coachman can be counted on to do that."

"My mission could be dangerous—even life-threatening," Liam said, feeling it his duty to warn O'Riley what he could be getting into. Though, in truth, he liked the idea of the plucky little Irishman guarding his back.

"All the more reason I should be with you, milord."

"Very well then, if I cannot talk you out of it, get yourself a few hours' sleep, then join me on my fishing smack, *The Wayward Lady*, that's anchored in Lynmouth Harbor. Any of the locals can give you directions."

A puzzled frown knit O'Riley's brow. "If memory serves me right, 'twas a vessel by that name you told me you captained when you plied your trade. Is it smuggling we'll be doing then, milord?"

"Smuggling it is, my Irish friend. But brandy will not be our cargo on this trip."

Chapter Fourteen

"The memory of last night will sustain me until I return," Liam had scrawled in charcoal across the square of foolscap Alexandra found when she awoke. She carried it in her pocket all through her busy day, and whenever she thought of the night they'd shared, her body tingled as if his magical hands were still caressing her.

She was determined that by the time he returned from his mission she would have one small section of the castle in livable condition so they could spend the summer in Exmoor. She knew Liam would like that, and so would she. For it was here in this ancient land of lonely moors and wave-lashed cliffs that he had awakened her slumbering sensuality—here she had first realized that she was deeply and irrevocably in love with her husband.

She would surprise him with a painting of The Aerie and the wild, Exmoor countryside surrounding it, but first she must put his beloved castle in order. To that end, she instructed the "army of servants" she had hired from the nearby village to sweep the cobwebs from the ceilings and dirt from the floors of the great hall and the rooms adjoining it, then scrub those floors until the stone gleamed.

Meanwhile, she conscripted John Coachman to help her employ Liam's method of housecleaning to the ten bedchambers directly above the great hall—five of which she assigned to Colin and Emmy O'Riley, the two outriders, and the duke's coachman. An inspection of what had been the servants' quarters in the old earl's time convinced her they were not fit for man or beast.

The only room she left untouched was the one she could see had been the old earl's bedchamber. It was a strangely impersonal room despite his clothing still hanging in the armoire and other personal possessions lying scattered on the chiffonier. From the look of it, Liam had never been inside the room since his father's death.

One odd thing—a square of wallpaper shades lighter than the rest of the room indicated a large painting had been removed from the wall directly opposite the bed. She wondered if it had been a painting of the earl in his prime that had become too painful to view when he'd become old and debilitated. Once again, her heart went out to the old man, who had apparently lived alone and died alone in his great, gloomy castle.

Once the musty bed hangings and coverlets were removed from the bedchambers, John Coachman built a huge bonfire in the courtyard to dispose of them, while the village girls swept and scrubbed the floors. By the time darkness descended and the day help left for home, the living quarters in the central section of the old castle were respectably clean, and gallipots of sugar and vinegar sat in every corner of every room.

With a satisfied smile, the new Countess of Stratham surveyed the results of her first day as chatelaine of The Aerie. Tomorrow she would set the village girls to applying beeswax to the hodgepodge of chairs and tables, highboys, lowboys, chests, and desks acquired by the Earls of Stratham over at least six different historical periods. Liam's predecessors had obviously been a frugal lot who never discarded anything.

Weary to the bone, she wanted nothing so much as to wash her face and hands, crawl into bed and dream of the glorious night she had spent with Liam. But she had left Emmy, with Jamie as interpreter, to supervise the village girls who were cleaning the kitchen. She felt duty-bound to check on them.

As was the custom in medieval times, the kitchen was not in the castle itself, but in a one-story brick-and-timber building reached by a covered walkway. However, contrary to Liam's dire predictions, it had been modernized in the old earl's time and contained such nineteenth-century conveniences as an open range, a brick bread oven and a copper-lined washtub with a pump for washing vegetables.

All it had needed was a good cleaning and a competent cook. The one was already accomplished; the other Alexandra hoped to find in the village on the morrow.

With a stab of guilt, she remembered that lunch had been a paltry thing consisting of the bread, butter and tea they had brought from the inn. Jamie must be starved, and she feared dinner would be even more sparse.

But to her surprise, a savory aroma wafted from the open door of the kitchen, and once inside, she found a brace of chickens simmering in a pot on the range and a bowl of custard pudding setting up on the hob of the fireplace.

"We are going to have a grand dinner, and I, for one, vote we eat it right here at this table," Jamie said, looking up from the peas he and Henry Pippin were shelling. "Henry and I fetched the chickens and vegetables from a farmer he knows—and eggs and milk as well. But Emmy is doing the cooking because Henry's mouth is watering for a woman-cooked meal."

A happy grin spread across Jamie's face. "I can't remember when I have had such a bang-up day, tramping the countryside with Henry and Dawg. Now Henry is telling us about when he sailed with Liam. You wouldn't believe the daring things Liam did."

"Oh, yes I would," Alexandra said, thinking of the dangerous mission on which her husband was embarking even now. Exhausted, she dropped onto a chair opposite the two peashellers with nary a qualm about the lady of the house sitting in the kitchen with the servants. Jamie was not the only one learning bad habits.

Henry Pippin split open a pea shell and scraped the peas into the bowl. "As I were saying afore ye come through the door, mistress, I sailed with the cap'n till I were too old to do me part. Then he bought me a fine ale house in Fowey. Took every last farthing he had, but that were the cap'n's way.

"A rare one he were—known and liked in every port in Devon and Cornwall. The other gentlemen landed up the coast and hid their goods in caves. But not the cap'n. He'd put into Cawsand Harbor bold as brass of a midnight and by the time the sun come up, every female in the town would be 'swollen with child'."

Alexandra gasped, too shocked by the old man's tale to do anything but gape at him in stunned silence.

"Waddling up the hill to St. Anne's church them females would go, their great bellies filling their skirts like wind billowing a sail. Many's a fancy cove in Plymouth-town raised a toast to the Gentleman from Exmoor the night after Cap'n Campbell's ladies 'give birth to his bastards'."

Jamie's eyes widened. "The ladies carried the kegs of brandy under their skirts?"

"That they did, lad, and right past the nose of the excise men, too. Yes sir, onct the word got out that the pregnant ladies of Cawsand was going to church, there were a steady stream of young bucks wanting to put a crown or two in the vicar's collection plate."

Alexandra released the breath she hadn't realized she was holding. "Good heavens, wasn't Liam afraid of being apprehended by the excise men?"

"The cap'n afeared?" Pippin scoffed. "He never heard of the word—and as for them thieving tax collectors, he'd as soon spit in their eyes as give them the time of day."

He chuckled. "Too smart for them, the cap'n was. He had a different way of delivering his goods in every port. Pull up any fence post outside Fowey, and ye'd find a keg of the cap'n's brandy beneath it. In Polperro, it were under gravestones. But best ye put the proper blunt in its place if ye know'd what was good for ye. The cap'n didn't take kindly to being cheated."

Alexandra pressed a hand to her heaving bosom, afraid to ask what retribution Liam had exacted on those who shortchanged him.

"I recollect onct when a couple of excise men catched us driving a wagonload of goods from Mousehole to West Looe," Pippin continued, obviously pleased with his audience's reaction. " 'Stop in the name of the law,' the blighters ordered and obliging-like, the cap'n yells whoa to the mules. But turns out, he'd taught them stupid fleabags all their commands backward to what they should've been, and the mules took off down the road like they was shot out of a cannon."

Jamie howled with laughter. "I'd no idea Liam was such a daring fellow."

"The cap'n don't fear nothing or nobody," Henry Pippin declared, "especially when he be at the helm of *The Wayward Lady*. I've seen him sail her so close to a revenuer he'd fair scrape the paint off her hull. And onct when he were in a hurry to get back to Moll . . ." He flushed. "Back to Exmoor, I means, he sailed right between a Frog ship and one o' ours as was firing cannon balls at each other. It's like he feels most alive when he be thumbing his nose at death, if you knows what I mean."

"Gadzooks!" Jamie exclaimed, his green eyes solemn.

Alexandra, on the other hand, felt numb with fear. She dreaded to think what reckless kind of derring-do Liam might resort to in order to rescue his friend from the Corsican's clutches.

And who was this "Moll" who had inspired such foolish behavior on his part? Another of Liam's friends—or had she, as Henry Pippin's slip of the tongue implied, been much more than a friend? A flash of feminine intuition alerted Alexandra that this woman from her husband's past was somehow connected with the dark secret he guarded so zealously.

Quickly, she put the disturbing thought aside. Whatever Moll may have been to him, Liam had not chosen to marry her. He chose me, Alexandra reminded herself. But a nagging thought crept into her mind. Liam had pursued her relentlessly until he had his ring on her finger, and once married, he had shown her time and again that he desired her. But he had never told her he loved her—not even when she'd confessed her love for him.

But of course he loved her. Surely their wondrous night together had proved that. He was just not good with words. She drew his endearing little note from her pocket to reassure herself. *The memory of last night will sustain me until I return.*

For the first time, the note seemed depressingly impersonal. He hadn't even bothered to sign his name—merely grabbed the first scrap of paper he could find and scribbled a succinct note. Her curiosity aroused, she unfolded the paper and found four lines penned randomly across the page in Liam's bold hand, almost as if he had taken hasty notes during a conversation.

There was nothing remarkable about the first two lines:

Exmoor Solicitor—Daniel Higginbotham, Ilfracombe
London Solicitors—Waltham, Osgood and Prine

She knew nothing of Daniel Higginbotham, but Messrs. Waltham, Osgood and Prine had been guests at her wedding—guests to whom Liam had instructed the vicar to give a copy of the marriage lines for safe keeping.

Her gaze slid to the two lines in the center of the page:

Henrietta Henning, Viscountess Hardin
Daughter—Alexandra—before first day of May

"First day of May" was underlined.

She blinked and read them a second time, but still she could think of no reason why Liam would have scribbled the odd collection of words.

Emmy chose that moment to put the platter of chicken on the table, and Alexandra had no choice but to refold the paper and put it back in her pocket. But even as she choked down the delicious food Emmy had prepared and listened to more of Henry Pippin's tales, the two lines in the center of the page burned like hot coals in her brain.

She told herself there must be a logical explanation for them; she reminded herself that every problem Liam and she had encountered in their marriage so far had stemmed from a simple lack of communication. She would not panic. But the minute he returned from his mission, she would demand—no request—an explanation of why and when he had made his puzzling notation. In the meantime, she vowed to keep so busy she would have no time to let her vivid imagination run away with itself.

By noon the following day, the army of village girls had waxed and polished every stick of furniture in the section of the castle Alexandra had designated as family living quarters. They had even polished the oak railing of the gallery rimming the cavernous great hall, beaten the dust from the three bearskins on the stone floor in front of the fireplace, and scrubbed out the old chamber pots beneath the beds in the ten bedchambers. In Alexandra's opinion the coins jingling in their pockets when they departed for home had been well earned.

She had kept the two most promising girls as day maids, and engaged a cook as well—a jolly, apple-cheeked woman who knew how to bargain with every farmer and shopkeeper in the district.

At last Alexandra was free to begin her painting of The Aerie, and she refused to let her mind dwell on anything else. She talked Jamie into helping her determine the best angle from which to paint the old castle. They walked the full circle around the mammoth stone edifice and finally decided she should set up her easel on the small rise where they had first viewed The Aerie. From that vantage she had a sweeping view of the castle clinging to the edge of the cliff, the rocky beach below, and the Bristol Channel beyond that.

She made a preliminary charcoal sketch while still on the rise. By teatime she had added the finishing touches to the drawing that would be her guide when she took up her watercolor brush to produce the painting she had in mind.

Laying her pencil down, she studied the sketch, imagining Liam's face when he saw the final painting. Maybe she would hide it away and have it framed as a Christmas present—or a birthday present. She shook her head, aware she had no idea on which day of the year her husband had been born.

"I love this place," Jamie declared, standing at the window of the library, where they had shared a pot of tea and one of the cook's poppy seed cakes. "I wish we could stay here forever."

Alexandra smiled. "I doubt you would find a medieval castle all that comfortable in the winter. Can you imagine trying to heat the great hall in cold weather, even with that gigantic fireplace?"

"I suppose you're right. Besides, the castle is exciting, but it wouldn't be any fun without you and Liam. I don't even want to explore the rest of it until he can be with us." Jamie chuckled. "I want to see his face when we find the dungeon and the skeletons of his ancestors' enemies."

He tapped a restless tattoo against the windowpane with his fingertips. "I miss him. I'll be glad when he finishes his business and comes home."

"So will I, Jamie."

As suddenly as it had begun, the tattoo stopped, and Alexandra looked up to find her brother's nose pressed against the glass. "It's Liam. He's coming home," he cried. "He just rode over the rise."

She leapt to her feet. "Are you certain? I didn't expect him so soon."

"He's too far away to see his face, but there is no mistaking his flame-colored hair." Jamie rushed from the room, and she heard his shoes clatter across the stone floor of the great hall. "Liam is home, Henry," he yelled. The massive door creaked open, and a moment later, she heard the old man's shuffling steps as he, too, crossed the great hall to follow Jamie into the courtyard.

Alexandra sat back down, picked up her charcoal and added

a line or two to her sketch. She would not rush headlong into Liam's arms, as if she had been waiting breathlessly for his return. She had questions she needed to ask him, and she would wait for him to come to her.

After an anxious few minutes, she heard footsteps cross the hall and looked up, expecting to find her husband. She found instead a disgruntled-looking Jamie. "It wasn't Liam," he said sourly, "but a great, ugly, red-haired brute named Stegin Hobart, who claims to be his half brother."

"I didn't know he had one."

"He has a good many of them, according to Hobart. If they are all as unpleasant as he is, I can understand why Liam has never mentioned them. As far as I can see, the only thing this half brother has in common with him is the color of his hair."

Alexandra frowned. "Where is he now and what does he want at The Aerie?"

"He's in the courtyard talking to Henry, who doesn't seem all that happy to see him. But he came looking for Liam. Claims he heard a rumor on the Ilfracombe docks that a crew was being recruited for *The Wayward Lady* and he wants to sign on." Jamie turned an accusing eye on Alexandra. "Did you know Liam was planning to put out to sea?"

She hesitated, uncertain what she should tell her young brother.

"You did! I can see it in your face. And you didn't tell me? Why would he go to sea without me when he has to know I would like above all things to sail with him?"

"It is not a pleasure voyage, Jamie, but one of a serious and very possibly dangerous nature. You would only be in the way."

"Listen to yer sister, laddie." The booming voice filled the small salon, even as the great hulk of a man filled the doorway in which he stood. "A puny scrap like ye would do nothing but heave up your guts on a run across the English Channel, and I'll wager me best pair of boots that be where *The Wayward Lady* be bound."

Alexandra's first impression of Stegin Hobart was that he was a grotesque caricature of Liam. She saw a vague familial resemblance, but it was as if Liam's finely chiseled features had been pummeled and flattened into something unspeakably coarse and ugly. Furthermore, where Liam's eyes were a golden amber, Hobart's were a muddy yellow; where Liam's hair was a gleaming mantle of red-gold silk, Hobart's stood out from his head like a flaming bush.

In a word, this particular bastard of the Earl of Stratham fit to a tee the description she'd heard of the old earl himself. A shiver crawled her spine, and she acknowledged she had judged her mother unfairly; any woman would have good reason to fear such a man. Henry Pippin seemed to shrink to half his size just standing beside him.

Alexandra rose to her feet. "I am Lady Alexandra Campbell, the Countess of Stratham," she said in a tone of voice reminiscent of her mother addressing the boy who scrubbed pots in the Henning town house kitchen.

"I knows who ye be, missus, and I knows why Liam Campbell married ye, so don't be putting on yer airs fer me."

"Hush yer jawing, ye great bumbling ox, afore ye ruins everything," Henry muttered.

"Oho! So that be the way of it." Stegin Hobart's eyes gleamed with an unholy light. "Didn't ye know then, missus, that Liam Campbell had to marry ye or forfeit his ill-got fortune?"

Alexandra stiffened and clutched the back of a nearby chair for support, her heart a great, heavy rock in her chest.

Hobart's laugh had a cruel ring to it. "I can see from the look on yer face I surprised ye. Why else did ye think the clever rogue would give up a lusty wench like Moll Blodgett fer a scrawny piece of London baggage?"

Henry clutched Hobart's arm. "Belay, Stegin. Liam will kill ye if he hears of this."

Hobart pushed him aside. "Let him try it, and we'll see who ends up dead and buried. Scammed me out of me due, he did. If me pretty-faced half brother hadn't showed up at The Aerie when he did, I knows the title and fortune would be mine, signed and legal, and ye with it, missus—for all ye looks to be half the woman yer mam were."

"You lie. Liam was the Earl of Stratham's chosen heir," Jamie cried. "And how could someone like you know our mother, the Viscountess Hardin?"

"Didn't say I did. But I seen her picture plain enough hanging in the old man's sleeping room—and I heard him plot to get even fer what she done to him. His very words was, 'Nothing could shame the bitch more than to see her daughter married to one of me bastards.' "

"Don't listen to him, Alex," Jamie pleaded. "Liam would never be part of such a horrid scheme."

"The lad be right, missus. Stegin Hobart be a small, mean man for all his great height." Henry Pippin's mouth was a thin line in his ashen face, but Alexandra noted he didn't refute Hobart's claim. Not that it would have mattered if he had. From Henry's earlier slip of tongue and Liam's odd notation—to the missing picture in the earl's bedchamber, the evidence was too overwhelming that the dreadful fellow's story was true.

The shock of that truth left her strangely numb and incapable, for the moment, of grasping the full reality of Liam's deception. Only one thing was clear—at long last she knew the dark secret that haunted him. She heard herself order Henry to show Stegin Hobart the door. She heard Jamie's heartbroken whimper, but she was no more capable of comforting him than of comforting herself.

With careful deliberation she walked up the staircase to the chamber that had been the scene of Liam's greatest betrayal— because, quite simply, she could think of no place else to go.

Only then, when she fell facedown on the bed in which she'd lain naked in his arms, did the pain inside her burst forth in terrible, wrenching sobs of shame and disillusionment.

The Wayward Lady was as seaworthy as Liam could make her, and one seasoned sailor, known as Abel, was already aboard. Only Tommy Yarrow, his old shipmate, was missing, and he should be along any minute. All that was needed was a change of tide and he could put out to sea.

But for once, the siren call of the sea was lost on him. He felt no exhilaration at the thought of a rolling deck beneath his feet and a sail unfurled above him. Nor did he feel the usual rush of heat in his blood at the thought of the danger ahead. He would sail to France in search of Yves Durand as he'd promised, but his heart would remain at The Aerie with his wife.

His wife. The words had taken on a new meaning since the night Alexandra and he had spent together. Now she was as much a part of him as the blood that flowed in his veins and the breath that filled his lungs.

He had read once that love made fools of all men. If so, then

he must be the greatest fool of all, for love had taken him un-
awares. It had crept upon him in disguise and captured his heart
before he could think to raise his defenses. He smiled to himself, thinking how eagerly he embraced his captivity. For his
was a beautiful and passionate captor who had freely admitted
she loved him, even as he loved her.

Anxiously, he watched the activity on the busy dock—wondering what was keeping Yarrow. Tommy had always been reli-
able in the past. All at once he spied a familiar head of flaming
hair towering above the rest. He cursed under his breath. He
could think of no one he less wanted to see at that moment than
Stegin Hobart. The man was a blight on humanity. Wherever he
walked, trouble soon followed.

"Ho, *The Wayward Lady*, permission to come aboard," Hobart called out, a foot already on the gangway.

"We sail on the tide," Liam answered, hoping to discourage
the bothersome fellow.

"Ye sail short a man then, for I bring word of Tommy
Yarrow. The poor fellow got himself a broken head in the alley-
way back of the Bell and Anchor."

"The devil you say!"

"I've come to offer me services. 'Tis the least I can do for
me own blood."

Liam wondered if Stegin had somehow arranged Yarrow's
accident; the devious fellow was not above employing such a
tactic to get something he wanted, and jobs were scarce for the
men who plied the smugglers' trade these days. But he had neither the time nor the means to prove his suspicion.

He considered his alternatives—sail short a man or sail with
one he neither liked nor trusted. He chose the latter. A short
crew could spell disaster if they ran into trouble in French waters, and for all his faults, Stegin was an excellent seaman.

"Come aboard and welcome," he said finally.

Stegin stepped onto the deck, his hand outstretched. " 'Tis
glad I be to see ye, brother. Ye be a hard man to track down."

Liam flinched at the word "brother." He could not bring
himself to think of any of the old earl's bastards as his brothers,
least of all this one. "Adam told me you came to the farm looking for me."

"Aye, that I did. And I just now left The Aerie. Met yer
pretty little wife, I did." A lascivious grin spread across Ho-

bart's heavy features. "I be thinking 'twere not so bitter a pill ye had to swallow to get yer hands on a fortune."

Stegin's sly yellow eyes lingered on Liam's face. "If ye be wondering how I knows about your arrangement with the old earl, I listened to him hatching it. It might have been me was his bloomin' heir if ye hadn't showed up when ye did. I be thinkin' ye owes me since ye wouldn't have knowed about the offer of fifty quid to all his bastards if I hadn't tipped ye to it."

Liam felt his skin crawl at the thought that if he had refused the Earl of Stratham's offer, Alexandra might have been forced to wed the miserable fellow. Still, he had to admit Stegin had a point. "I suppose I do owe you something, if you put it that way," he admitted. "We will discuss it when this trip is over. But whatever I agree to, I will pay it but once."

"That be all I could rightly expect, brother." Stegin's shaggy ginger brows drew together in a frown. "I be thinking, since ye're such a kind and generous fellow, I owes it to ye to be honest, no matter how it shames me to do so."

The vague uneasiness Liam had felt since first spotting Hobart on the dock instantly magnified tenfold. "By all means, let us have honesty between us," he said dryly, though he doubted Stegin knew the meaning of the word.

"Aye, well here it be then. 'Tis possible, through no fault of me own, I could have caused ye a mite of trouble."

"What sort of trouble?"

"Well, there I were, blabbering away friendly-like to yer missus about how lucky it were she be such a fine-looking woman—seeing as how ye had to marry her to get yer hands on the old earl's fortune—"

"You slimy devil!" Liam planted Hobart a facer before the bastard could finish his damning confession.

"Now what'd ye do that for?" Hobart asked from where he lay sprawled on the deck. "How was I to know ye was flim-flamming the chit? That old fool, Henry Pippin, should've warned me." Hobart rubbed his chin where Liam's fist had struck it. "It weren't till she turned all stiff and white that I knowed she were upset. 'Show Mr. Hobart the door, Henry,' she says, like she were the Queen of England."

Liam was too conscience-stricken to find fault with Hobart's reasoning. For in truth, he had been flimflamming Alexandra from the very first; Hobart's gaffe had merely exposed him for what he was. Nor could he afford to toss the whoreson off the ship, as he would like to. There was no way he could locate another competent seaman in time to sail as planned.

But he might be able to salvage his marriage. He did a quick bit of calculating. His mare was stabled behind the local blacksmith's shop a short distance down the dock. If he rode hell-bent-for-leather to The Aerie, he could devote a few minutes to begging his wife's forgiveness for his sins before he had to ride back to ready the ship to leave on the tide.

It was not enough time, considering the enormity of his offense, and God only knew what he could say. But unless he made the effort, he stood to lose the only woman he had ever loved.

The last thing he heard as he galloped away from the dock was Stegin Hobart's annoying voice. "Luck be with ye, brother."

Less than a quarter of an hour later Liam clattered into the courtyard of The Aerie, tossed his reins to one of the duke's grooms, and strode through the open door of the castle into the great hall. Once his eyes adjusted to the gloom, he realized Henry Pippin was sitting on the bottom step of the stairwell, his head in his hands and Dawg at his feet. They both looked up as he approached. It was hard to tell which of them looked the saddest.

Henry wiped his eyes on his sleeve. "Stegin Hobart were here."

"So I heard."

"I failed ye, Cap'n. Me wits is a mite slower than they onct was—and he talked so fast. Before I could stop him, he'd told Mistress all about the bargain ye struck with the old earl."

"I know. He searched me out and confessed. Though I've a feeling it was more to torture me than to give me a chance to make things right with my wife. Where is she, by the way?"

Henry dropped his head into his hands again. "In her chamber, crying her heart out last time I listened at the door."

Liam took the stairs two at a time, tried the knob and found the door unlocked. Squaring his shoulders, he strode into the room to find Alexandra curled in a tight little ball in the middle of the bed. From her mottled face and swollen eyelids, it was obvious she had cried herself to sleep.

He sat down on the edge of the bed and gently touched her arm. "Wake up, sweetheart. We need to talk, and I can only stay a few minutes."

She opened her eyes, took one look at him, and scooted to the head of the bed. "Don't touch me. Never touch me again."

"I know you are angry at me, my love. You have every right to be. I admit my reason for pursuing you in the beginning was less than honorable. But that has nothing to do with how I feel about you now."

"Money—that is all I have ever meant to anyone. Sir Randolph saw me as a generous allowance; to Papa I was the money that would keep him out of debtors' prison. Mama was willing to sell me to the bastard son of the man she hated to save her own social career. All this I knew and accepted. But fool that I was, I thought you were the one person who wanted me for myself—even if the wanting took the form of lust."

Liam felt as if she had stabbed him in the heart and, with each word she said, gave the knife another twist. "It is true I first wanted you to secure the old earl's fortune. I doubt you could understand how miserable it is to be poor," he said gravely. "And God knows I lusted for you; I still do.

"I married you for all the wrong reasons, my darling. But I want to stay married to you for the right one. I love you, Alexandra. I have never said those words to any other woman."

"Not even Moll Blodgett?"

"Least of all Moll Blodgett." *Damn Stegin Hobart's eyes. How had that subject come into the conversation he'd had with Alexandra?* Liam vowed that one way or another he would make the black-hearted devil pay for every hurtful word he had uttered.

Surreptitiously, he moved a few inches closer to where she was curled against the carved headboard.

"Don't touch me." She raised a hand as if to ward off a blow. "I could not bear to have you touch me."

"You bore it very well two nights ago, Madam Wife. As I recall, you also told me you loved me."

"That was before I knew you for what you were."

Liam's heart sank. His time was almost up and he had made no progress whatsoever toward convincing Alexandra he was a changed man. "I want the chance to win back that love," he said desperately. "Promise me you will be here when I return. Give me that chance."

"I will promise you nothing."

"Then I will sit here until you do, instead of readying my ship for departure, as I should be doing this very minute. I shall miss the tide and be trapped in the harbor another twelve hours—which means my friend stands that much more chance of being apprehended by the evil men who search for him. I hope you can live with a good man's death on your conscience, Madam Wife."

"Oh! You are a wicked man, Liam Campbell—a man who will do anything to get his own way."

"I have never denied that, my love. Well, what is it to be? The choice is up to you."

"Go, for heaven's sake. Rescue your Frenchman. I promise I shall be here when you return. But it will do you no good. I have learned my lesson. Love is not for me—and even if it were, you would be the last man on earth to whom I would trust my heart."

Chapter Fifteen

She had done it! Alexandra had burned her bridges as far as
Liam was concerned and she felt nothing but relief. Or so
she told herself as she stood at the window of her bedchamber
and watched him disappear over the very rise from which she
had planned to begin his painting.

He had begged her to give him another chance. To do what?
Lie to her . . . deceive her . . . pretend to love her, when all he
really loved was the money she represented? She had let him
know in no uncertain terms that his chances with her had run
out.

Too long she had been an unwitting pawn in this game of
greed and revenge the old earl had instigated. She wished the
spiteful devil to Hades, and his handsome bastard with him.
She would feel no compunction whatsoever about demanding
the London town house and generous allowance Liam had
promised her. She had earned it with her naive heart and her
willing body, and by all that was holy she would have her due.

Then she would surround herself with artists, writers, com-
posers—men and women of intelligence and integrity—as she
had always hoped to do before Liam Campbell disrupted her
plans. It would be a pleasant lifestyle, and a safe one, for she
would never again be so foolish as to love any man.

A violent pounding on her chamber door interrupted her ruminations, but even as she moved toward it, the door burst open
and Emmy catapulted into her. The girl's eyes brimmed with
tears, her breast heaved and she flailed the air in wild gestures
Alexandra could not begin to comprehend.

Frantically, Alexandra looked about her for a piece of paper
and a pencil, but remembered she had left her sketch pad and
pencils behind her when she fled the salon. "What is wrong,
Emmy?" she demanded. "What are you trying to say?"

Emmy's lips worked in a desperate effort to speak, and finally a sound between a word and a wail spewed forth. "Jaaaammmeeee," the girl cried, her fingers biting into Alexandra's arm.

"Jamie? Is that what you're saying?" Alexandra felt as if her heart had stopped. Something terrible must have happened to shock Emmy into breaking her long silence. "Where is he?" she demanded. "What has happened to him?"

"Gonnnnnn," Emmy managed, then tented her hands. Alexandra racked her brain. "Is that a sail you're portraying?"

Emmy nodded vigorously and waved her arm in an undulating motion graphically depicting the waves of the sea.

"Good heavens, never say Jamie is planning to stow away on Liam's ship!"

Again Emmy nodded her head and clasped her hands beneath her chin in an attitude of prayer.

"Of course I'll go after him. But what in the world is he thinking? Jamie never does such outlandish things."

With Emmy at her heels, Alexandra ran down the stairs. "Where is Liam's ship moored?" she demanded as she passed Henry, sitting on the bottom stair.

"In Lynmouth Harbor, mistress, but he'll not take kindly to your going there. Women and ships don't mix."

Without comment on that ridiculous statement, Alexandra flew out the open door and across the courtyard. "Has Master Jamie requested a horse this afternoon?" she asked one of the duke's grooms lounging in the doorway of the ancient stable.

"Aye, milady. Not half an hour ago he had me saddle the bay I rode from Kent. I told him it was too big for a lad his size to ride comfortable, but there was no stopping him."

"Then ready my mare faster than you have ever done before."

The young groom took her at her word, and but a few moments later, she urged the piebald over the Lynton Road toward the spot where it intersected the road to Lynmouth Bay.

The first thing that caught her eye as she rode into town was the blacksmith's forge with a stable directly behind it. A young boy was walking Liam's lathered chestnut, and a glance at the stable revealed the bay in one of the stalls. Jamie was here then, as Emmy had reported. She wondered if Liam knew this.

"Could you tell me where *The Wayward Lady* is moored?" she asked the blacksmith.

The smithy lowered his sledge long enough to point to a ship docked at the first pier on his right. "That's the *Lady*, ma'am, but if you're wanting to see her off, you'd best hurry. She's due to leave on the tide. S'truth, I'm surprised she's not already drifting out of the bay with the lads hoisting her sails as she passes the bar."

Without another word, Alexandra dismounted, tossed the reins to the smithy and took off on a run. As she neared the ship, she could see a small knot of men at the bow, Liam among them. She hurried toward the gangway, praying no one would notice her. Then, lifting her skirt, she started up it, only to be halted midway by a familiar voice.

"Stop, milady! You cannot come aboard. We're about to set sail."

Alexandra looked up to find Colin O'Riley on the deck above her. "I have to find Jamie. Emmy told me he was planning to stow away."

"The divil you say! 'Tis the hold where he'd be then, the young rapscallion." O'Riley cast a furtive glance toward the bow. "I'll take a look, but 'twill have to be a quick one. His lordship just ordered me to haul up the gangway."

"I'll come with you. Two sets of eyes are better than one."

O'Riley looked dubious, but he didn't argue, merely lifted the hatch cover and backed down the ladder into the hold. Alexandra followed his example and found herself in a vast, dark chamber with no light but that from the open hatchway.

Except for two large open tanks and a coil of thick rope, the area appeared empty. Jamie would have no place to hide unless he were crouched in some deeply shadowed corner, which she doubted considering his aversion to the dark. Just in case, she called out his name in a hoarse whisper, but got no answer.

"That's that then," O'Riley said. "The lad's not here. There's but one other place he could hide and that's the captain's cabin. Surely he'd not be so foolish as to try that."

"Still, I must check." Alexandra moved to the foot of the ladder just as a shadow loomed over the hatchway opening.

"Is that you in the hold, O'Riley?" Liam's voice was an impatient growl.

"Aye, milord." O'Riley scurried up the ladder and onto the deck. Alexandra froze in place, uncertain what she should do. She prayed O'Riley would have the sense to draw Liam off so she could take a quick peek into the captain's cabin before she left the ship.

"What the devil were you doing down there? I told you to haul in the gangway." Liam no longer sounded impatient; he sounded coldly furious. Alexandra shuddered. Poor O'Riley must be shaking in his boots, and it was all her fault.

"Now get to it," Liam continued. "Close the damn hatch and haul in the gangway. The dockmaster's men are waiting to cast off the lines. If we tarry any longer we'll miss the tide."

"But, milord—"

"Move, O'Riley. I'll tolerate your impudence on land, but not on my ship. Here my word is law."

"Aye, milord, but—"

"One more word out of you, Irishman, and I swear I'll toss you into the bay. Do I make myself clear?"

To Alexandra's horror Liam didn't wait for O'Riley to close the hatch. He slammed the heavy cover into place himself, leaving her in total, unrelieved blackness. Terrified, she crawled up the ladder and beat her fists against the thick slab of wood. "Help," she cried. "Let me out of here."

But all her pounding and yelling were to no avail. From the sound of shouting men and running feet on the deck above her, everyone was too involved with getting the ship under way to hear her puny efforts.

But where was O'Riley? Surely he wouldn't let Liam put out to sea while she was still locked in the hold—and Jamie possibly in the cabin. Moments later, the rocking motion of the ship told her he had done just that. She could scarcely blame the poor fellow; Liam had made it impossible for him to do otherwise.

She clung to the top rung of the ladder, wondering how long it would be before someone discovered her—and how she could explain her presence when they did. Her nails bit into her palms as she fought the panic that threatened to engulf her. The darkness was terrifying enough, but she distinctly remembered reading that all ships were infested with rats. What she could not remember was whether or not rodents were capable of climbing ladders.

Once the ship had cleared the harbor and was under full sail, Liam turned over the helm to Stegin with orders to hug the coast until Land's End was in sight. He then retired to his cabin to chart a course to a spot on the French coast he only vaguely remembered.

But his mind was not on his task. He was haunted instead by the sight of his wife recoiling from his touch—and by his last glimpse of the Lynmouth dock and the sad-looking lad who had watched the ship depart. Like his sister, Jamie had evidently been privy to Stegin Hobart's shocking revelation and shared her bitter disillusionment.

Sick at heart, Liam contemplated the disastrous turn of events. In a way, it seemed oddly appropriate that the greed and betrayal for which he was so deeply ashamed should have been brought to light by Stegin Hobart. He had always had an eerie feeling that his despicable half brother somehow embodied the dark side of his own nature.

Born but a month apart, they had been at swords' points since, as small boys, they had first recognized the ties of blood that bound them. Now, it appeared that without knowing it, he may have robbed Stegin of his chance of gaining the great fortune he coveted. He wondered if the ugly devil could possibly guess how effectively he had revenged that loss with his careless words. For it occurred to Liam that his fortune would mean nothing to him without Alexandra—and Jamie—to share it.

A knock at the door of the cabin interrupted his bitter ruminations. He ignored it, certain it must be O'Riley. Stegin was at the helm and Abel would never think of presenting himself at the captain's door. But the knocking persisted and he finally growled, "Enter."

"Beg pardon, milord, but there's a bit of a problem I think you should know about." O'Riley's ruddy complexion had faded to a sickly gray, and they were scarcely out of the harbor. Liam groaned. He should never have listened when the fool begged to go to sea with him.

"If your stomach is your problem, I cannot help you," Liam said impatiently. "I cannot put back into Lynmouth and set you ashore."

"'Tis not me stomach, milord, although the poor thing is roiling something wicked. 'Tis about the mistress."

"Alexandra? What about her?"

"She came looking for Master Jamie. It seems he told Emmy a bit of blarney about stowing away. But, as you could see, the young scalawag changed his mind."

"My wife came to the ship? Why didn't you tell me?"

O'Riley looked highly indignant. "Faith and wasn't I trying to when you threatened to throw me overboard if I said one more word. I had no choice but to shut me mouth for I cannot swim a stroke. So how could I be telling you the mistress was in the hold, looking for a lad who was still on the dock?"

"But she was gone from there when I closed the hatch cover."

"And why would you be thinking that, milord?"

"She had to be. We set sail immediately after . . ." Liam leapt to his feet. "Good God, are you saying Alexandra is still in the hold?"

"I fear so, milord. With those two spalpeens you've hired as a crew, I feared for her safety should she show herself on deck without your protection."

"Neither of them would dare touch my wife. But you were right to keep her presence a secret. But devil take it, Alexandra must be terrified; she told me herself she hates the dark."

Liam thought for a moment. "Luckily the hatch is but a few feet from the door to my cabin. If you can create a diversion, I'll sneak her in here, where no one will see her."

"Consider it done, milord."

Liam waited until he heard O'Riley begin spinning a tale about spotting a Selkie off the bow before he lifted the hatch cover. He found Alexandra on the ladder beneath it, white as the sails overhead and trembling from head to toe. It was a measure of her terror that she welcomed him with a joyful cry and allowed him to lift her in his arms. "I heard them," she cried as he laid her on his berth, slipped off her shoes and covered her with a blanket.

"Heard who, love?"

"The rats," she said and burst into tears.

Liam's heart ached for her. The poor darling had suffered such a fright, her brain had become addled. Without further ado, he lay down beside her and took her in his arms. Willing his warmth to still her shivering, he held her while she wept and confessed her terror, then wept again when he assured her that Jamie was safe on land—probably riding toward The Aerie as he spoke.

Darkness crept into the cabin, and Alexandra slipped into a restless sleep. Still he held her, every fiber of his being aching to make slow, sweet love to her until the passion they shared supplanted every memory of her ordeal. But in his heart he knew if he took advantage of her vulnerability now, he might well lose her forever.

He heard Stegin Hobart shout to Abel to light the candles in the lanterns that served as their running lights, and he was glad he hadn't given into the urge to throw the scoundrel off the ship. Hobart might be a born troublemaker, but his seamanship couldn't be faulted.

Furthermore, this particular trouble the blackguard had caused might be a blessing in disguise. If Alexandra and he could survive this threat to their marriage, they could build a relationship based on love and trust, with no dark secrets left to haunt them. Could it be that in this most unexpected of ways a benevolent God was giving him the chance he needed to win back his lady's love?

But now he, too, needed his sleep. As always, he would take his turn at the helm, and his was the midnight-to-dawn watch. For as long as he'd been before the mast, he had never tired of watching a sunrise at sea.

He drew his wife closer and buried his nose in her sweet-smelling hair—the scent of moorland wildflowers on the high seas. He smiled. What more could a man ask of life than that?

Alexandra slowly opened her eyes and found herself in a strange room and a bed that was stranger yet. An odd contraption, it stood flush against the wall on one side and was framed by two stout posts on the other. Like a flash of lightning, it all came back to her. *The ship. That dreadful, dark hold. Her terror. Good heavens,* she must be somewhere at sea if the rocking motion of the ship was any indication.

She had a vague memory of falling asleep in Liam's arms once he'd assured her Jamie was safe. She suspected she might even, at one time during the night, have nestled her head on his shoulder while he ran his fingers through her hair. A fine way to begin the life of fierce independence she had chosen for herself!

Well, there was nothing to be done about that now, except make certain it never happened again. Slipping from beneath the blanket that covered her, she stood up and took a moment to gain her sea legs. Then she located her half boots, made use of the chamber pot and smoothed the worst of the wrinkles from her gown. But since the tiny cabin contained no mirror, she could do nothing with her flyaway hair except pull it back from her face and tuck it behind her ears. Once that was done, she decided she was as ready as she would ever be to face Liam and his crew of ex-smugglers.

She was just about to go on deck when she spied Liam's note lying on top of what looked to be some sort of map.

Alexandra—I am at the helm. Do not under any circumstances leave the cabin—Liam

So now she was restricted to the cabin like a naughty little girl sent to her bedchamber. She marched to the door, tempted to fling it wide and dare him to stop her from taking the morning air. But at the last minute, she changed her mind and cracked the door just enough to peek out.

Liam was standing, legs wide, braced against the wind, with his hands on the wheel of the ship and his hair streaming behind him like a flaming banner. Even more than the moors, it was obvious the sea was his natural element. She felt as if she were truly seeing him for the first time, and the thought of eliminating this vital man from her life was like cutting her heart from her breast.

Yet, how could she do otherwise? Every word he had uttered, every touch of his lips on hers—the very act of joining their bodies in the ultimate intimacy—had been part of a monstrous lie he had perpetrated to gain . . . money.

She might have learned to live with a marriage arranged solely to secure a fortune; such marriages were common in the *ton*. But Liam had made her believe his lies. For that she could never forgive him.

As she watched, a crewman came to spell him at the wheel. A seaman's cap covered the fellow's hair, and not until he took his place at the wheel did she recognize him—Stegin Hobart. There was no mistaking his ugly face. She shuddered, remembering the vicious pleasure with which he'd torn her foolish dreams asunder. She wondered how he had talked Liam into hiring him; she wondered if Liam had any idea how much the man hated him.

Not a moment too soon, she closed the door and seated herself on the edge of the narrow bed. Liam strode into the cabin, bringing the salty scent of the sea with him.

"Ah, you are awake, Madam wife," he said, his amber eyes raking her with a provocative look that would have melted her bones twenty-four hours earlier. Now it only served to remind her of his perfidy. "I'll bring you some bread and cheese and a tankard of ale to break your fast. It is the best I can offer since *The Wayward Lady* has no galley."

"Do not put yourself out, my lord. Surely O'Riley or one of your seamen can see to my needs."

"O'Riley is suffering from an acute case of seasickness. I should never have let that Irish landlubber talk me into bringing him on this voyage. He is worse than useless. As for the other two members of the crew, they are not aware of your presence, and I hope to keep it that way until we reach France. They are both ex-smugglers, and smugglers are notoriously superstitious about a woman on board a ship. The last thing I need is trouble with the crew."

Alexandra stared at him, utterly dismayed. "You expect me to journey to France with you? I had hoped you could put me ashore at Plymouth."

"I would like to and O'Riley with you to see you safely to The Aerie. But I cannot do so. Here. let me show you why on this chart." He moved to the cabin's only table and reluctantly Alexandra followed him.

"My destination is a hidden cove on the tip of the Cap de la Hague, where I have reason to believe Yves Durand may be hiding." He pointed to a spot on the French coast. "Ordinarily I would hug the coast of England as far as Bournemouth before I crossed the Channel. But I cannot take such a leisurely route on this trip, as time is my enemy.

"We should round Land's End shortly after nightfall, and I intend to strike out across the open Channel from here." He tapped a jut of land designated as Lizard Point. "This way, I cut the distance in half. Furthermore, there should be no French patrol boats this far west in the Channel."

"And during all this, I am supposed to stay hidden in this cabin?"

"I'm afraid so, my love. But I shall do my best to keep you entertained."

Alexandra bristled. "I am not your love, and if you so much

as touch me, I will scream loud enough to alert your superstitious smugglers that you have a woman on board."

"Ah, love, are we back to that again? I had hoped you would be more understanding about my one attack of unrestrained avarice. How long must I pay for succumbing to the temptation an evil old man offered?"

He gave her one of his devastating smiles. "Think of it, sweetheart. Fate has decreed that we shall be confined together on this ship for a good many hours—a perfect opportunity for another delayed honeymoon."

"Go to the devil, Liam Campbell."

His eyes twinkled. "That, I fear, is a foregone conclusion. But I had hoped to enjoy myself prodigiously before I sailed the fiery sea." He shrugged. "Ah well, if I cannot interest you in . . . whatever, perhaps I should provide you with pen and paper so you can practice your drawing. A poor substitute, in my estimation, but at least your time will not be a total loss."

So saying, he unlocked a drawer in the cabinet attached to one wall of the cabin and produced a sheet of paper, a bottle of ink and a half dozen nicely sharpened quill pens. These he laid out on the chart table before he pulled her to him, kissed her thoroughly and departed the cabin.

Alexandra's knees buckled and she sat down abruptly on the edge of the bed. But even as her senses reeled from his kiss, she remembered how the pistol tucked in his belt had pressed into her flesh. She shuddered, more aware than ever of the dangerous nature of this mission and the dangerous man determined to carry it out.

Her hours of confinement passed faster than Alexandra had expected, thanks to the drawing materials Liam had provided her. She spent the entire day working on a reproduction, from memory, of her sketch of The Aerie, complete with the jagged cliff, rock-strewn beach and a lone seagull circling overhead. She was still feathering in the details when the light began to fail and Liam came to report they would round Land's End within the hour.

His eyes lit up when he saw the drawing. "You have an extraordinary gift, Madam Wife," he said softly. "With your permission, I shall have this framed."

Alexandra shook her head. "It is only a sketch. I'll take it with me to London and use it to render a watercolor painting suitable for framing. I shall send that to you if you wish."

Liam's expression darkened at her implication that she planned to leave him, but his voice held no hint of what he was thinking. "The winds will be ferocious as we tack from sou'west to sou'east when we round Land's End. Luckily you appear to have a seaman's stomach, as the ship will pitch and toss like a bucking stallion. I pray O'Riley survives it. I've never seen a man as ill-suited to the sea as my Irish valet."

Without further ado, he withdrew a length of rope from the bottom drawer of the cabinet. "Now, Madam Wife, please sit down on the bed. I need to tie you to one of the bedposts so you won't be flung about like a rag doll."

Too startled to protest, Alexandra submitted meekly, then watched him roll up her drawing and lock it, together with the pens and ink, in the cabinet drawer from which they had come.

That done, he bent down and cupped her face in his strong fingers. "Do not be frightened if the ship sounds as if it is falling apart; I promise you it will not. Think of this instead." His lips captured hers in a kiss so exquisitely tender that in spite of her resentment toward him, she felt her eyes fill with foolish, sentimental tears.

Then he was gone. But once again, he had worked his magic. For when the floor of the cabin heaved beneath her and the wind howled through the rigging above her—when the ship itself screeched and moaned like a mortally wounded animal, she felt no fear. Her mind was still too occupied with the seductive taste of Liam's wind-chilled lips and the fresh, salty scent of his sun-bronzed skin.

Chapter Sixteen

To Liam's relief, Alexandra suffered no ill effects from the violent turbulence they encountered rounding Land's End. His dainty little wife was a lot tougher than she looked.

O'Riley survived, but that was all that could be said for him. In truth, the Irishman's usually ruddy complexion took on a hue not unlike the color of his beloved shamrocks, and he gave up all pretense of doing anything but curl up in a ball of misery until he once again stood on English soil.

Once the course was set across the Channel, *The Wayward Lady* had clear sailing. But tacking across the more than one hundred miles of open water separating the French and English coasts at the west end of the Channel was a slow, tedious business. The sun had already set when Liam finally sighted his destination—the small cape just west of Cherbourg. From there, it would be an easy matter to find the quiet inlet and Durand's hidden cave.

"What be this place?" Stegin asked. "I've landed many a time up the coast, but I've never taken on brandy here."

"We are not here to pick up brandy. We are in search of a French Royalist who was instrumental in helping Lord Wellington defeat Bonaparte," Liam said, feeling it was at last safe to reveal the true reason for the voyage. "With the Corsican on the rampage again, it is essential we get this brave man out of France immediately."

"I've nothing agin that, Cap'n. For I lost two brothers in the war with Old Boney," Abel said. "But where be the profit in this trip for Stegin and me then? I'll be in for more trouble than we ever give the Frogs if I goes home to me old woman without a farthing in me pocket."

"I fully intend to pay the two of you what would be your fair shares of a normal smuggling operation."

Abel gave Liam a toothless grin. "Then I'll rescue the devil hisself if ye wants me to."

Stegin, on the other hand, had gone strangely silent and white around the mouth at the mention of the French Royalist. Why, Liam couldn't imagine. But he vowed to keep an even closer eye on his troublesome half brother if and when Yves Durand came aboard.

However, Stegin seemed willing enough to take the helm while Liam acted as lookout as they inched their way up the coast, looking for the odd-shaped rock that marked the entrance to the inlet he sought. He recognized the stretch of beach where he had run afoul of the French patrol and, not for the first time, wondered how the Frenchman had managed to carry him all the way to the hidden cave.

Twice he thought he had found the rock he sought; twice he was disappointed. But at last he spotted it—a great, black slab of granite rising from the waves like some ancient sea monster guarding the entrance to the inlet. Situated as it was, it allowed nothing larger than a small cockboat to enter the tiny bay.

The moon had risen by the time they dropped anchor. Liam would have been happier with a darker night. He knew the ship would be clearly visible to anyone hiding within the bay, and prayed that if eyes were watching him, they belonged to Durand.

He found Alexandra perched on his berth, her hands clasped in her lap when he returned to the cabin. She looked unusually pale and her huge, fear-filled eyes seemed to swallow her face. "You have anchored the ship," she said quietly. "You must have found the inlet where your friend might be hiding."

"I have, and I am about to row ashore."

"Alone?"

"Yes. It is a job best done alone." Liam unlocked the weapons' cabinet and lifted out two pistols. He drew back the flintlock mechanism on one and squeezed the trigger to test the flint spark. Satisfied, he poured powder down the muzzle and tamped a patch and lead ball into the bore. Again, he drew back the flintlock, primed the flash pan and laid the pistol on the bed beside her.

"I have no reason to expect you to have any trouble while I am gone. I shall be away from the ship no more than an hour or two, since there is only one place Yves could be, and if he's not there now, he never will be. Furthermore, O'Riley and Abel are both good men, and scoundrel that he is, Stegin has never been known to harm a woman. But on the odd chance that you should need to, I want you to be able to defend yourself."

"Thank you. I appreciate your consideration, but I'm afraid I haven't the slightest idea how to fire the nasty thing."

"It is loaded and the flintlock in place. Just hold it out with both hands at arm's length and pull the trigger," he said as he repeated the procedure with the second pistol, added it to the one already in his waistband and put a bag of powder and shot in his pocket.

Alexandra stared at the bulge beneath his jacket. "I take it you *do* expect to encounter trouble. Else, why do you find it necessary to arm yourself with two pistols?"

"Because, my clever wife, now that I have family responsibilities, I feel the need to be cautious." Liam smiled down at her. "I could also use a kiss for good luck, if it would not be asking too much."

Her answering smile looked a bit tremulous. "I think that could be arranged," she said softly, "as long as you know—"

"That I am the last man on earth to whom you would trust your heart. I am well aware of that, my love." Though in truth, he felt encouraged that she appeared frightened for his safety. However, he made no move to kiss her. For once he would let her take the lead.

She stood up, caught the lapels of his jacket in her slender fingers and drew him to her. Her mouth sought his with the delicacy of a butterfly lighting on a flower—a gentle, ladylike kiss. But the instant their lips joined, passion flared between them—wild and hot and head-spinning. With a throaty cry, she deepened the kiss in the sensuous manner he had taught her during their one night together.

He was the one to finally end it. He had to; another second and he wouldn't be able to leave her. "Keep that thought until I return, Madam Wife," he whispered. "Now bolt the door after I leave and shoot anyone who tries to force his way through it."

In a daze, Alexandra threw the bolt on the door as Liam had directed, then crossed to the chart table and climbed onto the stool. He was gone, and for all his bravado, she sensed he was well aware of the potential danger of rowing alone into an inlet in what was once again enemy territory. "It is a job best done alone," he'd said. What he'd meant was he would risk no life but his own in this chancy endeavor.

She couldn't have stopped him if she'd tried, but neither could she just sit and wait for him to return. She would go mad with worry unless she kept busy. For much as she might deny it, she loved the charming rogue with all her heart—and nothing he had done, including marry her to ensure his inheritance, would ever change how she felt about him.

Resolutely, she took up her pen and began to sketch Liam's face. First she outlined his broad forehead, then the finely chiseled contours of his cheeks and chin and the flowing lines of his shoulder-length hair. Soon his bold eyes stared up at her from the paper, and the corners of his sensuous mouth tilted in a knowing smile.

Deep in thought, she traced the shape of that tempting mouth with the tip of one finger. Liam was not the only one to employ magic to get what he wanted. In re-creating his image, she had consciously willed him to return safely—and with each stroke of the pen, she felt more positive that he would once again walk through the doorway and kiss her witless.

Her concentration was broken by the sound of something heavy hitting the deck outside her door and voices raised in anger. She couldn't make out the words, but one voice was definitely Stegin Hobart's low growl, the other Colin O'Riley's higher pitch. She listened, pen in hand, but the voices stopped as quickly as they had started and all was silent again, until she heard heavy footsteps approaching the cabin door.

Horrified, she heard the door bang against the jamb as if the person on the other side were impatient at its being locked. Her gaze flew to the pistol lying atop the bed, but she froze in place, certain she could never bring herself to discharge it at another human being.

Too late, she realized that she need only threaten the intruder with the weapon. Even as she made a dash for the bed, the door crashed open, ripped off its hinges by the force of Stegin Hobart's massive body. "What the devil?" he thundered, raking her with his cold yellow gaze. "So this be why our pretty cap'n spends so much time in his cabin. Ye must be more of a woman than ye looks to be."

With humiliating ease, he wrested the pistol from her hand and stuck it in the waistband of his stained drill trousers. "Ye're an obliging chit, I'll say that for ye. I come in here to find a gun, and here it be, waitin' for me like ye read me mind."

Frantically, Alexandra struggled to free herself from his bruising grip, but to no avail. Stegin Hobart had the strength of two normal men, and from the sour smell of ale on his breath, he had been drinking heavily. *Why hadn't she listened to Liam and armed herself the minute she heard the ugly beast scratching at her door? If she came to harm at Hobart's hands, it would be her fault and hers alone.*

Grasping her upper arm with one massive hand, Hobart dragged her onto the moonlit deck and shoved her against the ship's railing with such force, she gasped for breath.

"What be ye up to, Stegin? With all the shoutin' and bashin' about, a man can't get a wink o' sleep." The raspy voice came from near the bow of the ship, and a moment later, a short, stocky man with thinning hair and bulbous eyes stepped from the shadows.

He stared at Alexandra, mouth agape. "Who be the wench and where did ye find her?" he asked when he recovered his voice.

"She be Liam's fancy London wife. The muckworm's been tumbling the baggage in his cabin whilst you and me sleeps on deck."

"He be the cap'n," the seaman said. "Cap'ns sleeps in cabins. But he shouldn't of brought his woman aboard." The seaman shook his head. "Bad luck, it be, a woman on a ship."

Alexandra realized this must be the fellow, Abel, whom Liam had called a good man. She rubbed the spot on her arm where Hobart's fingers had dug into her flesh. "It will be bad luck for Stegin Hobart if my husband hears how he has treated me."

"She be right, Stegin. Cap'n will have your head if ye touches his woman."

"Not if he be feeding the fishes, he won't. Tricked me, he did. Made me think he were going smuggling when all the while he were plannin' to pick up some Frog count as spied for Wellington. Nobody japes Stegin Hobart and lives to tell of it."

"Kill the cap'n? Have ye lost your mind? I'll have no part in that piece of dirty work, nor in worryin' his woman neither. And how come ye to know the Frog be a bloomin' count? Cap'n never said such a thing."

Stegin started, as if suddenly awakened from a dream. "Ye knows me, Abel. I were always one to shoot off me mouth with no meaning behind it." His hail-fellow-well-met act was so false it made Alexandra's blood run cold—as did his threat against Liam.

For how had Hobart known that Yves Durand was a French count unless . . . ? Her breath caught in her throat. He could only have learned it from the English traitor who had divulged Yves Durand's true identity to Bonaparte. Stegin Hobart must be the one who had smuggled the traitor into England and blamed Liam for it. Intuition told her he hated Liam enough to do such a thing.

Like a child's picture puzzle, the pieces fell into place one by one. No wonder Liam's unscrupulous half brother panicked when he learned Liam intended to rescue Yves Durand. He must fear the Frenchman could recognize him and send him to the gallows.

She had to find a way to warn Liam before he returned to the ship. For one wild moment, she contemplated jumping overboard and swimming to the inlet, but quickly discarded the idea. She hadn't swum a stroke in ten years—and even then she had barely kept her head above water in a placid lake. She would have no chance of surviving the cold, choppy waters of the Channel.

This simple fellow, Abel, was her only hope. Somehow she must alert him that Stegin Hobart would have to kill everyone on the ship to keep his guilty past a secret. But dear God, how could she do so with Hobart looking on?

As if in answer to her prayer, she heard a faint moan and instantly realized it had to be O'Riley. In all the excitement, she had all but forgotten him. Heart pounding, she stared about her and for the first time saw a pair of feet poking out from behind a large wooden water barrel.

Before Stegin could stop her, she rushed to where the little Irishman lay, trussed up like a Christmas goose ready for the roasting pan, a dirty rag tied across his mouth and a lump the size of a cricket ball on the back of his head. She dropped to her knees beside him and cried out his name, but his eyes remained closed.

"What the devil be going on here?" Abel asked, peering over

her shoulder. "Why have ye coshed the Irishman, ye great bully."

"Because he be an Irishman, that's why," Stegin growled.

Alexandra had a sudden insight into the way Hobart's evil mind worked. "And because, Mr. Abel, he needs someone to blame for the murder of my husband—and the Frenchman who can identify him as the man who smuggled a traitor into England."

"Smart little chit, ain't ye," Hobart sneered. "And who's to say the Irishman didn't do in Liam and his Frog friend? For that be what I'll tell the harbormaster when we puts into Plymouth town. As every Englishman knows, the bog-trotters be naught but a pack of murderin' crazies."

"Have ye forgot the cap'n's woman knows the truth of it?" Abel asked. "I cannot believe ye'd kill a woman."

"Of course he would," Alexandra said, "and he'll kill you, too, once you've helped him sail the ship to Plymouth."

"Shut your whining mouth afore I shuts it for ye." Hobart yanked Alexandra to her feet and sent her careening back against the rail.

He drew his pistol and waved it in Abel's face. "As for ye, me old friend, it's into the hold for ye until I needs ye on deck. And think well on this while ye're down there. Ye've but to give me your promise ye'll go to your grave with nary a word of this to a living soul and I'll gladly send ye back to your woman as hail and hearty as ye left her."

Abel leveled a contemptuous look on the larger man. "I be as likely to believe that as I believes I'll be invited to drink tea with the bloomin' queen in bloody Buckingham Palace."

With sinking heart, Alexandra watched the seaman go into the hold without further protest, no doubt hoping against hope that his captain would somehow manage to turn the tables on Stegin Hobart.

Hobart slammed the hatch cover shut and shot the bolt. Then without so much as a blink of his eyes, calmly announced, "Now, bitch, we waits for me pretty brother to return."

Chapter Seventeen

It took all of Liam's strength to pull the oars of his small boat against the strong Channel current. But once past the sheltering black rock and inside the inlet, the water was as calm as a lake. Shipping one oar, he wheeled around, then sculled toward the beach, bow first, preferring to see what lay ahead of him. He had never before entered the inlet by water; Yves had carried him here from the spot two miles down the beach, where he'd been left for dead by his crew.

Still, with each dip of the oars, he found himself more inclined to think this was the most harebrained thing he had ever done. It had been pure wishful thinking on his part when he'd assumed Yves Durand would recall a promise made half in jest nearly six years earlier. He, himself, had completely forgotten it until Baron Ogilthorpe's remark about "the safest place in all of France" had called it to mind.

At last the keel of the boat scraped rocky shingle. He stepped out into ankle-deep water, pulled the craft onto the beach and surveyed the silent crescent of shoreline. Directly ahead of him stood the cliff that housed the cave where Yves had tended his near-fatal wound. Surely if the Frenchman were anywhere near, he would have shown himself by now.

More convinced than ever he was on a fool's mission, Liam started to shove the boat into the water—then changed his mind and pulled it back onto dry land. Anxious as he was to return to Alexandra, he knew he would never be satisfied he had done all he could to locate Durand unless he explored the Frenchman's former lair.

Luckily, he'd thought to bring a small flint box and candle. Searching out the entrance to the cave, he entered it with lighted taper in hand. He had progressed but a short distance into the dark, tunnel-like cavern when he stopped in his tracks. Was it his imagination, or had he caught a faint whiff of smoke?

Cautiously, he moved forward, and the smell of smoke grew noticeably stronger. Another few feet and he came to the bend in the tunnel that he remembered had immediately preceded the spot where Yves and he had hidden out so long ago. He blew out the candle, pulled one of the pistols from his belt and slowly worked his way around the bend. The first thing he saw was a small fire burning in a circle of rocks; the second, a gun barrel leveled at a spot directly between his eyes.

"*Bon soir*, Englishman. I was beginning to think you would never get here." The gaunt-looking man lounging by the fire lowered his weapon and favored Liam with a strained smile.

"And I had about given up hope of finding you when you were not on the beach to greet me. But incredibly, you did remember my promise!"

"And you remembered to keep it—which is even more incredible, to my way of thinking," Yves Durand remarked in his beautifully accented English. Grimacing, he raised himself to a sitting position and laid the pistol beside him. "You would not by any chance have any food with you? I have had little to eat this past month and nothing at all in the last three days, since I have been unable to hunt or fish."

He grimaced again. "Clumsy fellow that I am, I managed to break my leg while escaping two of Minister Fouché's *gendarmes* who were waiting for me at the top of this cliff."

"The devil you say. Where are they now?"

Yves shrugged. "Let us say they wait no longer—at least not in this world."

Liam pulled a small paper parcel containing a chunk of bread and a small wedge of cheese from one of the many pockets in his nankeen fisherman's jacket and handed it to his friend. "I brought this just in case. As I remember it, you were always hungry."

While Yves made short work of the sparse repast, Liam knelt beside him to cut away his left trouser leg and examine the injured limb. The break was halfway between the knee and ankle and the flesh was puffy and discolored. "It needs setting, but it is too swollen to do so now, even if I could find something with which to splint it. Best we get you home before we try it."

He surveyed his friend closely. Yves had changed a great deal in the past five years. Not only was he thin to the point of emaciation, but the devil-may-care fellow who had once laughed so boldly at life now seemed enveloped in an aura of deep, impenetrable sadness.

"I should have no trouble carrying you to the boat," Liam said quietly. "You are nothing but a bag of bones."

"Which you were not, *mon ami*, when I carried you five years ago. *Mon Dieu*, how I was tempted to leave you face-down in the sand." Yves shrugged. "Now it can be told. I probably would have done so had I not believed you were the smuggler for whom I had been searching many months."

"I was a smuggler, Yves. I made no secret of that."

"But, as I soon deducted, not the one who was providing transport between our two countries for Bonaparte's English spy. Not the one from whom I might learn the identity of that spy."

Anger blazed within Liam like a newly lit torch. He had been accused of that ugly crime by an enemy; he had not expected to hear it from a friend. "Why would you have thought me that?" he asked between clenched teeth.

"Because you fit the description of the black-hearted devil—a description I was given by a dying friend who had been betrayed by the traitorous Englishman. The smuggler I sought was a tall man with a head of flame-colored hair."

With silent efficiency, Liam edged his little boat up against the hull of *The Wayward Lady* and secured it to the bottom rung of the ship's ladder. He had experienced some spine-tingling moments during his days as a smuggler, but he realized now that he had never really known fear—certainly not this cold, paralyzing emotion that gripped him at this moment. For now it was not he who was in jeopardy—but Alexandra.

Thanks to Yves Durand's shocking disclosure, he finally understood to what desperate measures Stegin Hobart could be driven by his insatiable greed. He would never forgive himself for leaving Alexandra within the monster's grasp, with only a seasick Irishman and a slow-witted seaman to defend her.

Heart pounding, Liam worked his way to the bow of the boat, intending to carry Yves up the ladder. But with a wave of his hand, the Frenchman indicated he could haul himself up. With Liam close behind, he did so rung by painful rung until at last the two of them stood together on the deck, Yves leaning on the rail for support.

An eerie silence greeted them. "Something is wrong," Liam whispered. "I feel it in my bones. I can only pray that Alexandra is safe in my cabin."

"Your instincts are, as usual, correct, *mon ami*," Yves whispered back, "and I fear the age of miracles may be a thing of the past." He pointed to what appeared to be a body lying beside one of the ship's water barrels.

Liam took a closer look and found the body was his trusty valet, very much alive, but bound and gagged like a victim of the press gangs that recruited sailors for His Majesty's navy. "O'Riley? My God, man, what has happened here?" he demanded, crouching down to whip the filthy rag from the Irishman's mouth.

O'Riley spat, cleared his throat and spat again. "Faith, 'tis that crazy shirttail relative o' yours, milord. The blighter's run amok. He laid his shillelagh aside me head and locked Abel in the hold. But worst of all, he broke into the cabin and found the mistress."

Liam stood up, O'Riley's bonds forgotten. "Stegin Hobart dared lay his hands on Alexandra?" The tension that had been building since he'd left the cave exploded in a terrible, icy rage. "Then devil take him, the miserable coward has drawn his last breath this side of hell." He pulled both pistols from his belt, and out of the corner of his eye saw Yves draw his weapon as well.

"Brave words, brother." Stegin Hobart stepped from behind the cabin, one beefy hand gripping Alexandra's arm, the other holding a pistol to her temple. "But unless ye wants to see your pretty little wife's brains splattered from here to kingdom come, ye'll slide them pistols across the deck to me, nice and easy, and tell the crippled Frog to do the same."

"Don't do it, Liam. You will just be playing into his hands," Alexandra cried. "He means to kill us all; he has to because he knows Yves Durand can prove him a traitor."

Liam noted Alexandra's deathly pallor and terror-stricken eyes, and knew that if he could get his fingers around her captor's thick neck, he would choke the life out of the evil fellow with no compunction whatsoever. But as long as Stegin had a gun trained on her, he had the upper hand.

Calmly, Liam laid his pistols on the deck. "Noooo!" Alexandra wailed. "Save yourself. He can only kill one of us now. Don't give him the power to kill you and Durand as well."

"I told ye onct to shut your bloomin' mouth," Stegin snarled. "Open it again and ye'll feel the back of me hand."

Liam clenched his teeth, but with outward calm, he collected Yves' gun and placed it beside the other two. "God give you a steady hand, my friend—and tell my wife I loved her," he said in a voice so low only the Frenchman could hear it.

Yves took a firmer grip on the railing with his left hand and balanced himself on his one good leg. The look in his dark eyes said more clearly than words that he knew exactly what Liam planned to do.

Liam placed the toe of his boot behind one gun. "Release my wife and give me your promise that no harm will come to her, and the weapons are yours," he said with a straight face, though he knew Stegin's word was as worthless as a ship without a rudder.

"Don't do it, Liam. Give him nothing," Alexandra pleaded. "Can't you see that promise or not, he will have to kill me. I know enough about him to send him to the gallows."

Liam smiled at his brave wife for what might well be the last time. He longed to kiss her just once more—longed to tell her how proud he was of her. Instead, he said softly, "This is the least foolish thing I have ever done, my love. I would give my life ten times over for the merest chance that you might live."

He moved his toe an inch closer to the pistol, tempting Stegin with a promise of success. The cocky fool took the bait as eagerly as a fish snapping at a worm. "Give me one gun as a show of faith and I'll turn your woman loose," he said, just as Liam had known he would. The devious workings of Hobart's mind were amazingly predictable. With two weapons in hand, he believed he could kill both men who faced him before either could retrieve one of the pistols still lying on the deck. Little did he know that either man was capable of terminating his miserable life in an instant without aid of firearms once Alexandra was out of his grasp.

Liam moved his boot to where the toe rested against the pistol. "Again I say, release my wife and this is yours."

"Agreed. But remember this, I'll have me gun pointed at the chit's head until I have the other one in me hand."

"Fair enough," Liam said and with heartfelt relief watched Stegin give Alexandra a shove that sent her sprawling across a nearby coil of rope. With the blackguard's pistol still trained on her, Liam had no choice but to send the promised pistol sliding across the deck.

Stegin snatched it up as fast as a hawk might snatch a moorland hare. "Ye should have listened to your wife, Liam. She be a smart one for a woman. For 'tis true. I cannot let anyone live who knows me past." With a look of unholy glee in his yellow eyes, he straightened up and pointed the barrel of one gun at Liam, the other at Yves.

"One thing, smuggler—a last request if you will. I would know the name of the English traitor who paid you to carry him across the Channel." Yves rubbed the back of his neck, as if he had a raging headache. But Liam saw his long, slender fingers grip the hilt of the knife he always carried strapped to his back.

Stegin shrugged. "The bloke never give me his name and I never asked it long as he paid me the blunt I asked. It weren't like we was chums, what with him being a high-and-mighty milord."

Durand's question had given Alexandra time to get to her feet and watch Liam send the pistol sliding across the deck. *What was he thinking?* Liam was no fool. He had to know he was giving his half brother the weapon with which to kill him.

She saw a telling look pass between him and the Frenchman, and as if he had shouted his plans to the heavens, she realized the crazy daredevil was planning to launch himself at Stegin Hobart to give Durand time to grab one of the remaining guns and kill the evil fellow.

But the chances of a man in Durand's condition moving fast enough to do his part in the scheme were slim at best—and what would it matter anyway? Liam would already be dead. Tears misted her eyes as the last words he had spoken to her rang through her head. *I would give my life ten times over for the merest chance that you might live.*

Dear God! Didn't he know how bleak and empty a life it would be without him? With that startling realization, the terror that had gripped her for the past two hours instantly metamorphosed into white-hot rage. The very idea that a despicable traitor like Hobart could murder four decent people to keep his ugly past a secret was too obscene to be endured. And endure it she would not.

She watched the ugly devil aim his lethal weapons—one at Liam's heart, the other at Yves Durand's. She saw the look of grim determination on her husband's face and knew the moment of truth was at hand. Gathering every ounce of strength she had, she let forth a bloodcurdling scream and hurled herself at the villain who dared threaten the life of the man she loved.

Even as he lunged toward Stegin Hobart, Liam heard Alexandra's scream and saw the little idiot run headlong at the very man from whom he was trying to protect her.

He heard the twin explosions of Hobart's pistols, but thanks to the impact of Alexandra's body, the blackguard was thrown off balance. One bullet whizzed past Liam's ear, the other embedded itself in the mast. A second later, Hobart staggered backward and toppled over the ship's rail into the sea, the handle of Yves Durand's knife protruding from his throat.

The nightmare was over. With a cry of joy Liam caught Alexandra in his arms and crushed her to him. The two of them clung together, laughing and crying and congratulating each other on being alive, until Liam remembered that his French friend was still propped against the rail and his Irish valet still bound hand and foot.

"We are forgetting our manners, Madam Wife," he said. "May I introduce my friend Yves Durand, a good man to have around when one is in trouble." He offered Durand his hand. "Thank you for saving our lives, my friend."

"We saved each other, Englishman, and if the truth be known, this delicate little wife of yours saved both our skins."

Alexandra's cheeks flamed. "But it was your skill with a knife that finally rid us of the villain," she protested.

A brief flash of fire lit Durand's sad dark eyes. "He was mine to kill, Madame Campbell. The greedy devil was in the pay of the English spy who killed the woman I loved."

Liam felt his friend's pain as if it were his own. He had come so close to losing Alexandra, he understood the depths of the Frenchman's despair. But he knew Durand well enough to refrain from insulting him with the usual platitudes. Alexandra followed his lead, though he could see her eyes were swimming with tears.

Quickly, he untied O'Riley and put him in charge of letting Abel out of the hold and settling Yves as comfortably as possible until they could reach England and find a doctor to set his leg.

Then he swept his courageous wife up in his arms and carried her to his cabin to at long last begin the honeymoon that would last them the rest of their lives.

For as it turned out, Yves Durand had been wrong when he'd judged the age of miracles to be a thing of the past. It was, in truth, only just beginning. . . .

Epilogue

"Must we return to London so soon? I wish we could stay here forever." Even as she asked it, Alexandra knew Liam's answer to her plaintive question. The chilly winds of autumn whistling through the drafty halls of The Aerie heralded an end to their stay in the medieval castle.

Always before she had looked forward to returning to the city and the excitement of the Little Season when her summer holiday was over. Not so this year. She hated to think of leaving Exmoor. Between long, lazy days spent painting the starkly beautiful moors and the wave-washed coastline—and long, blissful nights in her husband's arms—she had found true happiness for the first time in her life.

Liam looked up from the book he was reading. "Spending the winter in a medieval castle is not an experience I relish. But if it is your wish, my love, we shall return to The Aerie next summer. I am certain Jamie will be delighted with that plan. I've never seen the lad so happy as when he's tramping the countryside with Henry and Dawg."

Alexandra smiled, aware that her husband was reminding her how foolish she had been to attach so much importance to her brother's friendship with the Irish abigail. Though Jamie still spent his evenings poring through the dusty books in The Aerie library with Emmy, he seemed equally enthralled with the garrulous old man and his mongrel dog.

"If I have my way, we shall return to Exmoor every summer until we are both too old to make the journey," she said, secure in the knowledge that the love Liam and she shared would endure long after strands of smoky gray had threaded his flame-colored hair. In those terrifying moments aboard *The Wayward Lady*, a bond had been forged between them that was as strong as the stone walls of the ancient castle in which they had first celebrated their love.

With each day that dawned she found new reason to give thanks for that love and for the handsome rogue who had shown her that despite her mother's poisonous teachings, she was a deeply passionate woman who could delight in the intimacies of the marriage bed.

Liam had given her so much—security, freedom, adventure—all of them priceless. But the most priceless gift of all had been the awareness of her own true nature.

And now at last she had a gift for him—something so wondrous the very thought of it left her breathless. She felt a flush of heat suffuse her cheeks when she remembered the enlightening conversation she'd had with Emmy just that morning. Embarrassing it might be, but she had to admit the fifteen-year-old Irish girl was far more knowledgeable about the functions of the human body than she was. As the daughter of a village midwife, Emmy had instantly recognized the significance of missing one's monthly flux for the third time in a row, to say nothing of a mysterious digestive disorder.

She glanced at Liam, wondering how best to tell him her exciting news. As if he sensed her perusal, he laid his book aside. "These months at The Aerie have been happy ones," he said softly.

Alexandra nodded. "The happiest of my life. I've been thinking, we should take a souvenir back to London to remind us of that happiness—and particularly of the love we found here in the wilds of Exmoor."

"An excellent idea, Madam Wife. It will, of course, have to be something rather small."

"Of course," Alexandra said, pressing the palm of her hand against her softly rounded belly.

"And easy to carry."

"That goes without saying."

"Still, it should be precious, I think. Something tawdry would never do as a reminder of the four glorious months we've spent together."

"Something precious it is then, husband. Have you any idea what it should be?"

Liam shook his head. "In truth, I haven't a clue. From what I have seen so far, my ancestors appeared more inclined toward suits of armor and battle-axes than small, precious objects. But never fear, I shall begin a search of the castle this very afternoon, for I find the idea of a souvenir of our love most appealing."

"How kind of you to humor me," Alexandra said, managing somehow to keep a straight face. Rising from her chair, she crossed to where Liam sat and curled up on his lap, her head on his shoulder. "But I think I may be able to save you the trouble."

Liam wrapped his arms around her and buried his nose in her hair. "How so, my darling? Do you know of some secret treasure The Aerie holds that I've not yet discovered?"

Alexandra chuckled. "I do indeed, my lord husband, and I feel certain that once you learn my secret you will have to agree it is the one absolutely perfect souvenir to commemorate the miracle of our love."